THE ANGRY EARL

The Earl of Beaconswood was furious with Julia, and that fury flared in his voice. "You go out riding astride dressed like this? It is time you were taught a lesson you will never forget, Julia. A painful lesson."

"You did not follow me because you were outraged," she said. "Or because you saw me as an unruly child in need of chastisement. Be honest with yourself, Daniel. You followed me because I am a woman. More woman than you have ever encountered before. More woman than you know what to do with."

The words seemed to speak themselves. She listened, appalled, even as she stared defiantly into his eyes.

"My God!" he said, and then he acted.

Julia was quite blasé about the art of kissing. She had been kissed several times by more than one gentleman and knew all there was to know about it. But what followed was not just a kiss. It was something she knew nothing about—something that evoked the most powerful feelings she had ever felt. Indeed, she was learning a new lesson—a lesson in love . . .

Courting Julia

Courting Julia

by

Mary Balogh

A SIGNET BOOK

SIGNET
Published by the Penguin Group
Penguin Books USA Inc., 375 Hudson Street,
New York, New York 10014, U.S.A.
Penguin Books Ltd, 27 Wrights Lane,
London W8 5TZ, England
Penguin Books Australia Ltd, Ringwood,
Victoria, Australia
Penguin Books Canada Ltd, 10 Alcorn Avenue,
Toronto, Ontario, Canada M4V 3B2
Penguin Books (N.Z.) Ltd, 182–190 Wairau Road,
Auckland 10, New Zealand

Penguin Books Ltd, Registered Offices:
Harmondsworth, Middlesex, England

First published by Signet,
an imprint of Dutton Signet,
a division of Penguin Books USA Inc.

First Printing, November, 1993
10 9 8 7 6 5 4 3 2 1

1

"They'll come rushing from all corners of the globe as soon as I'm dead," the Earl of Beaconswood said to his granddaughter—to his *step*-granddaughter, to be more accurate. The earl's daughter had married Julia Maynard's father when Julia, the child of his previous marriage, was five years old.

"Oh, Grandpapa," Julia said, closing the book from which she had been reading aloud and frowning at the old man as he reclined back against his pillows and tried to smooth the sheet across his chest with gnarled and feeble hands. "Don't say such things."

"They'll come racing all right," he said. "And weeping pailfuls and roaring fury at you for not summoning them sooner, Jule. But we'll cheat 'em, girl." His chuckle turned into a cough.

"I meant don't say that about dying," Julia said, standing up to fold the sheet neatly and bending over him to kiss his forehead. His bushy white eyebrows tickled her chin.

"It's true enough," he said. "The body is worn out, Jule. Time to turn it in for a new one." He chuckled again. "Time to turn up my toes."

"You will be getting better now that the warm weather has come," she said briskly. "Though I still think we should let everyone know that you are poorly, Grandpapa. I have had to lie to both Aunt Eunice and Aunt Sarah in the past month, assuring them both in reply to their letters that you are very well, thank you. It is not right. They should know. And it would be a comfort to you to have a little more company."

"Bah!" he said, frowning ferociously from beneath bushy white eyebrows. "Company is what I don't need, Jule. Everyone tiptoeing around and whispering and looking Friday-faced. And bringing me this gruel to make me feel better and that gruel and the other gruel. Bah!" He paused and wheezed for breath.

"Well," Julia said after watching him in some concern until he had succeeded, "I am not going to change your mind about it, am I?" Though she would be the one blamed for it afterward. He was right about that but she did not express the thought out loud. After what? her mind asked and shied away from an answer. "Are you enjoying *Gulliver's Travels?*"

"No better than I did when I first read it fifty years or so ago," he said. "That Gulliver was a fool if ever there was one. No, I've been lying here thinking, Jule."

She clucked her tongue. "So I was reading for nothing," she said. "You were not even listening."

"I like the sound of your voice," he said. "Besides, you were reading for your own entertainment too, girl, or you are a fool for wasting a sunny afternoon sitting up here with a dying old man."

"It is not a waste," she said. "Grandpapa, you will get better. You were feeling quite spry yesterday. You said so."

"Feeling spry these days means seeing a pretty chambermaid and knowing that once upon a time the sight would have meant something," he said with another chuckle that turned into a cough.

"For shame," Julia said, sitting back down again. "I am not going to give you the satisfaction of blushing, Grandpapa."

"You ain't married," the earl said, frowning and looking keenly at his granddaughter from beneath his eyebrows. "You know what that will mean after I am dead, Jule."

She sighed. "Let's not start on that topic again," she said. "Would you like some tea, Grandpapa? Cook has made some of the little currant cakes you like so well. Shall I go and fetch some?"

"How old are you?" the earl asked.

Julia sighed again. Nothing would distract Grandpapa once he was launched upon his favorite topic. And he knew very well how old she was. "Twenty-one," she said. "Aged and decrepit, Grandpapa. And definitely a spinster for life. Don't start. Please?"

But he was already started and well launched. "You came back from your Season in London with your nose in the air and all your beaux rejected," he said. "That was all of two years ago. And you have turned up your nose at every respectable young man I have brought here for your inspection since. You'll be lucky if you really don't end up a spinster, Jule."

"I have never turned up my nose," she said indignantly, falling into the trap of arguing with him, as she always did. "I have just not met anyone I cared to spend the rest of my life with, Grandpapa. There are worse fates than ending up a spinster, you know."

"Are there?" he said gruffly. "You want to be turned over to the Maynards, Jule?"

No, she certainly did not. Her father's elder brother and his wife and five children lived far to the north, almost in Scotland, and they had always made it clear that they would not relish having to take responsibility for Julia. Though they would if they had to, of course. They were all the direct family she had.

Julia held her peace and glared sullenly at her grandfather.

"It'll be the Maynards after I am gone," the earl said. "You can't expect my family to take you under their wing, can you, Jule?"

Grandpapa's family consisted of two sisters and a sister-in-law on his side, and a brother-in-law and sister-in-law on Grandmama's side, plus spouses and numerous nephews and nieces. Julia had grown up as one of them. Only in recent years had she realized fully that in truth she did not belong at all. Grandpapa had kept her constantly reminded with his repeated attempts to marry her off.

"You had better take Dickson while I am still alive to give a dowry," the earl said. "He is steady enough, Jule. And respectable. I'll have him summoned tomorrow. He's less than ten miles away."

"You will do no such thing," Julia said crossly. "I would rather marry a frog than Sir Albert Dickson. If you won't have tea, Grandpapa, then it is time for your sleep. You are tired and you have been talking too much. You know what the doctor said."

"Old fool," he said. "I don't have too much longer to talk, Jule. It's Dickson or the Maynards, girl. I don't have time to find someone else for you."

"Good," she said tartly. "That is one small mercy, at least."

But he grasped feebly for her wrist as she stood up, and tears sprang to her eyes. His hand was a thin, bloodless claw. Grandpapa had always been robust.

"Jule," he said, "I wanted to see you settled, girl, before I go on my way. I feel an obligation to you because of your stepmother. She loved your father and you. And your papa left nothing. I love you as my own granddaughter."

"I know, Grandpapa," she said, swallowing tears. "Don't worry about me. It is time for your sleep."

He looked at her broodingly. "But I do worry," he said. "What is going to happen to you, Jule?"

"I am going to go from this room," she said, bending to kiss him once more, "so that you can rest. And then I am going to go outside for some air and sunshine. That is what is going to happen to me. Aunt Millie will look in a little later to see if you are awake and need anything."

"I'll be sure to be asleep, then," the earl said. "Millie always shakes my pillows until they are all lumps and kicks the bed with her slippers so that all my bones jangle."

Julia chuckled as she let herself quietly from the room. But amusement faded quickly. Grandpapa really was failing fast. She could no longer pretend, as she had all winter, that he would rally again once spring came. It was June, more summer than spring, and he was weaker than ever. He had not left his room since just after Christmas. He had not left his bed in three weeks or a month.

He really was dying, she thought, admitting the truth to herself for the first time. It was difficult to imagine the world without Grandpapa in it. And it was still difficult to realize that he was not really her grandfather at all. He had always treated her as if he were, perhaps because he had no grandchildren of his own. Her papa and her stepmother had died together in Italy three years after their marriage. There had been no children of the marriage. All they had left behind were debts.

Julia tapped on the door of Aunt Millie's sitting room— Aunt Millie was Grandpapa's maiden sister—opened the door quietly, and found her aunt asleep in her chair, her mouth open, her cap tilted rakishly over one eye. Julia closed the door softly. She would be sure to come back inside to check on her grandfather herself within the hour.

She proceeded on her way outside for a stroll in the formal gardens without stopping to pick up a shawl. It was a warm day despite the breeze. She breathed in the scent of flowers as she crossed the cobbled terrace and descended the wide stone steps to the gardens. It was going to be hard to move away, to have to stop thinking of Primrose Park as home. It had been home since she was five years old. She could not remember any other with any clarity.

Julia changed her mind about strolling along the graveled paths between the flower beds and box hedges and sat down instead on the second step from the bottom, clasping her knees and gazing across the colored heads of flowers. It seemed self-centered to be thinking about losing her home when Grandpapa was dying. As if her grief over what was happening had less to do with him as a person than with what he represented to her—comfort and security.

But she need not feel such guilt, she knew. She loved him dearly. He was the only parent figure she had known since the age of eight. There was Aunt Millie, of course, but Aunt Millie had always been all adither. Even as a child

Julia had felt protective of her, almost as if their supposed roles were reversed.

Perhaps for Grandpapa's sake, Julia thought, she should have made a more determined effort to choose a husband. She could have been reasonable about it, choosing the least objectionable candidate. But the trouble was that she could not choose a husband with her reason. She was a romantic. A foolish one. For in looking for romantic perfection she knew that she was very likely to end up as a spinster, as Grandpapa always warned. Indeed, she was one and twenty already. But no, even to please Grandpapa she could not have married anyone who had yet shown an interest in her—or in the dowry Grandpapa was prepared to offer with her.

She did not really believe his threats. Grandpapa loved her and would not doom her to having to go to live with relatives who did not want her. No, he would provide for her, she was sure. She did not know details, but she did know that Grandpapa was enormously wealthy and that a great deal of his wealth and some of his property—including Primrose Park—was at his disposal, to be left to whomever he chose. He would leave her an allowance sufficient to enable her to live independently. She knew he would. In fact, he would probably leave her even more than that.

She was not really afraid for her future but only depressed by it. Soon there would be no Grandpapa and no Primrose Park. And no husband either. No grand romantic passion to set her on the path to the happily ever after. Sometimes life seemed very dreary. And her mood was not improved at all by the fact that she had disappointed her grandfather. He would have liked to see her contentedly married before he died.

Julia's attention was caught suddenly by movement beyond the gardens. A carriage had emerged from the trees far down the driveway and was making its way toward the house. Not a wagon or a gig, but a fine traveling carriage. Who was coming? It could not be any of the family, surely.

Grandpapa had given strict orders that none of them be informed of the poor state of his health, and the family never came until July or August.

She stood up and watched the carriage approach the terrace, shading her eyes against the sun.

He felt rather like a vulture, the Viscount Yorke thought as the house came into view. Primrose Park, with its neat Palladian manor and well-kept formal gardens and picturesque park, was neither the largest nor the most accessible of the Earl of Beaconswood's estates, but it was the one where he had elected to live most of his life. And so it had become the focal point of family life, the place where everyone tended to gather during the summer months.

But the viscount, the earl's nephew and heir, had not been there for six years. He had been busy with his own estate and other responsibilities. And with his own life too. And so he felt a little embarrassed coming now, in June, without an official invitation. He felt like a vulture. Primrose Park was unentailed, unlike the earl's other estates. He could leave it to whomever he chose after his death. And the earl was dying, if the strange, apologetic, secretive letter sent the viscount by his aunt was to be believed. Probably it was. His uncle must be close to eighty years old. He was certainly years older than any other member of the family.

And so the viscount was coming at his aunt's request, though she had advised him in her letter with lengthy apologies for the presumption not to divulge the fact that she had written. He was supposed to arrive just as if he had taken it suddenly into his head after six years to call upon his uncle. Or just as if he had been passing through Gloucestershire by some chance and had decided to call to pay his respects.

But it would look, the viscount thought, as if he were coming to gloat over all that would soon be his and as if he were perhaps trying to ensure that Primrose Park would be his too.

He was coming because it was the dutiful thing to do. He was, after all, the earl's heir and if it was true that the old man was dying, then he should pay his last respects to his uncle. And of course it would be as well for him to be on hand afterward to deal with all the business of the funeral and the will. There would be many things to be done and Aunt Millie had never been a competent manager.

He had come out of duty, he thought, peering out of the window as the carriage turned onto the terrace and slowed before the marble horseshoe steps leading up to the front doors. But he could think of other things he would rather be doing. He would rather be back in London, though this was the first year he had gone there for the Season for many years. He had gone to begin to look about him for a wife since he was at that awkward age of twenty-nine and his mother's hints were becoming persistent.

And surprisingly he had found Blanche, a grave, sweet, and pretty eighteen-year-old, who suited him very nicely indeed despite her youth. The courtship was proceeding slowly but promisingly. He chafed at the delay this visit to his uncle was creating. And perhaps it would be a prolonged delay. Perhaps, he thought, he should have acted with less than his customary caution and made his offer to Blanche's father before leaving town. But he had not done so and it was too late now.

There was a woman standing on the steps leading down to the formal gardens. Aunt Millie? But he realized the ridiculousness of the thought as soon as his eyes focused properly on her. She was too young a woman. She was rather lovely, too, by Jove. She was not wearing a bonnet. The breeze was blowing her short dark curls back from her face. It was also blowing her light muslin dress against a very pleasing figure indeed. Shapely but not too voluptuous. Just very—feminine.

Good Lord, he thought, leaning forward suddenly. Good Lord, it was Julia. She had been little more than a child the last time he saw her. But of course that had been six years before. His lips thinned as he remembered all his former disapproval of the girl. Hoyden, daredevil, show-off, pest. And of course, Uncle's great favorite. The apple of his eye despite the fact that she was no direct relation but the daughter of an irresponsible adventurer.

Well, perhaps she had changed. He had not seen her for six years. By the time the carriage had come to a stop and the steps had been lowered and he had got out, she was standing on the lowest of the horseshoe steps, looking at him. Her eyes were almost on a level with his.

"Good afternoon, Julia," he said, touching his hat and inclining his head to her. "How are you?"

She was looking rather flushed, perhaps by the wind. "Hello, Daniel," she said. "How did you find out?"

Her manner was faintly hostile, he thought. And definitely aggressive. Her bonnetless state and the absence of a shawl that might have prevented the wind from doing such revealing things to her muslin dress—both details that had dazzled him before he realized who she was—suddenly seemed offensive to him. Typical of Julia. Typically immodest. He raised his eyebrows and made his tone deliberately frosty. "I beg your pardon?"

"How did you find out?" she asked again.

"Find out what?" he said, raising his eyebrows. "I was in the area. I decided to call to see how my uncle is. Is he well?"

"In the area!" she said scornfully. "What a ridiculous bouncer. And you know very well how Grandpapa is. It was Aunt Millie, was it not? She wrote to you."

"I did receive a letter from my aunt last week," he said. "Are you going to keep me on the steps for the rest of the afternoon, Julia, or am I to be permitted to go inside?" He let his eyes roam over her to make her aware of the impropriety of her appearance. But it was useless to try to embarrass Julia, of course.

"You had better turn around and go home again," she said. "He does not want to see you. He wants to be left in peace. He gave strict instructions that no one was to write to you. Or any other member of the family."

"Did he?" He was beginning to feel irritated. "Clearly my aunt felt the need of the support of another member of the family, though, Julia. You will excuse me?" He set one foot on the bottom step.

"You are not going to upset him," she said. "I will not allow it."

He disdained to argue further with her. He walked around her and up the steps. "Thank you for your warm welcome," he said. "It was graciously done, Julia."

"There is no need for the sarcasm," she said, trotting up at his side when it became apparent that she had lost her audience at the bottom of the steps. "He is very ill, Daniel. He is d-dying. I don't want him upset."

He is d-dying. It was a little too carefully done. He realized the truth immediately, of course. She had been quite clever. She had thought to have his uncle all to herself until his death. She had probably persuaded him that no one else cared to come to visit him when he was so ill. She had probably persuaded him to leave her something of a fortune in his will. Doubtless she had succeeded. She had always been the favorite anyway. Now she did not want him coming along and threatening to upset her plans.

He stepped into the tiled hall and nodded to the butler, who was hurrying toward him from the back stairs. The man recognized him even after six years and called him by name.

"How do you do, Bragge?" the viscount said. "You will see about having a room made up for me and having my bags sent up? I would like to pay my respects to my uncle without delay. Is he up?"

"No, he is not up," Julia said indignantly from behind him. "He has not been up for a month."

The viscount ignored her. "Is he awake, Bragge?" he asked. "Perhaps you will go up and see. I will follow you. You may announce me if he is."

"Grandpapa is resting," Julia said. "I shall go up, Bragge, and peep in on him. If by chance he is awake, I shall tell him of Lord Yorke's unexpected arrival. Perhaps tomorrow he will be feeling strong enough for a brief courtesy call before his lordship continues on his way to wherever he is going."

It seemed, the viscount thought, that they had got themselves into the ridiculous situation of communicating through a third party. "Thank you, Bragge," he said. "Miss Maynard will conduct me upstairs." He turned to her and indicated with one imperious hand that she was to precede him to the staircase. She glared at him for a moment and then turned abruptly and strode away. Oh, Lord, she *strode*. Was it any wonder that she was still unmarried? She must be—oh, twenty at the very least.

He followed her up the stairs, his eyes on the angry sway of her hips, and along the corridor to the master bedchamber. She turned to him and glared again and spoke in a pointed whisper.

"He will be sleeping," she said. "I will not have him woken up. Do you understand me? He was very tired when I left him half an hour ago."

"What do you think I am planning to do, Julia?" he asked, disdaining to whisper. "Invite him to waltz with me?"

She was not amused. But then neither was he. She whisked herself around and proceeded to open the door very slowly and without any perceptible sound. She opened it a little, stepped inside, and half closed it behind her back. He heard a deep, gruff voice and then hers. He set a hand flat against the door and pushed it open against the pressure of her hand on the other side. She glared at him yet again.

"Here is Daniel come to see you, Grandpapa," she said, and she hurried across the room to bend over the bed and fuss with the bedclothes. "He was in Gloucestershire and thought he would come to call on you."

"Actually," the viscount said quietly, stepping forward, his hands clasped behind his back, "I heard that you were poorly, sir, and came down without delay. I thought I might be of some use."

"Don't exert yourself, Grandpapa," Julia said, smoothing a hand over the sparse white hair on his head.

"Millie, I suppose," the earl said. "Dratted woman. There was no need for you to drag yourself away from the pleasures of the Season, Dan. Dying can be done just as well alone."

"But it is probably done a little more comfortably when there are family members close by," the viscount said. "I don't spend much time in town, sir. Usually I give the Season a miss altogether. It is no great hardship to be away from there." He thought of Blanche with a pang of regret.

"Hm," the earl said. "Well, I'll try not to keep you here long, Dan." He attempted a chuckle and coughed instead. "A few days ought to do it nicely, I think."

"Grandpapa." Julia dropped a kiss and a tear on his forehead. A nicely affecting scene, the viscount thought. "Don't talk so. Don't talk at all in fact. Didn't you sleep?"

"I'll be sleeping long enough, Jule," the earl said. "I have been thinking. I want to see Prudholm. Tomorrow. No later than tomorrow. Is he at the house?"

"He is staying in the village," Julia said. "Leave it for a while, Grandpapa. You need more rest."

"When a man is close to the greatest event of his life," the earl said, "he has more need of his solicitor than his rest, Jule. Tomorrow. In the morning?"

"Prudholm is your solicitor?" the viscount asked. "I shall see that he is here, sir, bright and early. Now if you will excuse me, I would like to wash and change and pay my respects to my aunt. I shall look in on you tomorrow if you are strong enough."

"If I am alive, you mean," the earl said, chuckling. "You may be an earl by tomorrow, Daniel. You will like that well enough, I daresay, eh?"

Julia was glaring at him again, the viscount saw before he turned to leave the room. Doubtless she thought he had come merely to gloat over the imminence of a new and grander title. Doubtless she was terrified that the summoning of the solicitor was a sign that the old man was going to change his will. Was she so confident that it was in her favor now?

"I shall see you at dinner, Julia," he said with exaggerated courtesy. "What time is it served?"

"Six o'clock," she said. "We keep country hours here."

He bowed and left the room.

The Earl of Beaconswood spent almost an hour alone the next morning with his solicitor, keeping his doctor waiting downstairs for all of half an hour. The doctor was with him only ten minutes before reporting to Julia and to the Viscount Yorke that his lordship was comfortable and free of pain provided he was given his medication regularly, but that he was weakening.

It was the same report as he had given daily for the past month.

The earl was civil to his nephew when the latter called upon him for ten minutes after luncheon. He barked at his sister and made her cry when she bumped against his bed while shaking pillows that he had protested did not need shaking. And he lay awake for an hour listening to Julia read the opening of *A Pilgrim's Progress*. It was a damned sight more entertaining than that Gulliver drivel, he gave as his opinion, though Julia had the impression that he had not been listening at all. He stared at her broodingly and she waited for him to start talking about Sir Albert Dickson again. But he did not do so.

The earl ate a little dinner when Julia coaxed him with some of his favorite delicacies, and he bade a civil good night to her and to the viscount and his sister. He even added that Millie had a good heart after growling at her again when it looked as if she was approaching his pillows. He took his medicine obediently before Julia left.

But he did his dying alone as he had wished to do, without either noise or fuss. His valet, who had dozed the night away in his master's dressing room, the door wide open so that he would hear the slightest noise, found his master dead in the morning when he tiptoed into the room to check on him in the early dawn light.

It looked for all the world, the valet explained to everyone belowstairs later in the morning, as if the old earl was merely sleeping peacefully. Everyone else agreed, even Aunt Millie, who had to be carried away by a stout footman when she had the vapors although she had insisted on viewing the body, and Julia, who wept soundlessly until Lord Yorke quietly directed the housekeeper to take her back to her room and call her maid to stay with her there.

It was the viscount—or rather the new Earl of Beaconswood—who, after consulting his uncle's solicitor, wrote to all his relatives to summon them to Primrose Park for the funeral if at all possible, but certainly for the reading of the will. It was the new earl who set in motion arrangements for the funeral.

Julia was left alone to grieve.

2

The older generation always came faithfully to Primrose Park during the summer. Rarely did any of them miss. The younger generation had all come too while they were still children. The summers had always been wild, delirious times for Julia. She had played her heart out and wondered how she had lived for ten months without them and without any significant companionship except that of her grandfather and Aunt Millie. And yet when summer ended and they all went back home again, she had always returned cheerfully and even gratefully to the quiet life of Primrose Park and the warm and active one of her imagination.

The cousins had not come so often since they had started to grow up, especially the male cousins. There were other things to entice them away, like Brighton or one of the other spas, or parties at the homes of school or university friends. And Susan had married two years before and now had obligations to her husband's family as well as her own.

But they all came at the news of the death—just as the old earl had predicted they would. Not one of them stayed away, except Susan's husband. Most of them arrived in time for the funeral, but they were all there for the reading of the will, ten days after the death of the old Earl of Beaconswood. The new earl summoned them and they came, shocked and grieving and rather angry at the fact that they had not been warned or given the chance to come sooner.

Aunt Sarah, the Viscountess Yorke, Daniel's mother, was the first to arrive with her daughter, Camilla. Aunt Sarah was clearly annoyed.

"The old fool," she said of her deceased brother-in-law in Julia's hearing, though she was talking to her son. "He could not have informed his closest family that he was ill, I suppose, and had the comfort of our presence here while he was dying. Sometimes I wonder why I married into such a strange family when I had other choices. And why did you not let me know, Daniel? I take it unkindly in you to come rushing down here without a word to me."

"Mama," he said soothingly, "you and Camilla were in Bath and I was in London. Besides, Aunt Millie urged secrecy."

Aunt Sarah made a sound indicating her contempt of her sister-in-law's urgings. She was, Julia had always found, an abrupt, forceful, rather unsympathetic person.

Camilla smiled and kissed her brother and hugged Julia, murmuring words of sympathy in her ear. Camilla was still nursing a broken heart over the death in battle of her officer fiancé two years before. She was twenty-four years old.

Aunt Eunice and Uncle Raymond, Lord and Lady Bellamy, arrived the day before the funeral as did Uncle Henry and Aunt Roberta, Lord and Lady Hemming, brother and sister-in-law of the late countess, with their son and daughter, Malcolm and Stella Stacey. Julia hugged Stella, two years her junior and always her playmate during their girlhood. Malcolm bowed over her hand but did not smile. Malcolm had never been a smiler. But then everyone knew that he was painfully shy.

Aunt Eunice spent the rest of the day in tears, exclaiming at the cruelty of a brother who had not sent for his own sister during his dying days. Uncle Henry set an arm about Julia's shoulders and sympathized with her on her loss. She must come back to live with him and Aunt Roberta, he said. His kindness succeeded only in dissolving Julia in tears. Again.

Poor Grandpapa. She shed many tears over him, most of them in private, during those days leading up to his funeral and during the few days following while they all waited for the remaining members of the family to arrive for the reading of the will. She missed him. She felt orphaned anew despite the fact that she was one and twenty years of age. Suddenly she felt as if she had no one left of her very own.

It was a bleak and rather a frightening feeling. And an unnecessary one, she supposed. Not only Uncle Henry, but also Aunt Eunice and Uncle Raymond had offered her a home. But of course they offered out of a kindness she could not accept. She could not become a charity case to people who had no real obligation to her at all. Especially when she was twenty-one years old. Grandpapa had understood that. That was why he had urged marriage on her so persistently.

It was equally bleak knowing that another man now held Grandpapa's title and gave the orders that Grandpapa had always given and commanded the type of respect and deference that had always been Grandpapa's. Daniel. Julia resented him. Unreasonably so, perhaps since he certainly did take charge of affairs that would have been difficult for her and Aunt Millie to handle alone. Daniel was extremely efficient.

Julia resented him nonetheless. But then she had always resented Daniel. Or almost always. He had always been old enough to despise her. When she was a child, he had been a boy and not at all interested in playing games of house or school or chasing. When she became a girl, he had been a young man and already, from the age of fourteen, a viscount. He had not been interested in his girl cousins and their squeals and giggles or in the sort of wild games the boys and girls played together. He had grown up fast. Too fast.

Daniel had always had a way of looking contemptuously at his younger cousins—especially at Julia. She could remember bristling with resentment at the way he had always looked at her when he saw her riding astride or swimming in the lake or playing cricket, her dress tucked up at the waist so that she would not trip over the hem. He had always given the impression that he would respect a worm beneath his boot more than he respected her.

So she had always resented him. And set out to shock him whenever she could. And paradoxically she had also tried to impress him. For despite everything Daniel had always been the older cousin, the very handsome older cousin. When she was fifteen she had often spent an age changing from one dress to another before her looking glass until she was satisfied with her choice and dressing and redressing her hair until it was just so. But the only time he had noticed her that summer was the time when she had come racing and giggling up onto the terrace a foot behind Gussie, her face flushed, her dress creased and dusty, her hair flying in all directions and Daniel had been standing there looking as immaculate as usual.

"Really, Julia," he had said, his eyes moving over her in disgust, "isn't it time you started to grow up?"

After he had strolled away, she had crossed her eyes and stuck out her tongue and made Gussie hold his nose in an attempt to stifle his laughter. And she had been glad when Daniel had not come back the next summer—or the next or the next. She was glad he had never come back. She wished he had not come back now. Conceited, cold, humorless— earl. She hated now to think that he was the new Earl of Beaconswood.

Frederick and Lesley Sullivan, sons of Aunt Eunice and Uncle Raymond, arrived the morning after the funeral, and seemed not one whit upset at having missed it. Or rather, Frederick did not. But then Frederick did not take anything very seriously. He was a rake. At least that was how Gussie described him and Julia had no reason to doubt the truth of it.

"Hello, Jule," he said when he and his brother strode into the hall on their arrival and Julia happened to be crossing it on the way to the library and some needed solitude. He took her hands in his and kissed her cheek. "By Jove, but you look appetizing in black. Doesn't she, Les?"

Lesley smiled and nodded his head more times than were strictly necessary. "Yes, she does, Freddie," he said. "Yes, you do, Jule."

"I am in mourning," she said pointedly. "For Grand-papa."

"And so you are," Frederick said, squeezing her hands and looking down at her from lazy, handsome eyes. "The old codger finally worried himself into the grave, did he? You miss him, do you?"

"Do you, Jule?" Lesley asked in his gentle voice.

"Yes, I do," she said indignantly. "I loved him, Freddie."

"Ah," he said, looking amused. He winked at her. "I always like them angry, Jule, and it never takes much effort, you know."

"But he don't mean to make you angry," Lesley said. "Do you, Freddie? You loved Uncle, Jule. Sorry he's gone."

"Thank you, Les," she said, releasing her hands from Frederick's and setting them on Lesley's shoulders so that she could kiss his cheek. He was perhaps an inch shorter than she and at least six shorter than his brother. She smiled at him, making sure that Frederick was looking at her as she did so.

He chuckled.

They had to wait another two days for the remaining members of the family to arrive. But Aunt Sylvia and Uncle Paul Craybourne, sister and brother-in-law of the late countess, had to come all the way from Yorkshire. They brought their daughters, Susan and Viola, with them. They brought their son, Augustus, too—always Julia's favorite.

And so finally were all gathered at Primrose Park and the final business connected with the passing of the old earl could be proceeded with.

The family assembled in the drawing room for the reading of the will, the library being a little too small to accommodate so many in comfort. There was a great deal of shuffling around, most of it occasioned by Aunt Sarah, who believed that they should be seated somehow according to their rank in the family. Her son, as the new Earl of Bea-conswood, should of course sit in the center of the front row and as his mother and widow of the late earl's only brother, she should sit beside him.

"After all, dear," she was heard to say to her son, "if your poor papa had survived your uncle, then I would have been the countess."

But then Aunt Eunice stirred up trouble by pointing out that Aunt Millie, as the elder of their dear deceased brother's sisters, should have the place of honor, or at least the place beside dear Daniel. And perhaps she, as the other sister, should sit at his other side.

The new earl settled the matter by seating his aunts together in the front row with his mother beside them, while he took a chair behind the three of them next to his sister. Anyone who was observing the incident would have concluded that he had passed his first test as head of the family with a cool head and good sense. Frederick Sullivan, lounging against the pianoforte and not yet seated, caught his eye, grinned, and winked at him.

Julia sat in the back row of chairs, between Viola Craybourne and Susan, Lady Temple. Viola was three years younger than Julia, Susan one year older. They also had been her playmates in former years, her friends more recently.

The servants, standing respectfully behind the chairs, were also jostling for position, though rather more quietly than the family.

"I don't know why we all have to be here, do you, Jule?" Viola whispered. "After all there can be nothing in Uncle's will to interest our generation. Everything will have been left to our parents. I would far prefer to be outside strolling toward the lake on such a lovely day. Are the boats ready to be taken out yet?"

"I believe it is customary," Julia said, "for the whole family to gather on such occasions."

Viola pulled a face. "Almost everything is Daniel's anyway," she said. "The title is his and Vickers Abbey to go with it and Willowbunch Court. Those estates account for the bulk of Uncle's fortune, according to Papa."

Julia felt herself fidgeting with a ring on her finger and stilled her hands. It was all very well for Viola to be uninterested in the proceedings and even bored by them. Matters were not so simple for Julia. She had no parents. And no fortune.

What would she do? she wondered. Where would she go? Would she stay with Aunt Millie? Perhaps Grandpapa had left Primrose Park to Aunt Millie and Julia could stay with her there. Or perhaps Aunt Millie would be going to live with Aunt Eunice, or perhaps even with Aunt Sarah. If that were the case, then Julia would not feel comfortable about going along with her. Grandpapa would have made provision for her, of course. She had no doubt about that. But where would she live? She was too young to live alone. Would there be enough money to buy or rent herself a small cottage and employ a companion to live there with her?

Her stomach was churning with nervousness as the family members took a veritable age to settle in their chairs and quieten down enough that Mr. Prudholm could proceed with the business of reading the will. She was foolish not to have accepted one of the three offers that had been made for her during the Season she had spent in London or one of the four offers that Grandpapa had arranged since her return home. Seven offers of marriage and she had not been able to see herself married to one of the men who had made them! There must be something wrong with her, she thought. At least she would be safe if she were married. Bored and dissatisfied perhaps, but safe. At this precise moment safety seemed a very desirable state.

Mr. Prudholm coughed and silence fell on the drawing room.

The reading of the will took forever, Julia thought a long time later. Viola's yawns became perpetual and peevish until Susan leaned across Julia and shushed her sister. A long list of servants had to be read through and the bequest to each described. Every family member had been left something, even Viola, who was merely a niece on the late countess's side of the family. Viola stopped yawning abruptly when the solicitor's voice announced that she had been left a hundred pounds. She clasped her hands to her bosom and smiled with delight.

"That is more than Papa has given me in pin money my whole life," she whispered.

She must come next, Julia thought. Everyone else in the family had now been dealt with since Viola was the youngest niece. Only she was left. Despite her conviction that her grandfather would have looked after her, her heart beat uncomfortably. No, it was not beating. It was thumping—against her chest and in her throat and against her temples and in her ears. She felt as if there were no air left in the room.

" 'There remains only Primrose Park and all its farms and rents,' " Mr. Prudholm was reading. He paused as he had paused so often during the reading of the will. The late earl's solicitor had something of a flair for the dramatic.

Only Primrose Park. That was all that was left to bequeath. The family waited silently and expectantly. And yet all of them had been named and dealt with already. All except Daniel, of course, who did not need anything from the will since he had already inherited the title and the bulk of the former earl's property. Who was to be named again as owner of Primrose Park? Aunt Millie? But Aunt Millie had already been left a handsome portion.

Julia's heart was beating so fast that she thought she must faint. She clasped her hands in her lap and looked down at them. Grandpapa had meant it, then, when he had said that she must marry or prepare to go to her own relatives after his death. He could not have left her Primrose Park. Could he? Even as her head denied the possibility, her heart raced with hope and the sure knowledge that there could not be hope.

" 'Primrose Park,' " Mr. Prudholm read in his slow distinct way, " 'will belong to whichever of my five nephews' "—Julia bowed her head, and closed her eyes and concentrated on holding on to her dignity—" 'can win the hand of my deceased daughter's stepdaughter, Julia Maynard, within one month of the reading of this will.' "

At first Julia did not react. There was a shocked murmuring about her, someone—Aunt Eunice?—was blessing her soul, and Julia's eyes gradually opened and focused on her clasped hands. What? *What* had Mr. Prudholm just said?

The solicitor must have been holding up a staying hand. The murmuring ceased rather abruptly.

" 'The announcement of a betrothal is to be made to my solicitor, Tobias Prudholm, in this very place one month from today,' " Mr. Prudholm's voice read as Julia's head came up to stare at him in disbelief. " 'If no such announcement is made, then Primrose Park and its properties and farms will be given to a charity of my choice, to be named on that same day one month from now. Julia Maynard will be sent, at the expense of my estate, to live with her paternal relatives in the north of England.' "

Julia was on her feet, clutching the back of the chair in front of her and forcing Uncle Paul to lean forward. "This is preposterous!" she said. "He must have been joking. He cannot have been serious. There must be some mistake."

Mr. Prudholm held up a staying hand again, but Julia did not sit down. "Miss Maynard," he said, quietly, reasonably, "your grandfather was concerned for your future. He wished to secure it for you as best he was able. I am sure you are aware, as your five male cousins must be, that Primrose Park is a remarkably prosperous estate. It has been your home for most of your life. It can remain your home for the rest of your days if you choose to accept an offer from one of your stepcousins within the next month. But there is no compulsion on you. Neither your grandfather's will nor I can compel you to accept any offer. The will makes provision for that eventuality."

Julia glanced about her blankly, hardly noticing the stares of uncles and aunts, some of them as blank as her own, some curious, one hostile. Her eyes locked with Frederick's as he leaned against the pianoforte. His lips were pursed and he was looking back at her from narrowed eyes.

It was impossible to know if he was amused or not. She turned her head and caught the profile of another cousin. Daniel. A sharp, handsome aristocratic profile. His dark hair was immaculately tidy as it always was. He was looking at the solicitor with polite interest just as if the clause of the will that had just been read had nothing whatsoever to do with him. She wanted to scream some obscenity at him but knew none.

Aunt Millie was turned in her chair and was nodding and smiling sweetly. "A wonderful idea, dear," she said to Julia. "I knew dear Humphrey would do something handsome for you and he has."

"Hush, Millie," Aunt Eunice said, patting her sister's hand.

A hand touched Julia's arm. "Sit down, Jule, do," Susan said quietly. And Julia sank back into her chair, feeling foolish and conspicuous. One just did not interrupt the reading of a will. Lesley was looking back over his shoulder from the row in front and smiling sweetly at her.

Mr. Prudholm drew the attention of the room's occupants again with his professional cough. "One other point, my lords, ladies and gentlemen," he said, "and then we will be finished." He returned his eyes to the earl's will and read. "'My whole family is requested or invited to remain at Primrose Park for the duration of the courtship of my granddaughter. It will be the last time I can be considered to be your host. Let it be a good month of family entertainment, then. No black clothes. I'll not have anyone in mourning here after today. You have all been wearing it for a week or longer. Put it off again tomorrow. That is my final command as head of the family.'"

"But we brought nothing but black," Aunt Roberta protested.

Uncle Henry squeezed her hand and told her that a carriage would be sent home to bring different clothes. The matter could be accomplished in two days.

Aunt Millie dabbed at her eyes with a large linen handkerchief borrowed from Uncle Raymond, and Aunt Sarah was heard to remark that her brother-in-law had been impossible. Quite impossible. Who had ever heard of anything so outrageous? It was not clear to which clause in the will she referred.

Julia stared at her hands and fought embarrassment and bewilderment. And panic. She concentrated very hard on not crying. He had owed her nothing. For sixteen years he had given her a home and all the comforts she could have desired. He had tried to secure her future. Most important, he had given her love. He had owed her nothing.

But she felt betrayed. And hurt. And very frightened.

The reading of the will was over. Mr. Prudholm was packing up his papers. The servants were filing out and clearly bursting with the need to return belowstairs as quickly as possible so that they could talk freely. The noise level in the drawing room was rising.

"Jule." Viola gripped Julia's hand and squeezed hard. "You lucky, lucky thing. Just a few words from Uncle's will and you have five beaux. You are going to be betrothed within the month. I wish—oh, I wish I were in your shoes."

"How foolish, Vi," Susan said. "It would not work for you. One of those beaux is our own Gussie, and Malcolm is our first cousin."

"But Daniel," Viola said with a sigh. "And Freddie. Oh, Jule! You could be a countess immediately or a baroness at some time in the future."

"And Les," Susan said. "Lesley is the sweetest of them all."

Stella had pushed her way through the crowd and set an arm about Julia's shoulders. "The lady of the moment," she said. "So you are going to be able to stay at Primrose Park after all, Jule. I am so happy for you. Mama and Papa were planning to bring you back home with us to live, and I would love that more than anything. But even so—to be able to stay on as mistress of Primrose Park!" She laughed lightly. "But you must choose Malcolm, of course. Then we will be sisters-in-law."

"Oh," Viola said. "Then it must be Gussie, Jule. You and Gussie have always been the best of friends anyway."

"Julia." Camilla had joined them unnoticed. She smiled with quiet sympathy. "That was very naughty of Uncle Humphrey. He has put you in a dreadfully embarrassing situation. I am so sorry."

"Sorry?" Viola's voice rose an octave. "Sorry, Camilla? When Jule has five beaux, including Daniel and Freddie? I wish you could be sorry for me for the same reason."

Aunt Millie caught Julia's eye from across the room and smiled and nodded as she had before. It looked as if she might leave her group at any moment and come to offer her congratulations too.

Julia felt sick. Mortified and sick and unaccustomedly tongue-tied. It was easy to see already what the month's favorite sport was to be. It would be a wonder if the men did not start up a betting book like the ones they were reputed to have at the gentlemen's clubs. Whom would the betting most favor? Daniel? Freddie? Gussie perhaps? Malcolm and Les would doubtless be long shots.

It was going to be a very entertaining month at least. Grandpapa was going to have his wish on that. Entertaining, that was, for everyone but her.

"Excuse me," she said, flashing a smile about on the group of her cousins. "I have to go somewhere." And she pushed past them toward the mercifully uncluttered doorway and beyond. She hurried onward, looking for a hiding place.

3

"I believe," Frederick said after summoning his brother over to the pianoforte with a lazy but steady look and a lift of the eyebrows, "our wisest course at present, Les, would be to hoof it out of here before Mama thinks to look about her for her two sons."

"Uncle made a very fair will," Lesley said, falling into step beside his brother, whose pace was much faster than his leisurely stride might appear to be. "Everyone got something. You can pay your debts, Freddie. That will be a relief to you."

Frederick chuckled as he led the way downstairs and out through the front doors. "With five hundred pounds?" he said. "It would be rather like trying to douse the fire engulfing a large mansion with a thimbleful of water. Besides, Les, how unimaginative it would be to use the gift of five hundred pounds to pay off debts. How are you planning to spend your money?" He clapped a friendly hand on his brother's shoulder.

"I need some new coats," Lesley said. "Mama says mine are threadbare at the seams because I keep forgetting to get new ones. I should go to Weston, do you think, Freddie? He is the best?"

"They don't come any better," Frederick said. "That's the boy, Les. You are learning fast. So what do you think of Jule's legacy, eh?"

"Very kind of Uncle," Les said. "Making sure she stays here where she belongs. I'm glad for her. I like Jule."

"We all do," Frederick said. "The point is, my boy,

which of us is she going to marry? One can never tell with Jule. She does not always do the obvious."

"Dan," Lesley said. "He will be the one, Freddie. He has everything else. He might as well have Primrose Park too. And Jule. She'll be a countess. I'll be glad for her. I like Jule."

"You don't think Dan has altogether too much as it is?" Frederick asked. "Besides, he never much liked her. And he has been paying determined court to the Morriston chit all spring. I think I might have a shot at Jule myself, Les. I have never failed to charm any woman I fancied into my bed. It would be strange if I couldn't charm Jule into matrimony."

"You don't want to marry, though," Les said. "Said so just the other day, Freddie."

"That was before I knew that Primrose Park could be mine with the small inconvenience of a bride," Frederick said. "Quite an inducement, isn't it, Les?"

"It would all be gone in no time at all, though," Lesley said. "Money goes through your fingers like water, Freddie. You always say so. Not fair to Jule. She wouldn't like losing Primrose Park."

"And still being saddled with me after it was gone," Frederick said. "She might reform me, Les. A very strong-minded woman is Jule. And not a bad looker either. It's hard to remember that she was as straight as a pole just a few years ago, isn't it now?"

"She's pretty," Lesley agreed. "I like her."

"Then you must try for her too," Frederick said, giving his brother's shoulder an amiable pat. "That was Uncle's will, after all. The five of us were to compete for her hand. She can award it—and Primrose Park—to whomever she chooses. I like it, Les. I like the odds. It won't be nearly as interesting if there is only me. But Gussie will probably have a try and Malcolm will be talked into it. And Dan will probably try despite everything. He will probably think Primrose Park is his due even if he must take Jule with it. Yes, I like it very well. But you must be in it too."

"Jule wouldn't have me," Les said. "I'm not as clever as Malcolm or as easy with the women as you or as handsome as Dan or as funny as Gussie. She wouldn't have me, Freddie."

"Don't count on it," his brother said. "She may choose sweetness and good humor, Les. You'll give it a try?"

Lesley looked doubtful.

"Just imagine," Frederick said. "If she marries Dan, she will as like as not be spirited away to one of his other properties and may never live again in the house she loves. If she marries Malcolm, she may live a dull life and never lure him outside his library. If she marries Gussie, she may find that after a few years he will be sorry for marrying so young and will want to sow his wild oats. If she marries me, she might lose Primrose Park altogether and she might have to share me with other women. What can you offer to save her from any of those four fates, Les?"

Lesley thought, his expression grave. "I would let her stay here," he said, "and do what she wants. I would let her manage the estate herself if she wished. She could do a better job than I could, I daresay. She is cleverer. Or I would let her choose a good steward. I wouldn't get in her way at all. I would just look after her."

Frederick threw back his head and laughed. "It might work with her too, by Jove," he said. "Good old Les. So you are going to do it. We are arch-rivals from this moment on. Will it come to pistols at dawn, do you suppose?"

"I could never hurt you, Freddie," Lesley said gravely. "Or Dan or Malcolm or Gussie. Besides, Jule wouldn't like it, you know."

Frederick laughed again. "Not unless she was wielding one of the weapons," he said. "I like the look of this summer more and more, Les. I must admit I was less than enamored at the prospect of having to put in an appearance here. And I might not have come at all if I had known we were to be here for a month. But after all it promises to be an entertaining few weeks. Most diverting."

"I just hope Jule is happy at the end of it," Lesley said, frowning again. "I like Jule."

Stella caught up to her brother as he was trying to slip out of the drawing room without anyone noticing him. She linked her arm through his and smiled up at him. She said nothing as he led the way aimlessly along a corridor in the direction of the ballroom.

"The devil," he said at last. "This is the very devil."

"I thought you might be dismayed," she said, squeezing his arm. "Are you running from Mama and Papa? But you know they won't push you into anything you do not want, Malcolm."

"They don't need to." He grimaced. "Sometimes, Stella, there's nothing worse than kind and understanding parents."

"I know what you mean," she said. "They offered Jule a home before the will was read. I am sure the offer will remain open so that she will have an alternative to the choice Uncle has given her."

"That makes it worse," he said. "It just makes it worse, Stella. The burden on my shoulders will be intolerable. And you know that Mama and Papa have got me to agree since my thirtieth birthday that I will start thinking about marriage. They will expect me to go for this one. They'll expect me to offer for Julia."

"Would it be so bad?" she asked, gazing earnestly up at him. "She is one of my dearest friends, Malcolm."

He grimaced. "And she has beauty and vitality and—oh, the devil, Stella. She has everything," he said.

"Malcolm," she said, "you are not ugly. And you have intelligence and learning and good sense. There is no foundation for your dreadful shyness. It is just that—shyness. There is nothing inferior about you. Jule would be fortunate indeed to have you for a husband."

He frowned at her. "Did Mama and Papa send you?" he asked.

"No." She punched his arm. "But I want you to be

happy, Malcolm. I am very much afraid that your shyness will keep you single for the rest of your life. And I don't think bachelorhood will suit you. You need a wife. And children." She smiled impishly. "I need a sister-in-law. And nieces and nephews. Will you try? Will you at least try to talk with Jule? She will not bite your head off."

He sighed.

"Think of the alternatives," she said. "Daniel and Jule have never liked each other. Freddie is—well, Gussie says he is a rake, and I believe it for all his good looks and charm. Or perhaps because of them. Les is—well, Les is Les. And Gussie is too young. You are the perfect choice, Malcolm. You could have a wife within the month and would no longer have to worry yourself into a decline thinking about how you are going to find one."

"I wish Uncle were still alive," he said. "I would rather like to throttle him, Stella. Mama and Papa are going to start in on me as soon as they find me. They will use far less direct persuasion than you are using, but they will be ten times more persuasive for all that. And how am I going to refuse? If all of us refuse, poor Julia will be without a decent home at the end of the month. She doesn't like her father's relatives, does she?"

"They don't want her," Stella said. "Her father was the black sheep, I believe. You will marry her, then, Malcolm? If she will have you?"

"The devil," he said. "I won't have much choice by the time Mama and Papa have finished with me. Though I don't think I'll be able to do it, Stella. I just won't."

She laid her head briefly against his shoulder. "I love you, Malcolm," she said. "I just love you."

"Sometimes," he said, "one could wish one did not have such a loving family. It would be so much easier just to please oneself." He drew a deep breath and expelled it slowly. "What man in his right mind would have made a will like that one?"

*   *   *

"I think it quite outrageous," Aunt Sarah said, seating herself on the pianoforte bench after leading her son away from the other groups still gathered in the drawing room. "That man—your poor dear papa's brother, Daniel!—should not have been allowed to get away with such behavior."

"There is nothing illegal about the will, Mama," the Earl of Beaconswood said. "And Uncle was careful enough to leave something for everyone, even the least of the servants."

"You know very well that I am thinking only of that one ridiculous clause," she said. "It is criminal, Daniel. You must contest it. Primrose Park should have been left to you along with everything else. The properties should not be divided up. The aristocracy of England is only weakened when such a thing happens."

"Primrose Park is unentailed, Mama," he said. "It was Uncle's personal possession, to be disposed of as he chose."

"It is yours," she said. "It is rightfully yours. But now you are going to have to marry Julia in order to get it. Not that I have anything against Julia, of course. But her father was not a frugal man and very little is known of her mother. And she herself has been known to be rather wild in her ways. Your uncle was altogether too indulgent with her. You are going to have to take her in hand, Daniel. I will help you, of course."

"Mama," he said, "I will not be marrying Julia."

"Not—?" She looked at him sharply. "Your reluctance does you credit, Daniel. But to my knowledge there is nothing vicious about the girl. She merely needs taming. And I suppose it is only right that after being an adopted member of this family for so many years she finally become a member in reality. She is pretty enough when she dresses well."

"One of the others will marry her, Mama," he said. "She will be as much a member of the family married to one of them. She will not be married to me."

"But Primrose Park—" she began.

"I don't need it," he said. "I already have more property and wealth than one man needs in this life."

"Daniel." She was becoming annoyed. "You have promised me that you will choose a wife soon. It is time, especially now that your uncle is dead and you have both titles. You owe it to yourself and to your family to provide the earldom with an heir. It would not be wise to delay longer."

"I will have a wife soon, Mama," he said. "She will not be Julia."

She looked up at him sharply. "You have met someone?" she asked. "In London, Daniel? And have not told me? Who is she?"

His look became guarded. "I have prospects," he said. "Unfortunately the Season will be over by the time I can leave here. But no matter. You will have your daughter-in-law before another year has passed, Mama, and a grandchild a year after that in all probability. Possibly a grandson."

She clasped her hands to her bosom. "I knew I could rely on you, Daniel," she said. "You have always been a dutiful son. I need to be able to turn my attention to Camilla. She shows no sign of choosing someone to take Captain Styne's place in her affections, God rest his soul. And she is twenty-four years old. Of course, now she is the sister of the Earl of Beaconswood and will appear that much more attractive to a prospective suitor despite her age."

"Camilla does not need such lures," he said. "She has both beauty and character, Mama."

"Yes." She sighed. "And no inclination to mend a broken heart. But I still believe you should marry Julia, Daniel. I would hate to see this property going to Frederick or Lesley. And Malcolm and Augustus are not even, strictly speaking, family since they are your late aunt's relatives."

"Mama." The earl looked down at his mother with the stern expression she had come to learn meant that further attempts at persuasion were useless. "I will not be courting

Julia. Or offering for her. Or marrying her. I will never be the owner of Primrose Park."

"Well." She sighed. "Your uncle should not have been allowed to get away with it, Daniel. That is all I have to say."

Augustus grinned rather nervously at his parents as they came toward him across the drawing room. He had not moved from his place since the solicitor had finished reading.

"Well, now," his father said jovially, "what are you planning to do with five hundred pounds, Augustus? Eh?"

"I'll think of something," Augustus said. "Something useless, you may be assured, Papa. I would hate to waste such an unexpected windfall on something useful."

"We would not expect you to," his mother said, laughing. "Would we, Paul? That reading lasted a very long time. Were you dreadfully bored?" She sat down beside her son.

"Marvelously entertained actually, Mama," he said. "How would you fancy your son being a staid landowner at the grand age of one and twenty? Do you think the image would fit?"

His mother laid a hand on his arm.

His father coughed. "We wanted to talk to you about that, Augustus," he said. "You are one of the nephews, certainly, but you must not feel yourself obligated by that particular clause of the will."

Augustus grinned again. "I thought it great fun," he said. "I didn't realize that Uncle was such a jolly good sport. Though I expect Jule to be hopping mad. She went flying out of here like shot from a gun when it was all over. I'm glad I was not in her path. I would surely have ended up with two black eyes before I could have got my fists up."

"Augustus." His mother covered one of his hands with hers. "It is not a game, dear. Whoever offers for Julia and marries her will be married to her for life."

"I think it would be fun to be married to Jule," Augustus said.

"Marriage is not fun," she said. "At least, it is much more than that, Augustus. Sometimes it is frustrating and occasionally tedious. Forgive me, my love?" She glanced up at her husband, who was smiling ruefully at her. "Always it is hard work if it is to survive with any degree of tolerability."

"Jule and I have always been the best of pals," Augustus said.

"And friendship is important in marriage," she said. "But it is not everything, Augustus. Oh, what we are trying to say—"

"What we are trying to say, son," his father said, "is that you are too young to be thinking of matrimony."

"But Jule isn't?" Augustus raised his eyebrows.

"That is different altogether," his father said. "Women are ready for marriage far sooner than men. It is because of the childbearing, you know."

"And because women mature very much sooner than men," his mother added.

"And that too," his father agreed. "Don't make a mistake you will regret, Augustus, my boy. Let someone else marry Julia. There will be other women for you to marry when you get older."

Augustus had lost his grin. His expression had become rather mulish. "What is wrong with Jule?" he asked. "Is her birth not good enough for the Craybournes?"

"That was uncalled for, son," his father said. "There is nothing at all wrong with Julia. We are fond of her, your mother and I, and always have been."

"But not as a daughter-in-law," Augustus said.

"We came here planning to offer her a home for as long as she needs one," his mother said. "We really are fond of her, Augustus, and with Susan married and gone we would be quite happy to fill the empty space in our family. And Viola has always been excessively fond of her, as have you. We do not object to her as your wife, Augustus. But not

yet. Not for at least three or four years yet. You have
scarcely finished university. You have had no chance to experience something of life."

"I know enough," Augustus said. "And I am of age,
Mama."

"Yes." His father sighed. "You are of age, my boy. And
so we cannot command, you see, only advise. We advise
you to wait, Augustus. We advise you very strongly."

"Because we love you," his mother said. "And because
we are fond of Julia too. We would hate to see either one of
you unhappy."

"I could make Julia happy," he said. "And she could
make me happy."

His parents exchanged helpless looks.

"Well," his father said, "we will say no more, Augustus.
Just promise us one thing, will you? Don't marry Julia just
to spite us, just to show us that you are a man now. Do it if
you must only because you truly believe it is the right thing
for the both of you. Promise me?"

"Augustus?" His mother looked anxiously into his face.

"Parents!" Augustus said in exasperation, blowing air
from puffed cheeks. "Do all parents believe their children
are infants in perpetuity, I wonder? Credit me with some
sense. All right, I promise. Besides, Julia may say no, you
know. I'm quite sure she is boiling mad over this whole
thing. I stole one look at her and I could tell."

His mother smiled tentatively at his father. They wisely
said no more.

Julia found a hiding place in the conservatory. It was her
rainy day refuge, a room that was all glass on three sides
and overlooked a rose arbor and a lawn beyond it that
sloped downward toward the trees surrounding the lake.
The lake was not visible from the house. This was no rainy
day, of course, but she needed to be alone. She sat on one
of the window seats and drew a curtain across in front of
her. She drew up her knees, clasped her arms about them,
and set her chin on them.

She tried to digest what she had just heard. And yet at the same time she did not want to think about it. He had let her down. Grandpapa had shown her that after all she was not one of his family. He had left her nothing. She was going to have to go to her uncle in the north of England. But perhaps she would try to get a position as a governess instead, she thought, so that she would not have to rely on his charity, as she had relied upon Grandpapa's all these years. It had been charity. She had no right to feel angry with him for leaving her nothing.

She did not feel angry, she told herself. Only hurt and very, very depressed. She would leave immediately, she had decided at first, when she was still in the drawing room, instead of waiting for a month. But her journey was to be paid for out of Grandpapa's estate. Probably Mr. Prudholm would not allow that payment to be made within the month. She could ask someone else to pay for the journey, of course. Uncle Henry would probably agree to do so, or Uncle Paul. Daniel probably would not—not that she would ask him anyway. But it would be charity again. It humiliated her to know that she did not have even enough money of her own to pay for a stagecoach journey to the north of England. She had never needed much money before. Grandpapa had paid all her bills, and she had never been extravagant.

That insane—competition, for want of a better word! Despite herself Julia started to feel angry. How could Grandpapa have humiliated her so?

How they must be gloating, the five of them. *Here is Julia, desperate for a husband and a home. Who will be the highest bidder or the most convincing liar? She will be grateful for anyone. Anyone! Poor orphaned Julia. Poor Julia, one-and-twenty years old and unmarried. No one wants her. She has to be offered along with Primrose Park. The house and estate at least are attractive.*

She was not angry, Julia thought. She was furious. If any of them tried to come near her with a gleam of triumph in his eye . . . If any of them laughed at her . . . If any of them affected to have fallen madly in love with her . . . Well, let any of them try and see what they got, she thought. She had not lost the ability to deal out bloody noses and stinging ears merely because she was one-and-twenty and supposedly a lady. Sometimes a lady had to defend herself.

If they wanted her to act like a lady, then they could jolly well treat her like one. They could leave her alone. Strictly alone for one whole month. She hated them all anyway. Freddie had had a smirk on his face while the solicitor had been reading. Daniel had been looking supercilious. Even Lesley had smiled when there was no occasion to smile. She had not seen Malcolm or Gussie, but she would wager that Gussie thought it all a huge joke.

Men! And Grandpapa too. What a cruel joke!

She could cry, Julia thought. Or scream. Or go galloping off on her horse, Flossie, in a straight line, dealing with hedges and gates and other obstacles as she came to them. The thought was enormously tempting. She might well have given in to it, but someone had found her sanctuary. The door had opened and someone had stepped inside the conservatory.

Julia sat very still for a few moments. But whoever had come in was not going out again in a hurry. She even heard a soft oath, the type of obscenity that Gussie liked to use, though it was not Gussie's voice. Curiosity got the better of her and she leaned forward to peer cautiously around the edge of the curtain. She sighed.

"I might have known you would be the first to find me," she said out loud, not even trying to keep the sarcasm and hostility out of her voice. "Well, here I am. Deliver your speech."

Then she flung back the curtain and swung her legs to the floor. She could not hide for a whole month after all. She might as well come out with fists swinging. Figuratively speaking, anyway.

4

The Earl of Beaconswood left his mother in the drawing room. But he would, he knew, run into other family members soon and they would all wish to share their impressions of the will with him. He would prefer to have some time alone. It irked him to know that he was stuck at Primrose Park for a whole month. He could, he supposed, leave and return to London for what remained of the Season. He did not intend to have anything to do with the courting of Julia, and there was nothing physically stopping him from just leaving.

But other factors prevented him from doing it, of course. Although he was not the owner of Primrose Park and never would be, nevertheless in the absence of a real owner he must consider himself the host since he was head of the family. It would not do for him to leave. It would be unmannerly to say the least, and he prided himself on his good manners.

And then, of course, his uncle had requested that they all stay for a month. It was a man's dying wish or dying command. Honor dictated, then, that he stay. Besides, there was Julia. He was under no obligation whatsoever to her. Yet his uncle had accepted her as a responsibility and he was his uncle's successor. He must wait to see that she was settled somehow into a secure and satisfactory future.

Even if he did go back to London, he thought, he would not be able to participate in any of the social events of the Season. He was in mourning. It was all very well for his uncle to command them all to put off their blacks the next day, and doubtless they would do so, improper as it seemed. Again it was a dying man's wish. But that would apply only within the privacy of Primrose Park. If he returned to London, he would consider it essential both to wear mourning and to curtail his activities as the man who had inherited the deceased earl's title and fortune.

And so he was stuck. He had thought at first when he had listened to the request that they all stay for one month that perhaps he would invite Blanche and her parents to visit Primrose Park. But the idea had died almost before it had been conceived. How could he invite them to a home that was not his own? How could he invite them to a family gathering that included no other outside guests? If he and Blanche had been betrothed, perhaps it might have been possible. But they were not.

By the time he returned to London, he thought, she would be gone. He would have to find out where she had been taken for the summer and pursue her there if he was prepared to make his intentions so obvious. Or he would have to wait for next year and hope that no one else attached her in the meanwhile.

He was not in a good mood as he sought out a quiet haven, somewhere where he was least likely to be interrupted until everyone had recovered from the initial excitement of hearing the will. The conservatory might be the place, he thought, opening the door gingerly and stepping inside. Yes, he was right. It was unoccupied. He closed the door gratefully behind him. He would give himself the luxury of an hour to himself. An hour that might have been spent with Blanche if he were in London. He swore softly.

Then a voice spoke and he knew that he was not alone after all. And if he could have chosen one occupant of the house whom he least wished to encounter at that particular moment it would have been the very person who spoke.

"I might have known you would be the first to find me," she said. "Well, here I am. Deliver your speech."

He could not see her at first. But then one of the partly drawn curtains was pulled aside and she swung her legs down from the window seat, showing a quite indecorous display of ankle and leg as she did so. He felt instant annoyance.

"Meaning?" he asked her.

"I suppose it *is* quite a carrot," she said. Her tone was not at all pleasant. To be fair, he guessed that she had been as intent on being solitary as he had been. "A beautiful house built less than a century ago, filled with treasures of art and furnishings and draperies and decoration. A large and lovely park. Prosperous farms and healthy rents. It would be quite the jewel in your crown, would it not, Daniel? But it comes with me. Inseparable and indivisible. A minor annoyance."

He should have been amused, he knew, at her presumption. Instead he was unaccountably angry. "Minor?" he said, making an effort to keep his voice controlled and icy. "I might have used another adjective, Julia. Perhaps it is as well that I believe my crown to be sufficiently studded with gems."

He was proud of the setdown. She sat and glared at him. Julia had never been able to control her emotions. And yet control was an essential quality in a lady, he believed. Or in someone bent on quarreling.

"Your choices are not quite as numerous as you might have imagined," he said. "But then you may find it easier to choose among four rather than five, Julia. I will not be a contestant."

She pursed her lips and regarded him through narrowed eyes. "That," she said, indignation making her voice vibrate, "is one small mercy. Does that mean we will be losing your company, Daniel? I for one will be devastated."

He was not quite sure why they hated each other so much or when exactly it had started. She had always been one of the children, deplorably noisy and badly behaved. But that alone would not have aroused hatred in him. He did not hate his other younger cousins who had been equally unruly once upon a time—the boys anyway. However, that was not a problem to be considered at this precise moment.

"I could help you narrow the field further," he said. "If you are willing to listen to advice, of course."

He expected to be told in no uncertain terms where he could go and what he could do when he got there, but she smiled. Unpleasantly. She set her hands flat on the window seat on either side of her and leaned forward, all apparent eagerness.

"Oh, by all means, Daniel," she said. "Advise me."

She was damned pretty when she was angry, the earl thought. Or when she was not angry for that matter. Though *pretty* was rather a tame word to describe her appeal. It was not just her face or the neatness of her figure. There was something very—well, very attractive about Julia. If she behaved more like a lady, he would not have noticed it. She had no business flaunting her sexuality.

"I would not accept Freddie if I were you," he said. "He is always in need of funds and would like nothing better than to gain possession of these farms and rents. But he would gamble it all away faster than the rents could come in. Besides, he needs more than one w—" The trouble with someone like Julia, he thought, as he stopped himself midword, was that she sometimes made a man forget that he was a gentleman.

She leaned a little farther forward. "The word could not have been *wife*," she said. "I have heard that Freddie can be a little wild, but I do not believe that even he would try bigamy. He needs more than one woman, Daniel? My charms would not be enough to hold his interest, you believe? How lowering."

She was toying with him. She was beginning to enjoy herself. His best course would be to leave the room without another word and go find himself another retreat. But he would be damned before he would leave the last word with Julia.

"And Malcolm is too old for you," he said curtly.

"Is he?" She raised her eyebrows and smiled at him again. "Nine years is too wide an age gap, you think, Daniel? But there are eight between you and me."

And eleven between him and Blanche. "Another reason why I will not be offering for you," he said. "I prefer maturity in women."

If he had hoped to wither her with the setdown he was to be disappointed. Her smile held. "Are we talking about physical maturity?" she asked. "You prefer ripe fruit?"

He willed himself neither to flush nor to lower his eyes from hers. "You are the only lady I know, Julia," he said, "who can always be relied upon to be vulgar."

She chose not to take issue with the insult. "It will have to be Gussie, then," she said. "You cannot have any objection to him, can you, Daniel?"

"Gussie is too young for you," he said.

"We are the same age." She stared at him blankly. "In fact he is four months and three days older than I. At one time we even knew how many hours, but I have forgotten."

"He needs time to spread his wings," he said. "He does not need the ties of matrimony yet." He was feeling thoroughly annoyed with himself. Why was he giving her this advice, anyway? Sound as it was, it was unlikely that she would pay it any heed. Besides, why should he be interested in protecting her from a poor marriage? What difference did it make to him? Except that he was his uncle's successor and he had always been damnably burdened with a sense of duty. But perhaps it was not Julia he was protecting, he thought. Perhaps it was his cousins. He would not wish Julia on his worst enemy. But the sheer unreasonableness of the thought made him frown and increased his irritation.

"Especially with me," she said. "Gussie does not need to be chained for life to me. That was your meaning, was it not? Your low opinion of me as a matrimonial prospect is devastating me, Daniel. That leaves Les. He is three-and-twenty, neither too young nor too old. I would lay odds that he does not gamble—oh, that was a strange turn of words—and I can't imagine Les needing more than one w—?" She pointedly left the word incomplete. "I believe he would be pleased to own Primrose Park. And he would be kind enough to be pleased to own me too. Yes, Les would be by far the most sensible choice. Thank you, Daniel. Your advice has been most helpful."

"Les is too sweet," he said, "and too slow. He would not suit you at all, Julia."

She sighed. "Because he would be unable to keep a tight enough hand on my reins?" she said.

For exactly that reason. "If you wish," he said. "The words are yours."

"Oh, dear," she said. "Perhaps I should save everyone a month of suspense here and recall Mr. Prudholm tomorrow. I should announce that none of my five male cousins will suit me. Or should that be phrased the other way around, Daniel? I would not suit any of my five male cousins. I could be on my way to my uncle's without delay." Her tone was bright and brittle. He sensed that she had perhaps moved a step beyond anger into something else.

"You are eager to go and live with your uncle?" he asked.

She laughed and got to her feet to turn her back on him and gaze out of the window. "Oh, of course," she said. "I can hardly wait. And I am sure that they cannot wait either. They have only five children of their own."

"They do not want you?" he asked, frowning. It would be just like Julia to make him feel guilty now, to make him feel that he had been ungracious and ungentlemanly, suggesting to her that she was not wanted in his family either.

"Do you expect me to admit that?" she asked, looking over her shoulder at him. "Shall I weep with abject misery and arouse your pity after all, Daniel? Could it be done, I wonder? But it would be mean of me to do so. In reality I am in an enviable position. For five gentlemen I am the key to the possession of a stately and prosperous estate. For the next month I am to have the affections of five men to toy with before I choose one of them and gift him with myself and Primrose Park—not necessarily in order of importance. Oh, pardon me, that is four, is it?"

He felt foolish for the flash of pity he had felt for a moment and angry that he had allowed her to manipulate him. "You will not take my advice, then?" he asked.

"That was no advice, Daniel," she said scornfully. "If I followed your advice I would be without a husband and without a home at the end of the next month. How foolish you are. I have lived here most of my life and I love this place. I have a chance to make it my home for life. A good chance. I am hardly likely to let it slip through my fingers. I will be betrothed at the end of the month—to Freddie perhaps. Or perhaps to Malcolm. Or to Gussie or Les. Or perhaps even to you." She chuckled softly. "Perhaps if you see me about to spoil the life of one of your cousins, Daniel, you will decide to behave with extraordinary gallantry and marry me yourself."

"It would have to snow in hell first," he said.

She laughed again. "If you will excuse me," she said, taking a step forward, "I must put an end to this delightful tête-à-tête, Daniel. This room is not large enough to hold two."

He held up a staying hand and bowed stiffly to her. "That at least makes good sense," he said. "But since you were the first here, I shall leave you to it. Never let it be said that I have no gallantry at all."

He left the room and resisted the urge to slam the door behind him. He felt uncomfortably hot. Good Lord, he had been scrapping with her like an unruly boy. He had allowed her to drag him down to her level by engaging in a spiteful quarrel with her. And the worst of it was, he did not know why. He did not know why the very sight of her—no, even the thought of her—could make him bristle.

He left the house by a side door and wandered in the direction of the stables. He had not even seen the woman for six years. Had he disliked her so intensely during those summers when he had always come to Primrose Park? But how could he have? She had been just a girl. The eight-year age difference had been far more significant then than it was now.

He could remember always disapproving of her, of

course. At a time when the other girls—his sister and Susan and even the younger Viola and Stella—had been quieting down and realizing that there was a difference between what a growing boy was allowed to do for enjoyment and what was expected of a girl, Julia had played with the boys with as much daring and abandon as ever.

He had always thought that Grandpapa should have spanked her a few times when she was a child and hired a stricter governess for her when she got older—one who would not have spared the rod. He had even told her so a few times. But had she made him burn with anger and even hatred as she did now?

There had been that last summer, of course, when she had been just as wild as ever, riding astride, swimming fully clothed, running foot races—all at a time when she was budding out all over. He could remember feeling furious—oh, yes, there had been some fury even then—when Freddie had witnessed the way he had been staring at her when she had emerged from the lake one time, her light dress plastered to her newly budding curves, and had dug him in the ribs with an elbow and laughed in that way Freddie had of laughing.

He could remember wishing at that moment that it had been in keeping with his twenty-three-year-old dignity to dive into the lake himself, fully clothed, to cool off. But he had been furious with Julia for embarrassing him, for flaunting herself, for being foolishly oblivious to the effect she was having on the twenty-year-old Freddie and even on Gussie.

He had been at a stage of his own development when he had thought that such feelings as he was experiencing were appropriate only in a brothel. It had horrified him to know that he had been aroused by his own cousin—or stepcousin to be more accurate. By Julia. Good God. No real lady would allow a man to feel that way about her. Julia was no lady. She was vulgar.

The earl had reached the stables, but he changed his mind about riding. It would be time to get ready for dinner soon. It would not do to be late for dinner in his new capacity as head of the family. He sighed. Sometimes it was a burden to have such responsibilities. He had had them in some form or another since his father's death when he was only fourteen. Now they were more than doubled. Occasionally it seemed to him that he had missed a youth. He thought of Blanche and sighed again.

And so yes, he could see now that the intense disapproval of Julia had been there even before she had tried to turn him back from her grandfather's door a little less than two weeks before. He had just forgotten, that was all. But it had not taken him long to remember.

It was going to be a long month, he thought as he turned back reluctantly toward the house.

Julia sat between Camilla and Uncle Paul at dinner and talked cheerfully about anything and nothing. She would not give anyone the satisfaction of seeing that she had been rattled by the events of the afternoon, she had decided when she was getting ready to come downstairs. She still wore a black dress, of course, since it had been agreed that mourning would not be left off until the next day. But she had allowed her maid to spend longer than usual brushing her curls until they shone and sat in a decent style.

She did not glance down the table to where Daniel was sitting. He had had the gall to sit at the head of the table, in Grandpapa's place. He was the new earl, of course, and he was the head of the family. But even so he was not the owner of Primrose Park and never would be. That honor would belong to her and—someone. She was very careful not to catch the eye of any of the male cousins either.

It was all dreadfully mortifying.

The complexion of things had changed, of course, since she had been foolish enough to quarrel with Daniel in the conservatory. She should know from experience that it was never safe to quarrel because she always lost her temper when she did and as like as not ended up saying or doing something rash.

Today she had been more reckless than usual. She had told him that she was going to marry one of the cousins, perhaps even him. She had thrown down the gauntlet. There could be no backing down now even though she had no wish whatsoever to marry any of them, even Gussie, her particular friend. In fact, the idea of marrying Gussie was downright embarrassing. But she would have to marry one of them just to prove to Daniel that she could do it. If she went back on her word he would doubtless believe that none of them had wanted to marry her.

So she was going to have to lure one of them into offering for her. She was going to have to betroth herself to one of them. She might break if off afterward, of course, if it proved to be just too intolerable, but for the next month she would have to play the game. It was a thoroughly objectionable thought.

And she had Daniel to thank for it all. She glanced along the table at him despite herself and grudgingly conceded that his slim, muscular figure showed to advantage in black. She had not noticed before just how rich a brown his hair was. Well, he was handsome, she thought crossly. That did not mean that he had a pleasant character.

"Julia," Camilla said when Uncle Paul turned to speak with Aunt Eunice at his other side, "you are upset, aren't you? I can hardly blame you."

"Upset?" Julia looked at her in surprise. She had scarcely stopped prattling and laughing.

"You are too bright, too cheerful," Camilla said. "I recognize the signs. I used to do it sometimes in the months following Simon's death when I was afraid that people were going to press their sympathy on me."

It was hard to imagine Camilla prattling and laughing. She was sweetly grave and had been even as a girl, even before she had met and become betrothed to her captain. Well, perhaps not quite so grave.

"You must not let it worry you," Camilla said. "As Mr. Prudholm pointed out, there is no compulsion on you to marry anyone. Unless you are dreadfully attached to Primrose Park, that is. Are you?"

"I am rather," Julia said. "But in the nature of things a woman expects to leave her home when she grows up."

"In order to marry," Camilla said. "Not just because the man of the house has died. Though it happens often enough, I suppose. But don't let any of them harass you, Julia. I don't think any of them will, though Freddie might. Just don't allow it. If I can help, do call on me. A female companion at your side will dampen anyone's ardor, you may be sure." She smiled.

"Thank you." Julia gave her first genuine smile of the evening. "It is all rather embarrassing, you know. Everyone is going to be watching me for the next month and wondering who will offer for me and whom I will choose. What if no one offers? That would be a little mortifying." She giggled rather nervously.

As if to prove one of her points Aunt Millie was nodding and smiling encouragingly at her all through dinner as she had done every time she had spotted Julia since that afternoon. And everyone was watching her curiously, Julia thought self-consciously looking about her and finding that almost no one was. She looked down at her empty plate and wondered how many courses had already been eaten and what they had consisted of.

But she need not have worried about the cousins ignoring her, she discovered when dinner was over. Stella and Viola called her to the pianoforte when the ladies adjourned to the drawing room and they took turns playing and singing. Frederick, Lesley, and Augustus joined them there when the men came in from the dining room soon after. Frederick leaned indolently on the pianoforte while Augustus turned pages of the music for Viola and Lesley sang once with Stella. He had a pleasant tenor voice. The earl wandered out onto the balcony close by the pianoforte, Julia noticed out of the corner of her eye. She was glad he had not joined them.

But things were not the same as they usually were, she

thought crossly after a while. She always enjoyed herself immensely when all the cousins were together. But now no one was behaving quite naturally, including herself. Freddie was lolling against the pianoforte, his dark eyes watching her from beneath lazy eyelids, one lock of dark hair down across his forehead. Les was smiling at her more than at any of the others. Gussie was avoiding her eyes and pretending she was not there. Stella and Viola were laughing a little too merrily and a little too loudly. And Daniel was standing silently out on the balcony. What noise she expected him to be making when he was out there alone she did not stop to ask herself. But she could feel his presence there almost like a heavy hand pressing against the back of her neck.

"Warm, Jule?" Frederick asked, smiling lazily at her.

"Yes, I am," she said. "There seems to be no air coming through the windows at all."

"Aunt Millie shut all except the French windows," Viola said. "You know how terrified she is of drafts."

"The air will be cool outside, though, Jule," Frederick said, his voice almost a caress. She looked sharply at him but he was still standing there being Freddie. "Come on. I'll take you out for a stroll in the gardens."

"All right," she said warily. Normally she would have accepted such an invitation with alacrity and without suspicion despite the fact that she had been aware of Freddie's reputation for a long time. But this was not a normal situation. However, a beginning had to be made somewhere. "Thank you, Freddie."

He pushed himself to an upright position with apparent effort. Lesley was frowning down at a piece of music. The girls pretended to have heard nothing. Augustus turned away to gaze nonchalantly at a picture on the wall.

"That is the best idea anyone has had all evening, Freddie," another voice said. "It is delightfully cool outside. I shall join you and Julia if I may. Stella, would you care to come too?"

He must have been standing out on the balcony with his

ear pinned to the curtain, Julia thought indignantly, looking at the very handsome form of the earl and noting with satisfaction that he must be all of two inches shorter than Freddie and his hair at least two shades lighter. And he did not have that interesting lock of hair across the forehead or the dark bedroom eyes that Freddie could use to such effect. Of course, he did have blue eyes, and he did have the aristocratic nose. But even so . . .

"I'll come too," Viola said. "Les?"

Frederick chuckled when the six of them had left the drawing room and he was leading the way downstairs, Julia on his arm. "I can guarantee you one thing, Jule," he said. "You are going to be better chaperoned during the coming month than you have ever been in your life. How are you going to like that, eh?"

She could hear the earl talking to Stella just behind them. What she would really like to do was turn and resume the afternoon's quarrel with him. She knew what he was about. He did not want to have anything to do with her himself, but he was going to make very sure that she had no chance with any of the other cousins either. He just could not bear the thought of her becoming one of the family. And he would die before he would see one of them become owner of Primrose Park. He would prefer to see it pass to Grandpapa's chosen charity.

Well, they would see about that, she thought.

"I always thought chaperons a foolish idea," she said. "Especially when one is at one's own home with one's own family. I don't think we should tolerate having chaperons about us, Freddie."

Which was a very bold and probably a very rash thing to say to Freddie of all people, she thought as he slanted her a grin.

5

That was an invitation if ever he had heard one, Frederick thought. A not very proper invitation from a lady who had been brought up to behave properly. But one could always expect the unexpected from Jule, bless her heart.

It had been rather like a blessing from heaven, that will. Not so much the five hundred pounds, which was a negligible sum, but the prospect of owning Primrose Park. And the competition could only whet his appetite, for gaming, gambling on the outcome of what was not at all certain, was the breath of life to Frederick.

If the stakes were high and if he had a good chance of winning and if he could not afford to lose—then a game became irresistible. This game was irresistible. Primrose Park was the prize. Winning Julia was something that could be done, if he exercised care. And he certainly could not afford to lose. He was in dun territory and only one step ahead of his creditors. His best way out of the mess—marrying a wealthy wife—had seemed not an option, given his reputation. Until his uncle had presented him with the chance of marrying Julia, that was.

And she had just issued an open invitation.

"How about a stroll to the lake and back?" he suggested when they were all out on the terrace and had gathered in a group. "I believe the air is warm enough."

There were murmurs of assent and they all set off along the terrace, past the rose arbor, down the sloping lawn, and in among the trees. Except that now, outside the house, Frederick maneuvered matters so that he and Julia brought

up the rear. And eventually, before everyone else reached
the lake, they were not even doing that. It was the simplest
thing in the world to dodge behind a tree, holding Julia by
the arm, move off to one side with her at a steady trot,
dodge behind a few more trees, and consider that the two of
them had well and truly lost the others. It was almost dark.
In a matter of minutes it would be fully so.

Julia was laughing softly. "Oh, well done, Freddie," she
said. "I always did believe that chaperons were made to be
lost. You did it almost too easily."

"What was Dan up to?" he asked, stopping to lean back
against a tree. He folded his arms across his chest and lifted
one booted foot to set flat against the trunk. "Protecting
your reputation, Jule? Or protecting his own interests?"

"Trying to spoil everything for me," she said. "He is
quite detestable, Freddie, and I hate him. He has always
been unbearably stuffy for as long as I have known him."

"You had better not marry him, then," he said. "You
would worry each other into an early grave, Jule. If I remember correctly, Dan's objection to you always used to
be that you were not nearly stuffy enough—though he did
not put it in quite those words. Do you remember the time
you fell into the lake out of a tree branch?"

"I *jumped* in," she said, "because you dared me to, Freddie."

"Did I?" he said. "It sounds altogether likely. I do remember Dan standing on the bank looking like a Bond
Street beau as you fished yourself out looking for all the
world like a drowned rat. He told you that it might have
taught you a lesson if your head had collided with a large
stone at the bottom of the lake."

"That was the time Gussie called him a pompous ass,"
Julia said. "After he was safely out of earshot, of course.
You boys were always a little afraid of Daniel's fists. I
thought it a fitting description anyway and have only been
sorry that it is not good manners for a lady to use such language in public."

He laughed. "I didn't bring you out here and dodge chaperons and trees only to reminisce about our growing years," he said.

Julia frowned. "Why did you bring me out here, Freddie?" she asked. "We might as well have it out in the open. You are not going to tell me that you have conceived a violent and undying passion for me, are you?"

"Since you put it that way, no," he said. "Decidedly not. I can see it would not work. You are too perceptive by half, Jule. I should be able to look at you like this"—his eyes gazed meltingly into hers from beneath drooped eyelids and then slowly roamed upward to her hairline and downward to her mouth—"and touch you like this"—one hand reached out so that his fingertips feathered along one side of her jaw and cupped her chin lightly while his thumb touched her lips—"and murmur that you have grown up under my very nose and become an enticing and a beautiful woman without warning. And then your knees should buckle and you should be my slave for life." He dropped his hand.

"How foolish," she said. "Do other women fall for it, Freddie?"

He chuckled. He was almost glad she had not. He did not like a game with high stakes to be too, too easy. "By the dozen," he said. "But you would be onto my game in a flash, wouldn't you?"

"You have no fondness for me, then?" She sighed. "What a shame."

"Oh, I did not say that," he said. "I am very fond of you, Jule. I always have been. And you really have grown up in the last few years. You are enticing enough to make any red-blooded male's pulse quicken."

"Am I?" She smiled at him. "And do you want to marry me, Freddie?"

He smiled at her lazily. "The thought has its appeal," he said.

"Because I am beautiful and pulse-quickening and you are fond of me?" she asked.

"But of course," he said softly.

"Not because of Primrose Park?" she asked. "And not because of the state of your pockets?"

He reached out one hand and cupped her chin again. "Who told you my pockets were to let?" he asked. "Anyone? Or has my reputation preceded me here and you have drawn your own conclusions? It is not true, you know. I like to gamble now and then but never more than I can afford to lose. Are you afraid I would gamble Primrose Park away?"

She looked steadily back into his eyes. "Yes," she said. "You would marry me for Primrose Park, wouldn't you, Freddie? Don't say no. I know you would be lying."

He removed his hand and touched one finger lightly to her nose. Julia was no one's fool. "I really am fond of you, Jule," he said. "You should know the truth of that. We would deal well together."

"I would deal well with Gussie too," she said. "Or even with Les. And perhaps with Malcolm too. Not with Daniel, I must admit. But with any of the others. What could you offer me more than that, Freddie? I am curious to know."

"A title one day," he said. "You would be a baroness, Jule. Not that I wish any ill health on my father, of course."

"I could be a countess with Daniel or a future baroness with Malcolm," she said. "What else, Freddie?"

He grinned suddenly. "I have been trying to avoid the obvious answer, Jule," he said, "because I am a gentleman. But if you insist, I will oblige. A damned good time in bed, that's what I can offer you. It's a promise. And don't pretend that the idea does not appeal to you at all. You are twenty-one years old, aren't you? You must have dreamed of being treated to a good time between the sheets."

"Oh, for shame," she said. "You never were a gentleman, Freddie. You never were. But you have never so blatantly tried to put me to the blush."

"I'll wager I have succeeded too," he said. "It's a pity it is too dark to see your complexion, Jule." He reached out suddenly and captured one of her wrists. He slid his foot down the tree trunk and set it on the ground. "Come here and let me show you something."

"What?" she asked warily.

"Let me show you how pleasant a kiss can be," he said.

"I know how pleasant a kiss can be," she said. "I am no green girl. Do you think I have never been kissed, Freddie?"

"Probably not as I am going to do it," he said. "If you want a preview of what I can offer you, Jule, come here."

Julia took a step forward at the same moment as the Earl of Beaconswood's voice spoke. "Ah, here you are," he said. "We lost you in the gathering darkness. You are wise to shelter here. There is a cool evening breeze coming off the lake. It would be as well to get back, I believe, before the ladies take a chill. Do you want to walk with Stella, Julia?"

Frederick was amused. Disappointed too, yes—he would have enjoyed kissing Jule both for the sheer pleasure of doing so and for the chance to begin his campaign in earnest. But there was plenty of time. And with someone as sharp as Jule it was as well to move slowly, cautious inch by cautious inch.

In no time at all they were all headed back to the house again, Lesley with Viola, Stella and Julia together, Frederick and the earl behind the others.

"Let me get this straight, Dan," Frederick said when the others had walked on out of earshot. "Are you trying to stop me from winning this competition because you want the prize? Or are you trying to stop it because you don't want anyone to win?"

"It was just not the thing," the earl said, "taking her off into the darkness of the trees without a chaperon, Freddie. Aunt Millie should have spoken up as soon as you suggested the walk. Or else my mother or one of the other aunts."

"Perhaps," Frederick said, "they remember that Jule is of age. Or perhaps they trust me not to hurt her."

"I know what you were about to do with her," the earl said. "I have both eyes and ears in my head, Freddie."

"I was going to kiss her," Frederick said. "Is it so strange for a twenty-six-year-old man to want to kiss a twenty-one-year-old woman when she is both lovely and willing? And when he intends to marry her?"

"Until this afternoon," the earl said, "you had no more thought of marrying, Freddie, than of entering a monastery. I won't have you toying with Julia's affections. She is not up to your experience."

"I would hope not." Frederick chuckled and clapped a hand on his cousin's shoulder. "I can't make you out, Dan. Do you want Jule for yourself? I can't quite imagine it. You seemed in a fair way to getting yourself a leg shackle in London no more than a couple of weeks ago. If you don't want Jule, then you should be happy to leave her for one of us. It's time she was married, and we are all fond of her, you know."

"And of Primrose Park," the earl said. "And of its rents."

Frederick tutted. "Now that was below the belt, Dan," he said. "I have yet to meet the man who did not feel that life was lived more comfortably when he was in funds. Of course I am fond of Primrose Park and its rents. That does not mean that I am not fond of Jule."

"Just don't step out of line with her," the earl said. "She can't look after herself. She does not have the sense. She never did. And since she doesn't, then I have to look out for her. I am head of this family after all. And she is one of it even if not by blood. Uncle made her one of the family. So watch your step, Freddie, or you will have me to reckon with."

Frederick looked at him sidelong and laughed with genuine amusement. "Well, well," he said. "This competition could grow very interesting indeed. Poor Jule. I wonder if she is enjoying herself."

The Earl of Beaconswood did not comment.

Very interesting, Frederick thought. If Dan was out of the competition, it would be more easily won. On the other hand, there would be less of a challenge. But perhaps the real challenge would be in determining whether Dan was in or not. And perhaps even Dan himself did not know.

Julia awoke very early the next morning and could not get back to sleep again no matter how much she tossed and turned. She was to put off her mourning that day, she remembered. No more wearing black. The thought brought relief with it—she hated wearing black. But it also brought grief. Was Grandpapa to be so easily forgotten?

She had forgiven him during the night, before finally falling asleep. It was a dreadful thing he had done to her, but she knew it had been done out of love. Grandpapa had always believed that she could find happiness only in marriage. And she tended to agree with him. But not in just any marriage. Only with someone she could love and respect and like. Grandpapa had tried to ensure beyond the grave that she would marry and that she would retain the home that had been hers from childhood. Not many men would have done as much for a granddaughter who was not strictly speaking a granddaughter.

Julia gave up the attempt to get back to sleep and sat up, swinging her legs over the side of the bed. She knew what she would like to do. She often did it on summer mornings. But only ever when there were no visitors at the house. The days of heedless youth were long in the past and had been succeeded by an almost decorous adulthood. But when she was alone at the house, with only Grandpapa and Aunt Millie for company, she had often run down to the lake early on a summer morning for a swim.

She could not do that today. The house was full of visitors. There was far too much chance of being seen and chided. She glanced at the clock on the mantel. It was a little before six. Even most of the servants were probably still in bed. No one else would be up for at least two hours, more probably three or four. She could be back from a swim in less than an hour.

She hesitated even so, but when she crossed the room to

the window and drew the curtains aside, it was to find the perfect day greeting her eyes. The early morning sun was shining down from a cloudless sky. It was going to be a scorcher, she thought. The very best time of such a day was now before the heat made the outdoors almost oppressive.

Just a short swim, she thought, peeling off her nightgown and dashing through into her dressing room to pull on some clothes without ringing for her maid and dragging the poor girl from her bed. She would be back well before seven, and she knew that she would feel fresh and invigorated for the rest of the day. An early morning swim was even better than an early morning ride.

She chose a part of the lake that was a little more secluded than the area where she usually swam. A weeping willow hung over the water and the stone boathouse, built like a Greek folly, stood close to it. The air was loud with birdsong. Perhaps she should be content with just sitting on the bank for a while, Julia thought, drinking in the beauty and peace of nature, and perhaps dangling her feet in the water. But the lure of the water, sparkling with the sunshine slanting across it, was just too strong. And it really was very early. She fetched a large towel from the boathouse, set it on the bank with her dress, and dived into the lake clad only in her shift.

She shook her head and blew out when she reached the surface again and trod water. The first shock of the cold water had taken her breath away as it always did. But it felt wonderful. She laid back her head and spread her arms, content to float and watch the few small, fluffy clouds above her doing the same thing. Swimming—or floating—had to be the most relaxing exercise in the world.

Grandpapa had always impressed upon her that she must never swim alone, that it was dangerous to do so. But how could one relax with a maid sitting demurely on the bank? Julia had always made sure that she did not worry her grandfather—she simply swam without his knowledge. Usually early in the morning.

It was glorious, she thought, rolling over onto her stom-

ach and doing a lazy crawl out farther onto the lake, away
from the shadows of the trees. She would not even think
about yesterday or last evening or about the month to come.
But that decision had no sooner been made than it was broken. For of course as soon as one had determined not to
think of something, one could think of nothing else.

She wished that Freddie had had a chance to kiss her last
evening before they were interrupted. She was curious to
know what his kisses were like. How did a rake kiss differently from the two gentlemen she had allowed to kiss her
during her Season in London? There were only so many
ways two sets of lips could be pressed together, were there
not? But she had no doubt that being kissed by Freddie
would be an experience not to be forgotten. He was undeni-
ably an attractive man with those bedroom eyes and that
truant lock of hair. He was just Freddie to her, of course,
but she could still begin to see him as other women must
see him.

Perhaps she would choose Freddie at the end of the
month. His motives for wanting to marry her were far from
romantic ones, of course, and she was not at all sure that
she believed what he had said about gambling and the state
of his finances. But at least he was being reasonably honest
with her. And she believed that he was fond of her and that
they would deal well together.

She would doubtless have to accustom herself to having
a husband with a roving eye, of course, and one who would
occasionally take mistresses. She turned onto her back
again and wrinkled her nose at the sky. Ugh! What a
ghastly thought. It was more likely that she would grab the
fire irons and bat him about the head with the poker the
first time she had evidence that he had strayed.

No, she could not marry so cynically. She sighed and
wished she were not such an incurable romantic. And
wished she could do with her mind what she wanted to do
with it. It was always the least controllable part of one's
being.

Julia turned and began to swim again. Soon she was

going to have to dry herself off and whisk herself back to the house so that her hair would be dry in plenty of time that no one at breakfast would suspect how she had begun her day.

Not even Daniel. Gussie's pompous ass. She smiled at the remembered name and her remembered glee at hearing such vulgar language from one of her cousins. Daniel would probably have a thousand fits of the vapors if he could see her now.

He had not slept well all night. And with the sun streaming through his window it was unlikely that he was going to get any more sleep. The Earl of Beaconswood sighed and sat up on the edge of his bed, rubbing his eyes with the heels of his hands and yawning. What he should do was go out for a brisk morning ride to put air into his lungs and energy into his body. Or better still, he should go for a brisk walk.

It was very early, he saw with a grimace when he reached his dressing room. Far too early to summon his valet, poor man. He would shave later, he decided, at a more decent hour for sending down for hot water. He dressed quickly, avoiding his black clothes with reluctance. It did not seem right to be donning a blue coat when his uncle had died less than two weeks before.

He breathed in deeply when he had let himself out of the house and was standing on the terrace. It was a lovely morning and certainly the right time to be in the country. It would not be a comfortable day to be in town. The smells would be considerably less pleasant than those here.

And yet, he thought, looking about him uncertain which direction to take for his walk, he would give a great deal to be in London right now, to be looking forward to seeing Blanche later in the day. Blanche could always be relied upon to behave with the strictest propriety and to remain sweet and feminine at the same time. He had never even been alone with her, except when driving her in the park with all the fashionable world there to act as chaperon.

He made his decision and turned to stride in the direction of the lake. He wished he could just snap his fingers and have the following month behind him. Not that he would not enjoy the company of his relatives. It was several years since he had been with them all together, and he had always been fond of them, even of those aunts, uncles, and cousins who were not strictly speaking close relatives since they belonged to his late aunt. But he had been brought up to think of them as close relatives.

As he had been brought up to think of Julia as a cousin. And Julia was the trouble with this whole month, he thought, feeling his jawline tense. Without her he would be able to relax and enjoy himself. But then without her there would be no necessity for any of them to stay there for the month.

If ever he wanted to identify the complete opposite of Blanche, he thought, it would be Julia without any hesitation at all. Even physically they were opposites. Blanche was small and slender and blond. Julia was rather tall with those long legs of hers—he could still remember seeing them clad in breeches when she was fifteen—and generously shaped and dark. But in every other way she was different from Blanche too.

He swore out loud when he remembered his feeling on arriving at the lake the evening before to find that Julia and Freddie had been lost along the way—or had lost themselves. It was dark and they were among the trees and she was with Freddie of all people. Did she not know Freddie's reputation? Or did she not believe that he could turn that fatal charm upon her to seduce her? And would she not believe him that Freddie was badly dipped and would grasp at the opportunity to enrich himself with a wise marriage?

Foolish woman. How could he stand by and watch a member of his family deceive and perhaps debauch a woman whom his uncle had treated as a granddaughter? He could not do so. It was as simple as that. Even though she seemed to know nothing about propriety and decorum. Even though she had been inviting Freddie's kiss the evening before. He had arrived just in time. He probably would have planted Freddie a facer too if Stella and Viola and Les had not been close behind him. He had been feeling white with fury.

He had reached the lake and turned to stroll slowly along the bank. He frowned. The fury was strange really, he supposed. What if Freddie *had* kissed her? What if he had compromised her by keeping her away from the house for far too long? What if he had therefore been forced into marrying her? It was what he wanted anyway. And probably what she wanted too. Freddie was undoubtedly the most personable of the five of them, and she did not have the good sense to care about his character flaws.

Why should he worry about protecting her? From what was she to be protected?

But he was not given a chance to answer his own questions. Someone was swimming out on the lake. Alone. That was a foolish thing to do. One of the servants, he supposed. He almost turned away to walk back in the other direction until he looked more closely and noted the slim arms that rose rhythmically and gracefully from the water. Good God, it was a woman. Asking for trouble if any of the menservants happened along. Or perhaps that was what she was hoping for. He could feel anger rising.

But of course, he thought suddenly, coming to a halt close to the boathouse. Oh, of course. Why had he thought even for one moment that that was a servant out there, swimming alone in deep water? The truth was so obvious that it was almost laughable that it had not jumped at him immediately. Except that he was not laughing. Anger progressed to fury in one leap.

That was Julia out there! At the same moment as he thought it his eye was caught by her towel lying in the grass close to the bank not far away and the dress dropped in a careless heap beside it.

Good God! What was she wearing out there? Or what was she *not* wearing? His heart felt suddenly as if it was beating at double time.

She was swimming with leisurely strokes to shore. His first instinct was to turn and hurry out of sight. But fury kept him rooted to the spot. What if it were someone else who had wandered to that particular spot to witness what he was witnessing? What if it were one of the menservants? One of the gardeners? Or one of his cousins? What if it were Freddie? She would be swimming toward a fate worse than death.

If he did not throttle her when she had hauled herself out of the water he would deserve a medal for restraint. But he had never craved medals and did not do so now. He would prefer the satisfaction of having his hands about her throat and squeezing.

The Earl of Beaconswood planted his booted feet slightly apart, clasped his hands behind his back, and waited.

6

She set her hands on the bank, drew herself up out of the water, set one knee on the grass and then one foot, and pulled herself upright—all in one fluid, graceful movement.

For one moment he thought she really was naked. But she might as well have been, he thought when he realized that she was wearing a shift. It clung to her like a second skin, leaving nothing at all to the imagination. His mouth went dry.

She lifted her arms and her face to the sun filtering at a slant through the trees and pressed her hands back over her hair, squeezing the excess water from it behind her head. Then without lowering her head she passed her hands flat down her body, pressing out some of the moisture. They began at her shoulders and moved downward with spread fingers over her breasts—full, firm breasts clearly outlined against the soaked fabric—into her small waist, down over shapely hips, down the tops of her long, slim legs.

She could teach the most accomplished of courtesans a thing or two about arousing a man, the earl thought as he stood very still and watched. Though he was not thinking clearly. His breath caught in his throat and he felt a tightening in his groin. He wanted to touch her. By God, he wanted to touch her. He wanted to circle those magnificent breasts with his hands. They would be cold to the touch. He wanted to warm them with his palms. He wanted to pinch those nipples visible through her shift until they were hard and peaked. He wanted to spread his hands over her hips and move them over her flat stomach. He wanted to touch her where the wet cotton clung between her legs. He wanted his hand beneath the fabric. He wanted to touch her. . . .

Probably only seconds had passed since she had set foot on the bank. She shivered and reached down for her towel. But she stopped and stiffened suddenly, her fingers not quite touching it. She raised her head slowly and looked directly at him as he stood in the shadow of the boathouse no more than twenty feet away. They stared at each other for several moments before she grasped the towel, straightened up unhurriedly, and held it bunched in front of her.

She was the first to break the silence. "Are you enjoying the show?" she asked. "You should have hidden more carefully, Daniel. I usually remove the wet garment before donning the dry one for the return to the house. I am sure you would have enjoyed watching that."

Her voice and the usual brittle tone in which she spoke to him broke the spell and he was cold with fury again. Colder. She had made him desire her, by God, just as she had when she was fifteen years old. Even now she had not covered herself with the towel. Or dived back into the water with shame and the need to cling to some shred of modesty. She was standing with bare feet planted apart on the grass, shoulders back, head high. As if he was the one in the wrong.

"Have you no modesty whatsoever?" The viciousness of his tone surprised even himself. "Will you flaunt yourself for the whole world to see? Will you so carelessly invite ravishment?"

"Modesty?" she said. "I have been bathing—clothed—at six o'clock in the morning. And for the whole world to see? This is a private lake on private land. And ravishment? Is that what you have in mind, Daniel? Do you want me?"

"Clothed!" His nostrils flared and he strode unwisely toward her. "Is this what you consider clothes, Julia?" He indicated the clinging shift with one expressive hand and let his eyes sweep down her body. "You might as well have removed that also and had two dry garments to put on when you came out of the water. What if a gardener had wandered this way?"

"He would have wandered another way again," she said.

"And what if it were someone else from the house who had come?" he asked. "What if it were Freddie?"

"If it were Freddie," she said, "he would have made some appreciative comments instead of hiding in the shadows, remarked on his good fortune, and flirted with me."

"Flirted." The word was spoken quietly. He was so furious that his anger could not even show itself openly without taking him entirely beyond control. He would do her some violence if he did not keep his temper tightly reined. "Do you have any conception of what form that flirtation would take, Julia?"

"Do you?" She laughed at him and raised the towel to rub at one side of her hair.

"You would no longer be wearing that shift," he said. "You would no longer be standing upright. You would no longer be in possession of either your virtue or your virginity, Julia. If you are still in possession of either, that is."

Her hand stilled and color rushed to her face. "You become offensive," she said. "I believe you should apologize for that, Daniel."

"My God, woman," he said, his fists clenched tightly at his sides, "do you have no understanding of life at all? Or of men?"

"Yes," she said, and he could see from the flashing of her eyes that she too was now angry. "Yes, I understand men, Daniel. Some men anyway. I understand that they can desire what they hate and despise. I understand that they can accuse other men of doing what they would like to do themselves. You would like to ravish me, wouldn't you, Daniel? But of course the thought horrifies you because you are the very proper Earl of Beaconswood. And so all the wrong must be mine. There is nothing improper in my swimming here early in the morning, but because you have seen me here and because you have desired me, then I must be a wanton. Perhaps even a whore."

He kept his hands in tight fists. He thought his knuckles would crack. "Have you ever heard of a tease?" he asked her. "Women were made to be desired by men, Julia. Thus is the human race perpetuated. A woman who bares her body to a man's gaze must expect that he will want to put himself inside her." Color rushed back into her cheeks. "There is nothing shameful in his desire, only in what he does with that desire. You are fortunate that you have been caught this morning by one who can control it."

"Ah," she said, "and so you are exonerated. A man to be admired. A man with self-control and a conscience. The blame shifts back to me. So be it, then. But you still owe me an apology."

"Julia." He reached out and grasped one of her wrists. Her flesh was cold. "Be more careful. You are no longer a child to be living the life of a hoyden. You are a woman. A lady. Don't invite this sort of scene with another man. He might be less scrupulous."

"Like Freddie?" she said. "You denied me a kiss from him last evening. I wanted him to kiss me. I am that much of a wanton, you see, Daniel. I am twenty-one years old and I wanted to be kissed. Dreadful is it not?"

He ought not to have touched her. He could feel warmth from his hand seep into her wrist. He could warm her body too if he held her tightly against him, if he rubbed his hands hard up and down her back, if he first of all peeled off the wet shift, if he gave her the heat of his mouth. His thoughts worked independently of his will. He dropped her wrist.

"You little fool," he said. "You do not realize how much you play with fire by encouraging Freddie, Julia. Do you think you could be happy with a gambler and a woman-izer?"

"Perhaps I can reform him." She smiled at him.

"Women do not reform men," he said. "Those who marry in that expectation end up miserably unhappy. Freddie is personable and charming and apparently very attractive to women, Julia. But you would make the biggest mistake of your life if you married him."

"And do you care?" she asked him. "Why would you, Daniel? If I am not a lady and am without virtue and without—without virginity, why would it matter to you whom I marry?"

"My uncle loved you and treated you like a granddaughter," he said. "I grew up thinking of you as a cousin. I have to feel the same sort of concern for you as I do for any other member of my family. I feel responsible for you, Julia."

"Don't." She snapped the word. "I am not your responsibility, Daniel, and I thank providence for that. My choices are very limited. I may choose to marry one of four men if they all offer—Freddie already has in so many words. Or I may choose to go to my uncle in the north of England. Or I may choose to seek a post as a governess or teacher or companion. Actually not so limited. I have choices. I will make them myself. Without help from anyone. Least of all you. Do you understand me? You may take your damnable stuffy sense of responsibility and shove it in the lake or any other place of your choice, Daniel. I am cold. Like a block of ice. I would like to dry off and change into my dress if you please. Or do you want to stand and watch?"

He gazed hard at her for several moments and then turned without another word and strode away. He should have been feeling relief. She had just done what she had every right to do. She had spurned his help and absolved him from any sense of family responsibility toward her. She had chosen to carve out her own destiny. Or her own doom.

He should have been able to free his mind and his conscience of her and turn to the prospect of a pleasant, if perhaps slightly tedious, month spent with his family. He should have been able to turn his mind to Blanche again and plan what he would do about her when he was finally free to leave Primrose Park. The thought of Blanche should have made his heart leap with gladness.

But his heart was still beating at not quite normal rate and his groin was still aching. And he could not rid his mind of the image of Freddie finding Julia as he had found her. And of Freddie touching her as he had wanted to touch her. And peeling off her shift and laying her down on the grass and penetrating her body with his and taking pleasure from her. As he had wanted to do.

God but she was beautiful. And desirable. And everything he most despised in a lady. She *was* no lady. If she were a courtesan, he would employ her. He would keep her as his mistress until he had had his fill of her. Not that he was in the habit of keeping mistresses or even availing himself of the services of a whore with any great frequency. But if Julia were on the market, he would buy.

The direction of his thoughts horrified him. Good God! She might be no lady, but she was very far from being the other. And to think of himself buying and using her services was sickening. He could only despise himself for such thoughts. He turned his steps toward the stables as he came out from among the trees. Perhaps he needed that brisk ride after all.

He remembered suddenly that he had not apologized to her. He had as good as called her a fallen woman and he had not apologized. He felt renewed anger against her for provoking him into such an unpardonable indiscretion.

Julia, he thought. So wild. And so dangerously innocent.

When Julia emerged from her room at a very decorous nine o'clock in the morning, she was relieved to find the breakfast room full of family members. They were in the midst of planning a picnic for the afternoon. Julia fell in with the plans with enthusiasm.

"The lake would be pleasant," Aunt Millie was saying. "There would be trees to shelter us and grass to sit on. And it is not too far to walk."

"We can stroll to the lake anytime, though, Millie," Aunt Roberta said. "How about the hill?"

"Too steep," Uncle Henry said. "All the food would have to be carried up by foot. We would do better to keep that in mind for a walk or a ride some other day."

"What about Culver Castle?" Julia suggested. "We always had splendid picnics there when we were children. It was one of Grandpapa's favorite places."

Aunt Millie raised a handkerchief to her eyes. "Poor dear Humphrey," she said. "He would have liked nothing better than to be surrounded by his family and to be going on a picnic."

"It certainly does not seem right to see everyone dressed in colors again," Aunt Sarah said. "I must censure Humphrey for having put that in his will. It is not proper."

"But we would die of the heat today," Julia said, "if we had to wear black outdoors."

"We would not even be going out on a picnic," Aunt Sarah pointed out, "if we were in proper mourning, Julia, dear. Daniel should have used his authority as head of the family and decided against our following Humphrey's instructions. I am sure he could not have been in his right mind when he wrote that particular part of the will. Mr. Prudholm should have talked him out of it."

Daniel, Julia had been relieved to see as soon as she had stepped into the breakfast room, was not there.

"Culver Castle sounds wonderful, Jule," Stella said. "Do you remember how we used to climb up to the battlements? I suppose the stairways are crumbling even more now than they used to do."

"And how we boys used to descend to the dungeons," Augustus said. "One hundred and thirty-two steps."

"And me," Julia said. "I always used to go down too."

Augustus smiled at her a little uncomfortably. "And so you did too, Jule," he said. "You were always one of the fellows."

"But she is a lady now," Aunt Sarah said firmly. "And I think that we all must see the castle only as a picturesque site for a picnic and not as something to be romped over. You are none of you children any longer."

Augustus pulled a face when Aunt Sarah turned her head away and grinned at Julia. The first natural smile he had exchanged with her since the reading of the will the afternoon before.

"Culver Castle it is, then," Uncle Raymond said, getting to his feet. "I'll see that the carriages are ordered out for the ladies."

"And I'll see Cook about the food," Aunt Eunice said. "Come with me, Millie?"

"Oh, I suppose so, dear," Aunt Millie said, flustered. "But Cook will be cross to have her day's plans upset. Oh, I do so hate it when she is cross." She pushed back her chair reluctantly.

Frederick winked at her. "Go to it, Aunt Millie," he said. "Go and give them hell in the kitchen."

"Freddie, dear," Aunt Millie said, shocked.

"Freddie!" his father said sternly.

Frederick chuckled.

Julia traveled in one of the barouches. Normally she would have insisted on riding with the men, and even today she watched them with envy as she sat demurely between Camilla and Aunt Sylvia. Sometimes she wondered what malevolent fate had decided that she would be female at birth since her inclination was for the freedom and uninhibited physical activity that only men enjoyed. But then if she were not female she would be unable to look appreciatively at men without being guilty of some heinous sin.

And men really were splendid creations, she thought. Far more splendid than women. All muscle and hardness instead of feminine softness. At least the better examples were. Like Freddie. And even Gussie. She had never really thought of Gussie as a man before, only as a cousin and close friend. But he was good-looking in his own way—his own very distinctive way. His face would be lined with laugh creases before he was forty, of course, and his very fair hair would be curly and unruly until he began to lose it as he inevitably would within the next ten years or so.

Uncle Paul was almost completely bald. Gussie had a graceful man's body even if he was not very tall.

Of course he could never match Freddie in splendor. Or Daniel either. Daniel was one of the picnickers, of course. She had been a little disappointed when she saw him, but it would have been strange if he had not come. Everyone else had, and Daniel was nothing if not meticulous about family duty.

Yes, he was a very handsome man too, she admitted grudgingly. And attractive, she thought even more grudgingly. She had wanted him that morning. The thought, verbalized in her mind in just those words, shocked her. *Wanted* him? She had wanted him to kiss her. The trouble with Daniel was that he was always at his most attractive when he was angry. And he had been very angry when he had stridden across the grass to stand in front of her. Angry at himself as much as at her, she had guessed. There had been something rather erotic in the contrast between his immaculately dressed person and her woefully undressed one.

She had wanted more than a kiss. Julia shivered despite the warmth of the day and the press of bodies in the crowded barouche. She had wanted to feel his hands on her. It was a dreadful admission. She had never wanted such a thing before nor ever thought to want more than kisses from a man. Even the desire for kisses had sometimes made her feel sinful. What had he said? His words had shocked her so much—as they had been meant to do—that she had suppressed the memory of them. What were they? Something about any man seeing her like that and wanting to put himself inside her.

Julia could feel her cheeks flame and twirled her parasol. She could feel an uncomfortable ache and throbbing between her legs, as she had felt then. She had wanted him— Oh, dear, she might as well complete the thought since no one but she would know it and she could not hide it from herself anyway. She had wanted him to put himself there.

The marriage act. At least she supposed that was what he had meant and what she had wanted. The joining of two

bodies. The type of intimacy that had always made her un-
easy before whenever she thought of it and made her shy
away from the thought of marriage. She did not want anyone being familiar or intimate with her body—not with
more than her lips anyway.

"A penny for them, Jule," Susan said from the seat opposite.

"You *are* unnaturally quiet, Julia," Aunt Sylvia said.

"Oh," she said. "Nothing. Just dreaming." *Just wondering what it would be like to have Daniel inside me.* She
could feel color and heat flood her cheeks.

Aunt Roberta, sitting opposite beside Susan, laughed.
"She is thinking that she has five strings to her bow," she
said. "And wondering which will make his move at the picnic this afternoon. It is both an exciting and a frightening
time when one is marriageable and choosing a husband, is
it not, dear? I envy you and pity you."

"Actually," Julia said, giving her parasol another twirl, "I
was thinking of Grandpapa and wishing he were alive and
here with us so that I could lure him up onto the castle battlements and push him over the steepest wall."

"Oh, goodness," Aunt Sylvia said, setting a hand over
her heart while everyone else laughed.

The earl, who was riding not far off, looked back over
his shoulder at the sound of the laughter. She hated him,
Julia thought. If he were a gentleman, he would have stolen
away as soon as he saw her swimming and left her to her
privacy. If he were a gentleman, he would have turned his
back at least until she could have got the towel right about
herself. If he were a gentleman, he would not have accused
her of loose morals merely because she liked to swim at
dawn. And he would have apologized. Profusely and ab-
jectly.

A man's thighs showed to definite advantage, she
thought, twirling her parasol absently again, spread on either side of a horse. If they were strong and well-muscled,
of course. As Daniel's were.

She wished he had tried to kiss or touch her. She could

have cracked him across the face and been feeling infinitely better now. She should have slapped him anyway when he had said that about her virginity. She had missed a golden opportunity. She would love to slap Daniel's face. And she would do it too at the first chance. Just let him try prosing on at her about propriety and decorum again. Or about the undesirability of her marrying Freddie. She would marry Freddie if she wanted to. She would do it to spite Daniel— if she wanted to.

"Ah, there it is," Camilla said, pointing ahead to the ruined Norman castle. "I always forget just how picturesque the setting is until I am back here. It must be a few years since we were here last."

Julia brought her mind back to the present. Culver Castle had been the scene of many happy childhood romps. Sometimes she wished they could all be young again. How foolish children are, she thought, always to be longing to grow up. Being grown up was not at all a pleasant business.

The uncles handed the ladies out of the carriages. The male cousins held back. Almost as if they were afraid of her, Julia thought, or afraid of one another. It made her wish again that they were all still children, that she could look at them as she always had instead of as prospective husbands. She hated seeing them this way. There was not one of them she wanted to marry.

Aunt Sarah had set the picnic site beside the river that formed a natural moat around half the base of the castle hill. There was grass there and a buttercup and daisy-strewn meadow behind with trees beyond it and some late-blooming bluebells. With the castle forming almost a storybook picture at the other side of the river, they had found the perfect setting for a picnic. Or so said Aunt Sarah, directing the placement of the blankets for them to sit on and suggesting several delightful strolls they might care to take to work up an appetite. The picnic baskets were to arrive later by a separate carriage.

But Julia did not feel like strolling or admiring the more delicate beauties of nature.

"Who wants to explore the castle?" she asked, raising her voice defiantly.

"I don't think, Julia—" Aunt Sarah began.

"I am going up there," Julia said. "I want to see the view. And I want to climb up onto the battlements. Is anyone coming?" She strode off in the direction of the arched stone bridge that had long ago replaced the original drawbridge, quite prepared to go alone if no one wanted to come or if she must be treated as if she had some particularly nasty infectious disease.

"Bravo, Jule." Frederick was chuckling. "We are going to storm the castle, are we? Lead the way, then, and your faithful cohorts will follow."

She threw him a grateful glance over her shoulder. But he was quite right. Others were following—most of the younger generation, that was, despite Aunt Sarah's frowns. Aunt Sarah had said no more, Julia could see, because Daniel was coming to the castle too. Drat! She wished she were still at an age when she could poke out her tongue. He was coming to spoil the afternoon for her.

"Wonderful idea, Jule," Lesley was saying. "Too wonderful a castle merely to be gazed at."

Augustus had caught up to her by the time she had reached the center of the bridge.

"I'll race you to the top of the hill, Jule," he said. "Do you want me to give you a sporting start?"

Julia, conscious of the ghastly change that had occurred in the family during the past day, grasped gratefully at a little bit of nostalgia. She caught her skirt up above her ankles with both hands, shrieked, and was off and running.

"I'll race you anyway, Gussie," she yelled. "With feet that size all you can do is trip over them."

The years fell away with exhilarating speed as she pounded her way up the hill with Augustus panting at her shoulder, waiting to make his move past her at the last possible moment. As he always did, the wretch.

*   *   *

Malcolm did not join the climb up the hill with the other young people. He stood looking after them—a thirty-year-old man caught somehow between the two generations.

Camilla paused, undecided whether to go or to stay. She felt sorry for Malcolm, too shy for his own good, too old to have been a playmate for any except Daniel and Freddie and her. Pushed into the background when the younger, noisier children began devising their own games. And now he was thirty years old, heir to a barony, and undoubtedly under pressure from both his parents and his own sense of duty to choose a wife.

And suddenly feeling trapped by the eligibility of Julia.

"Really, Millie," Camilla's mother was saying, "you should have had a talk with that girl a long time ago. At her age she should be married with a few children in the nursery, not rushing up a hill like a hoyden. It is quite unseemly."

And Camilla felt sorry for Julia too. Julia was very special, with vast amounts of energy and a great capacity to love. But no one to love—yet. The right man had not come along for her. Camilla sighed. Just as in twenty-four years only one man had come along for her—and been snatched away cruelly before she could even have the comfort of being his wife.

Daniel was not interested in Julia. He had never understood her need to break free from restraint on occasion since he had long ago suppressed all such need in himself. And there was no one else among the five cousins who was quite right for her. Certainly not Malcolm.

"Malcolm," she said, stepping up to him and touching him on the arm. He was very tall. A trifle too thin, perhaps, but thick blond hair gave him a claim to beauty. She had always been fond of him. "Would you like to stroll to the woods to see the bluebells?"

"I would, Camilla," he said, looking vastly relieved.

Malcolm stammered quite badly with many people, but he never had with her. They had been playmates as children. The first summer after Simon's death, when they had met at Primrose Park, he had sympathized with her and held her, and his own eyes had been not quite dry when he released her.

"We will let the children run and play," she said, smiling.

"There is no harm in it," he said as they strolled away toward the wood. "I like to see them enjoying themselves as they always used to do despite the fact of Uncle's death and despite the fact that they are all grown up now—even Viola—and are expected to behave soberly."

"I think Julia will see to it that they never do that," she said.

"I admire Julia," he said. "I hope she never allows people like Aunt Sarah to dampen her spirits. Oh, sorry, Camilla."

"Mama is sometimes harsh in her judgments," she said. She looked up at him with interest. "You want to marry Julia, Malcolm? Are you going to try to win her hand during this month?"

He looked a little alarmed. "I don't think she would look twice at me, Camilla," he said. "But I suppose I should try. My parents expect it of me and it is time I married."

"Just because of your age and who you are?" she asked.

"No," he said. "I want to marry."

"But it does not have to be to someone you feel obliged to offer for," she said. "There must be many women who would love to marry you, Malcolm, and whom you would wish to marry."

"But I would have to meet them and get to know them," he said. "That is more easily said than done in my case. What about you, Camilla? Are you getting over your grief?"

"Yes and no," she said. "I will always look back on Simon with regret. We had so little time together. But life cannot be lived in the past. Or it would be dreadfully wasted if it were. I am ready to live again."

"And love again?" he asked. "And marry?"

"If I were to meet the right man," she said with a smile.

"But he would have to be very special. After knowing Simon, I could not settle for less."

"You will find him, Camilla," he said. "There must be many men who would love to marry you."

"There. Now we have flattered each other and made each other feel good," she said with a laugh. "Should we pick some bluebells, do you think? Aren't they glorious? But they will not last all the way back to the house, will they? I suppose we might as well let them live out their span in the place where they belong and look best."

7

Nobody else had taken up Augustus's challenge to race up the hill. It was most wise of them, Julia thought as she collapsed, panting and laughing at the top. It was far too hot a day to do anything more strenuous than crawl.

"I wish you would not do that, Gussie," she said, the crossness of her voice belied by her laughter. "How many times have I told you not to? If you are going to pass me, do it early enough that I will not get my hopes up. I shall go to my grave with the ambition of beating you in a race blighted."

"I would let you win, Jule," he said. "But the only time I tried that you hurled yourself at me, fists and feet flying, teeth gnashing, and tongue wagging. It seems I was a little too obvious about it."

"I was ten years old," she said, "or thereabouts. Perhaps you should try it again, Gussie."

"No thanks," he said cheerfully. "Your feet and hands and teeth are bigger and your tongue longer. Besides, I offered to give you a head start."

She got to her feet and brushed herself down. "Let's go into the courtyard," she said. "I have just realized what a shocking display that was, Gussie. Aunt Sarah has probably swooned quite away, and Daniel is probably wishing that Grandpapa were still alive so that he could recommend me for a spanking as he always used to do."

"No, no, Jule," he said. "Be fair. He only used to tell you that you deserved a walloping. He never bore tales to Uncle."

"Grandpapa would just have laughed anyway," she said. "Oh, those were the days, weren't they, Gussie? I wish we could have them back. Don't you wish we could be children again?"

"Not particularly, Jule," he said. "On the whole I prefer to be an adult."

She sighed. "Well, that is where men and women differ," she said. "Men grow toward freedom while women grow into captivity. Life is the unfairest thing there ever was."

The others came straggling into the courtyard too after a few minutes. Only grass and a few stubborn mounds of stones remained of what must have been a bustling community in Norman times. But the shell was almost intact. A few round towers still stood among the battlements. And as always they were irresistible.

"Let's go up," Julia said. "I want to see the countryside."

"What you want is the thrill of danger, Jule," Augustus said. "You could see the countryside from the top of the hill."

"You want the romance of it, Jule," Frederick said. "You want to picture yourself as the lady of the castle gazing out at her lord's domain."

"The stairs are crumbling away quite badly," the earl said, strolling toward the group from one of the towers. "They look even more dangerous than they used to be. I would recommend not taking the risk of climbing them."

"Ah," Stella said, "then we had better stay down here. What a pity."

"I used to love going up there," Viola said. "But I always hated coming down. The stairs are so steep and winding."

"Gussie?" Julia looked at him eagerly. If anyone else had pointed out the danger of the stairs, perhaps she would have listened. Perhaps. But it had been Daniel.

"Yes, Jule," Augustus said, squinting up at the battlements. "I know you can't resist. Neither can I, actually. Let's go."

Julia was almost disappointed that the earl made no further attempt to stop her from going. She and Augustus went alone. The stairs, winding up inside one of the towers, fairly wide at the outside wall, narrowing to nothing at the center column, were indeed in bad repair. In one place the wider part of three successive stairs had crumbled away to little more than a heap of loose stones. They had to scramble up, using hands as well as feet. It would be very easy to lose one's footing and fall and fall and fall. One would be dead before hitting the bottom. Julia shuddered.

"Oh," she said, coming out into daylight at the top and flinging her arms wide, "this is wonderful." She peered downward over the stone parapet to the courtyard below. "This is wonderful," she yelled down. "You do not know what you are missing."

"It is going to be devilish tricky on the way down," Augustus said.

"We'll think about going down when the time comes," she said, and they strolled together around the battlements, gazing out over river and trees and fields into a hazy distance.

"Jule," Augustus said.

"Ah." Julia's shoulders slumped. "Reality intrudes. I can tell by the tone of your voice. What did you think of it then, Gussie? Stupid, was it not? Grandpapa did some very foolish things in his life but this must beat them all. I thought I had lost you for good. You have scarcely looked at me since yesterday afternoon."

Augustus coughed.

"Daniel is not in the hunt," she said. "Even the lure of owning Primrose Park will not induce him to take me on. There never has been any love lost between the two of us. And that is putting the case mildly. Freddie is a different story. He needs the rents. Daniel says he is dipped—is that the correct expression? The foolish man likes to play too deep. He says his debts aren't bad ones and that he is fond of me. I don't know, though. He is a rake, isn't he? I don't think I could share a man, even someone gorgeous like Freddie. But I am fond of him, you know. What do you think, Gussie?"

"I don't think Freddie is the one for you, Jule," he said.

"Don't you?" She looked at him briefly. "I have not heard anything yet from Les or Malcolm. But has anyone ever heard anything from Malcolm? I don't believe there could be a more silent man. And I can't imagine Les's being very interested in matrimony. Can you, Gussie?"

"Les doesn't have the brains," he said.

"For marriage?" she said. "Does one need brains for marriage? He is not exactly an imbecile, is he? Just a little slow. He gets where he is going eventually if one can just give him time. I am fond of Les. He is invariably sweet."

"He would drive you silly with boredom in a week, Jule," he said. "Or with impatience. You wouldn't be able to bear a man who would not stand up against you."

"No, I wouldn't, would I?" she said. "What would you suggest then, Gussie?" She flashed him a smile. "You? Shall I marry you?"

"I think it might be a good idea, Jule," he said. "We have always dealt well together, haven't we?"

"Yes," she said, "we always have, Gussie. But marriage? Can you seriously imagine us married?"

"I don't see why not," he said. "It must be an advantage to marry a friend."

"Must it?" She frowned. "Kiss me, Gussie."

"What?" He flushed.

She looked outward over the wall behind her and down toward the courtyard. "We are out of sight of everyone," she said. "Kiss me."

"Now?" he said, aghast. "Here, Jule? Shouldn't there be moonlight and—and a-atmosphere or something?"

"No," she said. "Only two people who are private together and who are considering marriage together. You don't want to, do you?"

Augustus stared at her.

"Are you a virgin, Gussie?" she asked.

"*Jule!*" He blushed furiously. "Only you would even dream of asking a man something so—so absolutely outrageous."

"Well, are you?" she asked.

"Of course I'm not," he said. "Good Lord, Jule, where did you grow up? In the gutter?"

"You are," she said calmly. "I thought you were. You're afraid to kiss me."

"I'm not afraid—"

"You are blustering," she said. "Actually it is not so much fear, is it, as embarrassment. I feel the same way. I can't quite think of you as a man, Gussie. Not in that way. And I am not being insulting. It is just that you are more like a brother. The thought of kissing you quite puts me to the blush. Why did you want to marry me?"

"Because I'm fond of you, Jule," he said.

She sighed. "Everybody and his dog is fond of me," she said. "Except Daniel. But why in particular? Primrose Park?"

"I was thinking of you, Jule," he said. "You need someone to look after you. I couldn't do it without Primrose Park. We would have to live with Mama and Papa and I would hate that. But it was mainly you. Because I am fond of you and because I can't see you being happy with any of the others."

"Oh, Gussie," she said on a sigh, "how kind you are. Oh, yes, you are. I believe you about your motive. And until now I really thought that you would probably be my best bet. But it wouldn't work, would it?"

"We could make it work, Jule," he said. "We could be content to be friends for a while. And as for the other . . ."

"The other is an essential part of marriage," she said. "Not just for children, Gussie, but for—oh, for completeness of life. For emotional satisfaction. I want the other. But I should die of embarrassment with you. As you would with me. We cannot even face the thought of kissing each other. How could we think of—well, *you* know. It would seem a little like incest, wouldn't it?"

He stared at her for a while. "It would rather," he said eventually.

She smiled a little sadly. "I think we had better settle for being pals for the rest of our lives, Gussie," she said. "Is it not a pity? It would be fun to live together at Primrose Park, wouldn't it? To belong there. Just you and me. But we are not children any longer. And that other part of marriage is important to me."

"Lord," he said. "Don't marry Freddie, Jule. No decent mama and papa will allow him within five miles of their daughters in London, you know. I don't know anyone with a worse reputation."

"But I like him," she said.

"Of course," he said. "He's Freddie and we have known him all our lives. But your life would be hell as his wife, Jule. You would be better off marrying me."

"We had better go down," she said, "before Daniel has a head-of-the-family anxiety attack thinking we have thrown ourselves off the battlements. I wish he had not come, Gussie. The last several summers have been bliss without him, haven't they?"

"He is a decent sort, Jule," he said. "At least he can always be counted upon to do what is right and honorable. A woman could look for worse in a husband."

Julia pulled a face. "I hope you are not suggesting what I think you are suggesting," she said. "Ugh!"

He grinned suddenly and looked like the old Gussie again. "Actually," he said, "I wasn't. He might be a good catch for you, Jule, but I would have to say you might be a disastrous catch for him."

"Oh!" She aimed a punch at his disappearing back and scurried after him along the battlements. The others were still down in the courtyard, most of them sitting on the grass. "I owe you for that one, Gussie. I'll get you for it, you may be certain sure."

Augustus only laughed and raised his hand to wave to their cousins down below.

He should have stayed down by the river, the Earl of Beaconswood thought. If he had not got up to answer Julia's challenge, probably no one else would have done so except Gussie and perhaps Freddie. And Les, of course, if Freddie had. But everyone else would have stayed. And she would have come to no harm with Gussie. Or with the others, either. There was always safety in numbers.

But no, he had had to follow her as he always had. There had always been Julia at Primrose Park, from his early boyhood on. Always madcap Julia and his strong disapproval of her and his equally strong need to be there just in case she went too far one day and got herself into real danger. He could not explain that latter need. He never had been able to do so. It had only ever brought him anger and frustration. And contempt from her.

Freddie was stretched out on the grass, basking in the sun, one arm thrown over his eyes. Viola and Stella sat beside him, talking. Les and Susan had strolled over to where one low wall would give them a view out over the countryside on the opposite side from the river. No one else was pacing, worrying that she would lean against the parapet and it would give way from the weight of her body and plunge her to her death. No one else kept glancing at the doorway into the tower after she and Gussie had been seen to be making their way back down, worried that she would miss her footing on the stairs and come plummeting down to her death.

Everyone else was fond of Julia and not one whit worried about her, he thought, clamping his teeth together. He hated the woman and could cheerfully shake the living daylights out of her for putting him through this anxiety— again. As she had always done. Always. If there had ever been a tree in Julia's path, it had been made to be climbed. Or a lake, it had been made to be swum. Or a horse, it had been made to be galloped at a neck or nothing pace. Or a dare, it had been made to be taken.

But she was not a child any longer. Or even a girl. Goddammit, she was a woman. A lady. The earl stopped himself when he realized that he was beginning to grind his teeth, and strode over to the tower. They were taking altogether too long to get down.

He heard her giggles long before he rounded the bend in the staircase that brought him in sight of them. It was a nervous giggle, he realized then. Three of the stairs were little more than rubble, the light from a slit arrow window slanting across them. Julia was on the stair above the rubble. Gussie was on the stair below it, trying to coax her down.

"You can reach my hand, Jule," he was saying. "I'll help you. Trust me."

"But I have no grip with these slippers, Gussie," she said. "It was all right on the way up but not on the way down. And if I take your hand, I will come down with a rush and bowl us both over. I may just be stranded here for life. You will have to toss food up to me. I will become a legend." She giggled.

"What is the problem?" the earl asked, though he could see very well what the problem was. Julia had frozen with terror and Gussie was not up to talking her down.

"Oh, dear," she said and giggled again. "Here comes Daniel. Now I really feel six inches tall. I am stranded, that is what the problem is. My slippers are too smooth to grip these loose stones and I can hardly take a run at them with at least fifty more stairs spiraling away below them. Can I?" Another giggle.

"Give me your hand, Jule," Augustus said, his voice a trifle impatient. "You can't stay up there forever."

"Oh, goodness," she said. "I feel remarkably stupid. Go away, Daniel, do."

"Sit down," the earl said. "Sit down on the step behind you, Julia."

"What?" she said. "Time for a rest? I suppose it makes as much sense as standing here." She sat.

"I can't pass you, Gussie," the earl said. "The stairs are too narrow. How far apart can you set your feet and still maintain good balance?"

"Eh?" Augustus said.

"Try it," the earl said. "Can you reach up and grasp Julia's waist? You are going to have to slide down, Julia, using your bottom and the flat of your feet."

"I don't think so," she said. Her voice did not sound quite steady. Her giggle sounded a little hysterical.

"Gussie is going to guide you," he said, "and keep a firm hold of your waist. He is going to pass you between his legs. I'll be here to catch you on the other side. I am not going to miss you and I am not going to be bowled over. You are quite safe. Ready, Gus?"

"Oh, dear," Julia said. "Whose idea was it to climb up to the parapets anyway? Yours, Gussie? You deserve to be hanged, drawn, and quartered. I'll not be able to look anyone in the eye when this is all over. I will be mortified in the extreme. That is if I am still in one piece to not look anyone in the eye. But if I take the two of you down with me, no one will ever know exactly what happened, will they? I might be seen as a martyr who died trying to rescue you both."

"Julia," the earl said, keeping his voice firm, "stop babbling. Edge down onto the step where you have your feet. Wait until Gussie's hands grip you and then move, slowly but steadily."

"I am not going to look very elegant, am I?" she said. "And my dress is going to be horribly covered with dust and rubble."

She was still babbling, but she was doing as she had been told, and Augustus was doing his part, saying nothing, but looking as solid as a rock.

She moved slowly for as long as she could brace herself with her elbows on the upper step. But when she had to move them too down onto the rubble, she came sliding in a rush that Augustus could barely control and with a little shriek.

The earl grasped her ankles and let his hands slide up her legs to her knees. Her dress, it seemed, was not moving as fast as the rest of her body. And then she was sitting on the step below Augustus, looking decidedly shaky and giggling again.

"Oh, dear," she said. "Oh, dear."

The earl acted without thinking. He took her by the

upper arms and brought her to her feet and against him, bracing himself against the outer wall. "You are all right now, Julia," he said against her hair. "Quite safe. I have you quite safe." He wrapped his arms right about her.

"Yes," she said, her face pressed against his neckcloth. Her teeth were chattering and she was shaking badly. He knew that for the moment at least she would be incapable of standing alone. "How many more s-stairs are there, D-Daniel? Did you count?"

"Thirty-eight," he said. "Not too many. Do you want me to carry you down?"

"No," she said, sounding more like her usual indignant self for a moment. "Absolutely n-not. I can go d-down on my own, thank you."

"In a few moments, then," he said. "When you have found your legs again, Julia." He glanced up at Augustus.

"We might have been here all day," Augustus said in disgust. "She got the giggles."

The earl was very glad suddenly that Gussie was there. Julia's tremblings were making him very aware of the shapeliness of her body pressed against his own. And the warmth and the softness of her. And there was the emotional relief they both felt after a few minutes of tension and danger. He began to feel hot despite the coldness of the inside of the tower. He was very glad indeed of Gussie's presence.

"Oh," Julia said, raising her face from his neckcloth at last and looking up accusingly into his face, "you will tell everyone, won't you, Daniel? It would be just like you to tell. And this is your perfect opportunity, is it not? I'll have no defense against you whatsoever."

Lord. Those full breasts of hers were heaving against his chest. He could not move her away. As it was she was balanced on the narrower part of the stair they were sharing.

"I'll not breath a word," he told her coldly. "And I am sure Gussie will not either. It would be an embarrassment to admit to having such a shatterbrained relative."

"Don't let the thought provoke you," she said. "I am not

really a relative, remember? Is that not a blessing beyond belief?"

"Yes," he said curtly. "I am going to go down first, Julia. Gussie will be behind you. Put your hands on my shoulders to steady yourself if you wish."

"I can manage on my own, thank you," she said.

But when he stepped down to the stair below her, moved her in against the wall, and finally let go of her, her hands came up to take his shoulders in a death grip, and she kept hold of them until a turn in the stairs finally brought them in view of the ground.

"Well," she said, "that was quite an adventure. And that is the very last time I will wear these slippers out of doors. Women's footwear is remarkably foolish. What I should have worn, knowing we were coming to Culver Castle, was boots and breeches."

Augustus snorted. "Aunt Millie would have been prostrate with shock," he said.

"There you are wrong," she said, setting her feet finally on firm ground and drawing a deep breath. "Aunt Millie has seen me in my breeches and she thinks them very sensible. One has to ride sidesaddle when wearing a skirt, you know. Now if anyone wants to talk about dangerous doings, let's talk about riding sidesaddle. I would prefer to wear breeches and ride astride and feel safe."

Good Lord, the earl thought. Good Lord!

"Oh," she said, "it was so cold inside that tower. My teeth will not stop chattering. And there is something wrong with my knees."

"It is called shock," the earl said. "You need to walk it off, Julia. Take my arm and we will stroll about the courtyard. Everyone might guess that you took fright on the stairs if you join them right away."

"I did not take fright," she said indignantly. "It was just these silly slippers."

"You might as well take a well-earned rest in the sun, Gussie," the earl said, nodding toward the group of cousins sitting a short distance away. "My arm, Julia."

She took it.

* * *

His arm felt blessedly solid. Her legs felt anything but. She was ready to scream with the humiliation of the last several minutes.

"Say it," she said. "Don't keep me in suspense, Daniel. And please don't feel that you must play the gentleman. Just say it and get it over and done with."

"Say it?" He looked down at her, his eyebrows raised.

"'I told you so,'" she said.

"Ah." He was maddeningly cool. He had been maddeningly cool in the tower too, directing operations just as if he were an army general in the midst of battle. "I told you so."

"I knew you were longing to say it," she said. If only it had been anyone but Daniel. Any of the uncles. Any of the cousins. But it had had to be Daniel. Good heavens, she could suddenly remember his hands on her legs and her knees. Her *bare* legs and knees. If she could only die of mortification, she thought, she cheerfully would. "You have been just waiting for something to go wrong with me so that you could gloat, haven't you? Well, gloat on. I shall wear different slippers next time."

"Next time?" he said quietly.

She had burrowed her head against his neckcloth and pressed herself against him as if he were the only solid and safe thing in an infirm and dangerous universe. Good heavens. Oh, good heavens, a man's thigh muscles were even firmer than they looked gripping the sides of a horse. And his chest muscles. At least Daniel's were. Oh, gracious heaven, what an idiot she had made of herself. The weak trembling female having to be comforted in a man's arms.

"Next time I shall wear the proper attire," she said, "and not have to trouble you over the small and stupid matter of slippery slippers, Daniel. Slippery slippers. It sounds like a very long snake, does it not?"

"Julia," he said, "you are regaining confidence by the second, aren't you? I know what is going to happen when we rejoin the others. Someone—probably Freddie—is

going to mention the dungeons. A few men are going to decide to go down there, right into the bowels of the hill so
that they might have the dubious pleasure of peering out
through the grate at the bottom onto the river and then
climbing all the way back up again."

"It is slimy with wet moss down there," she said.

"I know," he said. "I remember. Before they go, Julia,
someone—without a doubt Freddie—is going to dare you
to go down too."

"A dare," she said wistfully. But her knees threatened to
turn to jelly again at the very thought of being on any more
of those winding stone stairs.

"If you accept," the earl said conversationally, "I shall
throttle you. After which I shall sling you over my shoulder
and carry you back down the hill to the picnic site. Do I
make myself clear?"

Oh, dear, Julia thought, bristling inwardly, she did not
have the energy or the stamina at present to take him on. It
was a dreadful shame since the combination of a dare from
Freddie and a prohibition from Daniel would normally ig-
nite her into any adventure, however hair-raising. But no,
she was going to have to let this one pass.

"How foolish you are," she said disdainfully. "Who
would want to descend into dungeons when the food must
be arriving and it is well past the normal time for tea?"

"Who?" he said. "You, in short, Julia. But my threat
stands. Or to make it more realistic, let me put it this way. I
would not throttle you, of course. But I would tip you under
my arm and wallop your derrière. And if you do not believe
me, try me."

If it were possible to explode, she thought, she would be
raining down in a million pieces over the castle hill at this
precise moment. She smiled. "Lay one violent finger on my
person, Daniel," she said, "and you will be observing the
world for the next two weeks from two black eyes. It is a
promise."

"I believe," he said, guiding her to where all the other

cousins were congregated on the grass, "it is time to go down for tea."

She slipped her arm gratefully from his.

"Anyone for the dungeons?" Frederick asked.

"Are you mad, Freddie?" Julia replied. "When it is time for tea? I am starved. Anyone for a race down the hill?"

A foolish challenge, she thought a moment later, when her legs still felt as if they were missing a few essential bones. She was going to end the race an ignominious last. But it was better than appearing to be afraid to go down to the dungeons. A woman had her pride, after all.

8

It was two days later before Malcolm summoned enough courage to talk with Julia. All his life he had been quiet and painfully shy, finding consolation in the interior world of the intellect and the imagination. In the past several years, once he had passed the painful years of the early twenties, he had even reconciled himself to the fact that he would never be able to change his nature to be as outward going and charming as Frederick or as self-assured as Daniel. He had learned to accept himself for who he was. He had learned to be happy with himself.

They had decided to walk the three miles to the hill east of the house. Not all of them—Susan and some of the aunts and uncles had decided that the distance was too great. But there was a sizable party, all in exuberant spirits. The summers were associated in Malcolm's mind with Primrose Park and family and exuberance—and himself in the background watching like a spectator. Not unhappy exactly, but a little envious of Daniel and Freddie.

And a little afraid of Julia. She had always been the most exuberant and most daring of all—pretty, mischievous, sunny-natured Julia. Malcolm admired her and liked her immensely, but he had never felt that he could have any personal dealings with her. They were just too different in every way. But Uncle's will had changed all that.

He walked out to the hill with Camilla, the only cousin with whom he always felt comfortable. Perhaps because she was quieter than the others. Perhaps because she had suffered. But then he had always felt at ease with her, even when they were both children. She told him now about

Bath, where she had just spent a few months with her mother. He told her about some books he had been reading recently.

That was the good thing about being with Camilla, he thought when they finally lapsed into silence. He could talk to her about anything that came into his head instead of reaching around for some suitable topic, as he did with most other people. And he could even be silent with her without any feeling of discomfort.

This was very probably, he realized suddenly, the last time they would all be together at Primrose Park. Quite possibly he would never see Camilla again since they were related only by the marriage of his aunt to her uncle, both now deceased. He would be sorry not to see her. He hoped she would find the husband she was looking for and be happy. She deserved to be happy.

The others had reached their destination before them. The hill was surrounded by woods but was itself grassy and almost bare of trees. From the top there was a magnificent view of the countryside for miles around. It had been the site of many childhood games, Malcolm remembered.

Some of his relatives were sitting on the slope of the hill, resting after the long walk. Others were climbing higher. A few were wandering around the base of the hill to where a small stream trickled its way slowly toward the lake. Julia was standing alone at the very top, shading her eyes and squinting off into the distance. Malcolm led Camilla upward.

"What is it?" she asked, looking up at him suddenly.

"W-what?" he said.

She frowned slightly and looked above them to the top of the hill. "Oh," she said quietly, "you had better go on ahead of me, Malcolm. I am tiring anyway. You had better go and talk to her."

"I d-don't think it's the r-right time," he said.

"I think you need to," she said. "Both for your parents' sake and for your own, Malcolm. Do it now before you have time to think further. I'll walk up slowly after you to

see the view or perhaps to join the two of you." She slipped
her arm from his.

It was all wrong, Malcolm thought. Not Julia. Anyone
but Julia. He should not even have considered it or allowed
his mother and father to do so. But Camilla was expecting
him to go forward. And he knew he would despise himself
if sheer cowardice kept him away from Julia. It *was* cowardice. But cowardice sometimes had to be fought. He
strode on up the hill.

"It's a l-lovely view," he said, coming to stand beside
Julia. He rarely stammered any longer. So rarely that it took
him by surprise when it happened. He was thirty years old,
he reminded himself. Julia was his cousin, or almost so.
She was only twenty-one.

She turned her head toward him and smiled. No one had
a brighter smile than Julia. It always lit up her whole face.
Daniel had used to say that it was the most damnably mischievous smile he had ever seen.

"Hello, Malcolm," she said. "Yes, it is, isn't it? Well
worth the climb."

"Yes, indeed," he said. And reached about in his mind
for something else to say. There must be a million things to
say, a million commonplaces to mouth. No one else ever
seemed to have difficulty making small talk. He could not
think of a single thing.

"And such beautiful weather," she said. "The trouble
with us English is that we can never enjoy a warm sunny
spell like this. We are always wondering how we will have
to pay for it later."

"Yes," he said. "Yes, we are like that, a-aren't we? We
should e-enjoy it. Shouldn't we?"

She laughed suddenly and he twisted the hands clutched
at his back, mortified. "Malcolm," she said, "what did you
think of Grandpapa's will? Was it not dreadfully naughty
of him to provide for me as he did?"

"He w-wanted what was best for you, J-Julia," he said.
No, not this topic. She was not going to talk openly about

this, was she? But it would be just like Julia to do so. Julia always confronted issues head-on.

"Yes," she said. "Oh, I know. He was always trying to find husbands for me, you know. Or a husband, I suppose I should say. He longed to see me happily settled before his death. I disappointed him. I could never like any of the gentlemen who showed an interest in me. I should have tried harder, shouldn't I?"

"I-I d-don't"—Malcolm stopped and swallowed and unclasped his hands—"I don't know if you can or should force yourself to accept an offer you don't quite like," he said.

"Don't you?" She looked up at him, interested. "How should one choose, then? How can one know who will suit one for a whole lifetime?"

He opened his mouth and shut it again, staring at her blankly. How did one choose? How did one know? It might be easy to choose with the heart if one fell in love. Or with the head if one wanted to be sensible. But how could one use good sense on the future? Perhaps years and years of the future. People changed. All people changed. Both partners in a marriage would change in the course of years. How could one be sure that one would not change in different ways from one's partner? How could one be sure that even if they suited now they would suit ten years in the future? Or twenty?

Julia shifted from one foot to the other and flushed slightly. "You are one of the five cousins mentioned in Grandpapa's will in connection with my future," she said. "Does that fact have any significance to you, Malcolm?"

How did one answer such a direct question? With a simple yes? Should he try to explain? Did she want them all to be interested in her? Or did she feel trapped, rather as if she were being preyed upon by vultures? Poor Julia, he thought. Uncle should have left her Primrose Park. It would have given her the wealth and freedom to choose her own husband in her own time.

Yes, she was looking trapped. She was darting glances, pointed glances beyond his shoulder.

"I-I," he said. "Julia— That is—"

But blessedly someone had come to join them. Camilla. She must have been watching and realized that they both needed rescuing. Thank God for Camilla.

"Isn't the view lovely?" she said in her easy, quiet manner. "And such a wonderful clear day. Do you remember playing pirate ships up here, Malcolm? You always had to be the captain because you were the oldest."

"And you were the captured maiden in distress," he said.

"Borne off by that notorious cutthroat pirate, Freddie," she said. "Always Freddie. It was quite in character."

They both chuckled and Julia smiled brightly from one to the other of them. "I have the most dreadful urge to race down the steep side of the hill," she said. "We used to do it, I remember, and try to pull to a halt before plunging into the stream and getting soggy shoes, stockings, and hems. I am so glad that Aunt Sarah did not come today. Daniel is nowhere in sight, is he?"

"I saw him at the bottom of the hill walking with Uncle Paul and Uncle Henry," Camilla said.

"Good." Julia smiled that radiant, mischievous smile again, the one that Malcolm found so appealing. "Because here I go. I think Freddie and Les are down there. Would anyone care to join me?"

Without waiting for an answer, she gathered up her skirt, just as she had done at Culver Castle in order to run up the hill, and went racing off down the steep slope. She shrieked as she gathered speed.

Malcolm and Camilla looked at each other and smiled. "Some people," Camilla said, "seem able to resist the urge to grow up, don't they?"

"But she is not childish," Malcolm said. "She is delightful."

"Daniel would disagree," Camilla said. "But poor Daniel has not felt free simply to enjoy life since Papa died when he was only fourteen. I wish for both their sakes it could have been much later."

"Death is the one thing we have almost no control over," Malcolm said. "We can only make the most of life as it is presented to us day by day."

"Which is exactly what I have been telling myself of late," she said. "Do you remember all those games we played, Malcolm? You were always my great hero, you know, because you were six years older than I and always appeared dependable and strong. And then before I knew it you were too old to play any longer."

"But I continued to dream of rescuing you from dragons or highwaymen or quicksand or whatever danger presented itself to my imagination long after I stopped playing," he said.

"Did you?" She laughed and looked up at him with interest. "You always appeared so grave. I think a great deal more goes on inside you than ever appears to other people, does it not? It was no good with Julia, Malcolm?"

"I could think of nothing to say," he said ruefully. "I felt dull and tongue-tied. I *am* dull compared to someone like Julia, Camilla."

"Do you love her?" she asked.

He thought for a moment. "No," he said. "There has to be an emotional attachment, doesn't there? I admire her greatly. I always have. Am I a hopeless case?"

She laughed. "Because you can only admire a certain lady but not love her?" she said. "By no means. One day you will love, Malcolm, and you will feel neither awkward nor dull nor inferior. There is a lady somewhere who is just right for you."

"She had better find me, then," he said. "I am not sure I would have the courage to find her." He laughed, something he rarely did.

They strolled along the top of the hill and down the gentler slope, talking amiably about nothing in particular.

* * *

The three men were walking along beside the stream, enjoying the shade from the hot rays of the sun that the trees afforded. Though their minds were not really on their physical comforts. They were deep into a discussion of the desirability of parliamentary reform and the possibilities of its ever happening when the government was made up of men in whose interest it was to keep things as they were.

"Of course," Uncle Paul said, "there is always the danger of revolution along the French lines if the government proves quite implacable."

"I think not," Uncle Henry said. "Look what happened in France when it was tried, Paul. Englishmen are more sensible."

"Let's hope English gentlemen are too," the earl said, "and do something in the name of justice and fair play before it is too late. Reform must come, I believe."

But their discussion was broken into by the sound of a wild shriek and they all turned their heads to look up the hill.

"The children at play," Uncle Henry said with a chuckle.

"*Julia* at play," Uncle Paul said, laughing outright. "There is not another child in sight."

She was hurtling down the hill, quite alone, at a pace that was going to have her either losing her balance and tumbling down the steepest part of the slope at the bottom or else plunging headlong into the stream. The earl sprinted back the way he had come to save her from the latter fate, at least.

She almost bowled him off his feet. If he had not caught her by the waist and lifted her and twirled her right about, he would have been flat on his back and she would have been spread-eagled on top of him. She was laughing when her feet touched the ground again. Until she looked up and saw who her savior was.

"I might have guessed it," she said breathlessly. "It could not possibly have been anyone else but you, could it, Daniel?"

A small, soft, warm waist. Those breasts heaving against

his chest again. If he dipped his head a mere few inches, he would be able to taste her lips. She would taste sweet. He would be able to taste the inside of her mouth with his tongue. And he could easily part company with his sanity altogether during what remained of the month at Primrose Park, he thought, coming back to his senses in the nick of time. He put her firmly away from him and dropped his hands. The uncles, he noticed, were walking on after yelling some witticism and doing a deal of laughing.

"I know what it is," Julia said, frowning up at him. "You have an identical twin, don't you? No, there have to be more than two. Quadruplets? Sextuplets, maybe? That's right. There are six of you, Daniel, aren't there? I have discovered your secret. For most of my time—oh, a little more than most—I am busy doing the most blameless, most decorous things. But whenever I do, on the rarest of occasions, decide to kick up my heels and show a little enthusiasm for life, there is one of the six of you to confront me with compressed lips and contemptuous eyes and a lecture two yards long and inches thick with dust. It is quite disgusting."

"If there are six of me," he said, "there must be twelve of you, Julia. Don't you realize how covered with bruises and cuts you would be if you had lost your balance?"

"But I did not," she said.

"Or how wet you would be if I had not caught you?"

"But you did," she said, "more is the pity. Did you have to be just here at just this moment, Daniel?"

"Did *you?*" he asked, glowering at her.

"Camilla rescued me at the top of the hill," she said, "bless her heart. And I was so relieved that I had to do something quite—"

"Reckless?" he said. "Dangerous?"

"Those are the words," she said, flashing him a smile.

"What did she rescue you from?" he asked. "A wild boar?"

"A very tame bore, actually," she said, laughing. "Though it is dreadful of me to say so and I feel quite ashamed for not being able to resist the pun. I am sure Malcolm is not really a bore. He reads and studies a great deal, does he not? He must know all sorts of interesting things. If he could only talk about some of them! I could get nothing out of him except stammerings and fixed stares. And yet he sought me out. I caught Camilla's eye and yelled out 'Help' silently. She came, and I rewarded her by abandoning them. Poor Camilla. It was dreadfully mean of me. Especially when she had to suffer his company all the way from the house."

"I take it, then," he said, "that Malcolm has not made you an offer yet?"

"Oh, dear, no," she said. "Though I am sure that was why he came to talk to me. Why else would he have done so? He never has before. But he could not get the words out. That water looks very inviting. I suppose you would be outraged if I removed my slippers and stockings and paddled in it. Wouldn't you?"

And find himself subjected to the view of her bare feet and ankles? Yes, he would be outraged. Very.

"Silence, just as with Malcolm," she said. "Though your answer speaks loudly from your eyes. Very well, I shall stroll with ladylike decorum at your side, Daniel, since I am sure you are too much the gentleman to go striding off and leave me alone here. I shall even take your arm since you are offering it. There. The thing with Malcolm is that one gets the feeling he is thinking all sorts of profound things, which he forgets to put into words. It is very disconcerting."

"So you have not made your choice yet?" he said. "I thought perhaps you were settling things with Gussie up on the parapets of Culver Castle a few days ago."

"Oh, don't remind me of that," she said. "I suppose you plan to do so every time we are alone together, don't you, Daniel? My great humiliation. I gave those slippers to my maid, by the way. They are a size too large for her, but she was quite delighted. No, I really could not marry Gussie, though he was quite willing to give it a try. He is far too good a friend to be my husband."

"Is it not desirable to be friendly with your husband?" he asked.

"Friendly, yes," she said. "But not bosom pals, Daniel. I would die of embarrassment when we . . ."

"Would you?" he said. "I thought you were incapable of feeling embarrassment, Julia. Except when you are caught out in some weakness, like being terrified to descend castle stairs, for example."

"I don't like the topic of this conversation at all," she said. "I suppose it is the topic of a large number of conversations these days, though, isn't it? Whom will Julia marry? I hate it. Let us turn the tables. Whom will you marry, Daniel? I suppose it would be entirely in your nature not to marry at all. I cannot imagine that it would be easy for you to find a woman worthy of your great dignity and consequence. But of course you will marry, nevertheless, because you are always dutiful and it is your duty to marry and set up your nursery someday soon so that the succession will be assured. Am I right?"

"You are right," he said curtly. His anger felt almost like hurt, he thought in some surprise. Must it be assumed that his sense of duty and responsibility made him a cold and an unfeeling man? Incapable of tenderness? He was not incapable of the finer feelings.

"Well," she said, "then you must be looking about you. You were in London for the Season when Aunt Millie summoned you, weren't you? Were you shopping at the marriage mart? And had you singled out anyone special, Daniel?"

Blanche. He did not want to discuss Blanche with Julia.

"Your silence speaks louder than words," she said. "What is she like? Is she pretty?"

"Small," he said, "and delicate. And blonde. Exquisitely lovely."

"Ah," she said. "My antithesis. But then she would have

to be. And is she worthy of you, Daniel? Is she very lady-like and proper? Will she make a perfect countess?"

"She is everything that is decorous," he said. "I would not know one moment of anxiety with her. Only pride."

"Ah," she said and was quiet for a while. "Do you love her, Daniel?"

Love Blanche? Did he love her? The word was not appropriate. It had nothing to do with anything. Blanche was everything that he wanted and needed. And she was more than pleasing to the eye. He could have a life of peace and contentment with Blanche.

"Let me put it another way," she said. "Do you want to put yourself inside her?"

"The devil!" he said, coming to an abrupt halt.

"You were the first to say the words," she said. "Beside the lake a few mornings ago, remember? You wished to shock me. So you cannot accuse me of saying something quite improper without accusing yourself in the same breath. Well, do you?"

"No!" he said. "Of course I do not— Julia, I could shake you. I could shake you until your teeth rattle."

"That makes a change," she said. "So you don't. I suppose that is not important when you are choosing a wife. A very proper wife. Only when you are choosing a mistress. Oh, don't look outraged, Daniel. I am not a green girl. I have heard of the existence of mistresses. But I don't think it would be a very joyful marriage if you could not take all the pleasures there are from it. Would it?"

He inhaled deeply. No other woman—no, not just no other *lady*, but no other *woman*—would think of holding such a discussion with a man. Good Lord, how did she come to know of the difference between respect for a lady and lust for a woman? And how did she come to disapprove of the fact that most gentlemen chose to keep the two quite separate in their lives?

"Won't your marriage be rather dull?" she asked.

"Julia." He was speaking through his teeth, showing her as he did not wish to do that she had him rattled. He breathed inward again. "The woman I choose to marry and the quality of my future marriage are none of your concern. None whatsoever. Do you understand me?"

"I hate that question," she said, "especially when it is posed in just that tone of voice. It is so despicably rhetorical. Do you enjoy the dull life, Daniel? Don't you sometimes long for adventure? Don't you sometimes long to break loose and do something quite—"

"Outrageous?" he said. "Daring? Dangerous? No, I don't, Julia. I grew up several years ago. I have no wish to revert to childhood."

"You grew up when you were fourteen," she said. "I can remember when I first came here with Papa and Stepmama that you were fun-loving and always laughing. You and Freddie both. I was very young but I can remember that. You were like two gods to me. I can remember looking for you one day and being told that you had been confined to your room for the rest of the day after a thrashing. I can't remember what mischief had provoked it."

"I was a child, Julia," he said. "Children get into mischief. It is part of growing up."

"But you grew up too soon," she said. "Fourteen is too soon, Daniel. Freddie was still having fun long after that."

"Freddie is still having fun," he said. "And a long way it has got him. I hope you have given up all thought of marrying him."

She sighed. "And so we are back on the topic again," she said. "He has kept his distance for the last few days. He just stands back and grins at me and looks at me in that lazy way of his and sometimes winks. I think he is waiting for everyone else to have his say before moving on to the next stage of his courtship. I look forward to seeing what it is. At least life is always exciting when Freddie is involved with it."

"If you marry him, Julia," he said, "I doubt you will be saying that to me in ten years' time. Or even five. Don't do it."

She smiled up at him. "The trouble with you, Daniel,"

she said, "is that you want to drag everyone else down to your level. You want us all to be sober and dull."

He felt that strange mixture of anger and hurt again. If they had not been moving away from the stream and rounding the hill and coming in sight of other relatives, he might have clamped her arm to his side and pulled her to a halt and turned her to face him. He might have had it out with her. Face to face, toe to toe.

He was not dull. His life was not dull. It was rich with meaning—with relatives and friends and duties and responsibilities. And there was marriage in his future—with Blanche if he was fortunate—and children. A wife and a family. People of his own. People to relax with and laugh with and love with and have f— Yes, and have fun with. Fun did not have to be daring and reckless. It could simply be fun. It must be years since he had relaxed and had fun. Fifteen years, perhaps? Could it be that long? Was he really twenty-nine? Had all his youth passed him by since the unexpected death of his father had catapulted him out of boyhood and into an early manhood?

"Never say," Julia said, "that you are going to let me have the last word, Daniel. How very disappointing you are sometimes."

"Perhaps you had better hope, Julia," he said, "that you only ever see me when I am sober and dull. Perhaps you would not wish to see me any other way."

If he had expected to silence her, he was to be disappointed. She looked up at him with widened eyes and smiled in that special way she had of smiling, everything in her that was mischievous and impish lighting up her face. "Oh, Daniel," she said, "that sounds so very interesting. For perhaps the first time in our lives you have piqued my curiosity."

And she slipped her hand from his arm and went tripping off across the grass to join Stella and Viola, who were with Freddie and Les. The earl drew one more steadying breath. He had to admit that she did light up a day. Not at all in the way one might want it to be lit up, perhaps, but she did it nonetheless.

Would life be dull with Blanche? But he put the thought from him before it could take root and bring him doubts that he had no wish to entertain.

9

Frederick had had rather a nasty shock. Though perhaps *jolt* would be a more appropriate word, he thought, since it was a fairly minor happening. But it might be symptomatic of things to come, and then life would become uncomfortable.

He had had a note and a bill from one of his creditors. A fairly insignificant one—a bootmaker to whom he owed the trifling sum of a few hundred pounds. But if one had discovered his whereabouts, the chances were good that word would spread fast, and then there might be a flood of such notes.

There was nothing new in it. He was quite accustomed to ignoring the bills when his pockets were to let and paying off some of his more persistent creditors when he was in funds. Sometimes after all he had a streak of good luck just as sometimes he had a string of losses. But it was one thing to receive and ignore bills when one lived in bachelor rooms in town and quite another to do the same thing at Primrose Park. Someone else might get wind of them. His father, heaven forbid. Or Julia.

Another frustration of being in the country, of course, was that it gave him little opportunity to bring his fortunes about. And it was high time they came about. His losing streak had lasted altogether too long this time. He was due for some good luck. Of course there was the one potentially lucrative and quite acceptable game in progress at Primrose Park. A game it was becoming increasingly imperative that he win.

"You have changed your mind, Les, have you?" he asked

his brother as the two of them rode their horses at a walk for the last mile back to the stables after a morning ride.

"Mind?" Lesley looked blank. "About what, Freddie?"

Frederick clucked his tongue and tossed a glance at the gray sky. "About what else?" he said. "Is there any other topic of conversation these days, Les? About Jule. Have you changed your mind about offering for her?"

Lesley frowned. "Offering for Jule," he said. "The thing is, Freddie, I don't think she would have me."

"You will not know unless you ask," Frederick said. "And you have been dithering for a week, Les. I want to get on to the next stage of my own campaign, but I also want to give you a sporting chance."

"I thought perhaps Gussie would be the one," Lesley said. "They've always liked each other, Freddie. Still do. He is with her more often than not. Always laughing, the two of them."

"And that is not a promising sign at all, my lad," Frederick said. "Not promising for Gussie, that is. It is very promising for you and me."

Lesley looked blank again.

"If those two are lovers," Frederick said, "I'll eat my hat, Les. Whichever one you choose to make me bite into. No, Gussie is not in the running. Neither is Malcolm. He got together with her once at the top of the hill several days ago and spent all of five minutes with her. Then she went whooping down the steep side of the hill like a schoolboy let out of school for the summer holidays. He has not been near her since to my knowledge."

"Dan?" Lesley said.

"Dan bristles with outrage every time he sets eyes on her," Frederick said. "And sometimes even when he does not. Someone only has to mention her name. Besides, he has the divine Miss Morriston panting for him in town. Or probably not panting exactly—the chit is made of ice as far as I can observe. No, Les, I think the serious contenders can be narrowed down to you and me."

"I like Jule," Lesley said. "Can't understand why Dan don't."

"For the very reason that we do," Frederick said. "Jule is not ashamed to show that she is alive. When are you going to talk with her? If you are not, then I am going to proceed to sweep her off her feet."

"You will anyway," Lesley said, "even if I offer for her, Freddie."

"Yes, granted," Frederick said with a grin. "But at least you will not be able to say that I did not give you a sporting chance, Les. But it is true that I have never yet failed to bowl over any female I set my mind to bowling over. And Jule is ripe for the picking, if you will pardon the lamentable mixing of images."

"But you never liked her in that way before," Lesley said, frowning. "Did you, Freddie?"

"Neither did you," Frederick said. "But she never came with Primrose Park before, Les. Only with a dowry. Dowries, no matter how generous, come to an end. Rents don't."

"I think someone should marry Jule because she is Jule," Lesley said after frowning in thought for a while. "Not because of Primrose Park."

Frederick chuckled. "And so someone will, my young idealist," he said. "You know I am fond of her. I'll give her all the affection she needs, Les. And all the pleasure she craves. And children too. Doubtless she will want some children and I suppose it would not hurt for me to have a son or two. Would it? Set up my dynasty and all that." He laughed again.

Lesley drew his horse to a halt outside the stables. He was still frowning. "But it is the rents that are most important to you, Freddie," he said, "not Jule. You wouldn't marry her without them, would you?"

"Les," his brother said, "this is the real world. This is not fantasyland. In this world money is necessary for survival."

"Papa gives you plenty of money." Lesley looked troubled. "He gives me plenty, Freddie, but he gives you more, I know. And you will inherit when Papa dies."

"Which may be a long time in the future," Frederick said. "Which I *hope* will be a long time in the future. In the meantime we both have to live. And you know that Papa is not the sort of person to whom one goes to ask for more blunt. For one thing it would be humiliating. And for another he would assume that sorrowful look he always used to have when we were lined up for canings. As if we had disappointed him beyond measure. As if the whipping was going to hurt him more than it hurt us. Gad, Les, he knows how to make one abject with guilt and misery."

"You really do have big debts, then, Freddie?" Les asked. "They can't be cleared with next quarter's allowance? Even if I give you some of mine?"

Frederick swung down from his horse's back and grinned. "Les," he said, "you can do it almost as well as Papa. Yes, dear brother, I do have big debts. Bigger. And next quarter's allowance has to be lived on. I'm afraid it is debtors' prison for me or Papa's sorrowful look or a political marriage—one of the three. On the whole I think the marriage is the best bet. And the fact that it is to be with Jule makes it a little more palatable than it would otherwise be. Actually the thought of a leg shackle is enough to make me break out in a cold sweat."

Lesley slid from his horse's back a little more slowly. "I think you should go to Papa, Freddie," he said. "He won't eat you, you know. And you are too old for a caning. Then you would be free."

Frederick laughed and handed the reins of his horse to a waiting groom. If Les only knew, he thought, how much of a dent the paying of his debts would put even in their father's fortune. "Until next time," he said. "I am afraid I have a compulsive and rather expensive habit, Les. Though my luck could change any day and I could end up as rich as Croesus. That is a pleasant thought to dream on, now is it not?"

"I don't think you should marry Jule," Lesley said, relinquishing his own horse to the same groom. "I really don't, Freddie. Not fair to her, you know. Jule deserves better."

"She will think herself the most fortunate woman in the world," Frederick said. "She will *be* the most fortunate woman. I'll see to it, Les. I intend to treat her well. I know how to treat a woman. It is one of my innate talents and practiced skills." He grinned again.

"You will give up all other women?" Lesley asked.

Frederick threw back his head and shouted with laughter.

"Then I think I had better talk with her," Lesley said. "I really do, Freddie. I'm sorry if she chooses me. Sorry for your hopes, I mean. I don't suppose she will, mind, but I think it would be best for her. I think I'll talk to her as soon as possible. Today."

"Why delay any longer?" Frederick asked, looking affectionately at his brother. "There she is now, Les, my boy, strolling in the formal gardens with Aunt Millie. I shall draw Aunt Millie away and leave the field clear to you. You see how much brotherly love I have? I'll blight my own chances by giving you an opportunity to make your offer. I do believe the rain is even going to hold off." He glanced up at the sky.

"All right, Freddie," Lesley said, drawing a deep and audible breath. "I'll do it. Let's go."

"That's the boy, Les," his brother said, slapping him on one shoulder.

And the thing was, Frederick thought, confident as he was of being able to win any woman he set himself to charm, and insignificant as Les's opposition might seem, there could be no certainty about the outcome. One could never tell with Jule. She might choose Les just because she was Jule and had a habit of doing the unexpected.

That was part of her charm. And part of the excitement of the game. For though he desperately needed to win, he would not enjoy the process of winning if it were a certain thing—if there were no gamble involved.

Perhaps, he thought, he was an incurable gambler.

*   *   *

"And you will keep the parterre gardens," Aunt Millie said as she strolled through them with Julia. "I know you will, dear, because you have always been fond of them. And I have never held with these new ideas of doing away with formal gardens and making parks look natural and green to the very doors of the house. If anyone wants natural landscape, I always say, then they should walk out onto common ground. Though much of that is disappearing to enclosures these days, is it not?"

"I love parterre gardens," Julia said. "I love order and symmetry in nature—before a house anyway. But I may have no say in what happens with these gardens, Aunt Millie. I may well be moving away from here at the end of the month."

"Oh, never say so, dear," Aunt Millie said. "One of the nephews will offer for you, dear, if not all of them. They are all fond of you, I am sure, though that is hardly surprising. So am I. And a fine lot of young gentlemen they are too. I might not have stayed single myself if I had had such suitors vying for my hand. As it was, there were only gentlemen I had no interest in at all." She sighed. "Though I regret not having had children. But then I was blessed with your dear mama as a niece to live in the same house and more lately I have been blessed with you, dear Julia."

Julia turned to smile at her and then extended her smile to Frederick and Lesley, who were striding toward them, still dressed in their riding clothes. Things had been quiet for several days. She and Daniel had managed to avoid each other quite nicely, Malcolm was giving her a wider than wide berth, Gussie was her dear friend again, and Freddie was still keeping his distance, and still grinning and winking whenever he caught her eye. She wished he had continued with the promising line of courtship he had begun the evening they had strolled toward the lake, but he had not. And Les had made no move at all.

"I thought two roses had escaped from the rose arbor," Frederick said when they were within earshot. "But when I looked more closely it saw it was Aunt Millie and Jule."

Aunt Millie threw up her hands and laughed merrily. "Oh, Frederick," she said, "how outrageous you are. Two roses, indeed. Perhaps Julia looks like a rose—indeed I am sure she is prettier than one. But I am just an old thing."

"Precious gems are usually old things too, Aunt Millie," he said. "And so are priceless paintings. And medieval tapestries. Now I swear that I saw a pink rose in the arbor this morning the exact shade of your dress. I am going to pluck it for you without further delay and thread it in your hair. It is an exquisite bloom. It will almost do you justice." He bowed elegantly and offered his arm.

"Shameless flatterer," Aunt Millie said, tapping him sharply on the arm before taking it. "It is Julia you should be taking to the rose arbor, Frederick. I don't know what an old thing like me wants with a rose in her hair."

"We will honor the rose," he said. "Besides, Aunt, Julia is wearing green and I did not see any green roses in the arbor."

"Foolish boy!" Aunt Millie said as she was borne off along one of the gravel walks.

Lesley smiled. "Hello, Jule," he said.

Ah, so this was what that little scene was all about, was it? Lesley was about to make his move, with Freddie's connivance. Julia smiled in return. "Hello, Les," she said. "Did you have a pleasant ride?"

"Yes, we did, Jule," he said. "The weather has turned cold but it was pleasant for a ride."

"I know," she said. "I rode early. Before breakfast." Having found that she could no longer bring herself to swim in the early morning, she had taken to riding instead. For the first two mornings she had been quite decorous about it, donning one of her riding habits and having a sidesaddle placed on Flossie's back. But she had met no one during those rides and for the last three mornings had worn her breeches and had been able to gallop and enjoy herself.

"Some females don't get up until noon," Lesley said. "They miss a lot. I like females who get up early. I like you, Jule."

"Do you?" She smiled encouragingly. But he was merely beaming back at her. "Just because I get up early, Les?"

He looked blank for a moment and then startled. Then he laughed. She had always liked Lesley's laugh. He always sounded and looked genuinely amused. "Oh, no," he said. "No, no, Jule. I like you for everything. I have always liked you."

"Thank you," she said. "I have always liked you too, Les."

"Thank you, Jule." He beamed at her again.

Dear Les, she thought, trying to decide quite irrelevantly if he really was an inch or so shorter than she was or if they were on a level. They looked on a level, but then he was wearing riding boots while she wore silk slippers. Les was going to need as much encouragement as Malcolm, she could see.

"What did you think of Grandpapa's will?" she asked him.

"Uncle's will?" His smile broadened. "Very generous, Jule. He was a kind man, Uncle, even though he didn't like anyone to know. Five hundred pounds was very generous. I was happy."

Julia was hard put to it not to laugh out loud. Oh, dear. Perhaps he would need even more encouragement than Malcolm. "He did not leave me five hundred pounds," she said. "He left me the chance to live at Primrose Park for the rest of my life if I marry one of his nephews. Do you think that was really like leaving me nothing, Les?"

"Nothing?" he said. "No, it was not nothing, Jule. Though you wouldn't own Primrose Park, would you? And if your husband said you were to live somewhere else, you would have to go, wouldn't you?"

"I would owe him obedience," she said.

"And if he lost Primrose Park," he said, "you would have nothing but a husband, would you, Jule?"

"Oh, dear," she said. "How would he lose it?"

"If he spent too freely," he said. "Gambled or something like that."

"Do you gamble, Les?" she asked.

"Me?" He laughed again. "No, not me, Jule. I can never remember how to play a card game from one time to the next."

They stood smiling at each other for a few silent moments.

"Let's go and sit by the fountain, shall we, Les?" Julia suggested at last and took his arm to walk along the two gravel paths that would bring them to the marble structure and the wrought iron bench that circled its base. "Did you wish to talk to me about anything in particular?"

"Freddie and I thought it would be a good idea if I suggested you marry me, Jule," he said. "Freddie said he would take Aunt Millie out of the way."

"Did he?" She smiled. "Freddie thought you should ask me?"

"Yes," he said. "He said he would give me a sporting chance before he asked you again. You are bound to choose Freddie, of course, Jule, but you can choose me if you wish. I think you would be better with me even though I don't seem as good a bargain."

"Why not?" she asked, releasing his arm to seat herself on the bench and patting the place beside her. He took it.

"I don't have the looks or the brains that Freddie has," he said. "And he is the older son. I don't know much about women except that I like them."

"And you like me," she said. "You said so a little while ago."

"And I like you, Jule." He beamed at her.

"Why do you want to marry me?" she asked. "Just because you like me, Les? Or is it Primrose Park?"

"It's Primrose Park, Jule," he said eagerly, and Julia felt her heart sink. "I love it here. Everything is always so well kept. And the farms are prosperous. It is always fun being here."

"Yes," she said quietly. "It would be something to own it, would it not, Les? Especially for a man who cannot expect to inherit his father's property."

He beamed at her. "I want you to stay here, Jule," he said. "I want it to stay as it is for you. This is where you belong. I don't want you to lose it. And I don't want you married to someone who will make you obey him and go somewhere where you don't want to be. I want you to be free, Jule. I think Uncle should have left it to you. Maybe there was a good reason why he did not, but I think he ought to have."

Julia leaned forward and set a hand over his. "Les," she said, "you are so very sweet. And kind. You would marry me so that I could be free to enjoy Primrose Park at my leisure? But what would you gain from the marriage?"

He gazed blankly at her. "I would be happy to see you happy," he said at last. "I would look after you. But I would stay out of your way. You would not need to worry that I would be underfoot all the time. I think that would annoy you. I would do whatever you wanted me to do, Jule." He flashed her a smile.

She squeezed his hand. "You would get very little pleasure from the marriage," she said. "Do you get much pleasure from living, Les? What would you like to do most in life? If you could do anything?"

He gazed at her until his eyes grew dreamy. "I would travel," he said. "All over Europe, Jule. Maybe all over the world. To see things. I can read about them but I can never remember them. I can't picture them in my head. But when I see things, it is different. I saw the Elgin marbles. I felt it all. Here." He touched a loosely closed fist to his heart.

"You could travel," she said. "The wars are over."

He stared at her. "Could I?" he said. "I had not thought about it, Jule. Only dreamed. But you would not like it, and I would need to stay here to look after you."

She patted his hand again.

"Will you marry me, Jule?" he asked. "I think you should. I'll look after you."

"I know you would, Les," she said. "I know you would make a most wonderful husband."

He looked gratified. "Do you think so?" he asked.

"I know so," she said. "But would I make a wonderful wife for you, Les? I would be marrying you just so that I could stay here and have a secure future. I could offer you nothing more than affection."

"Will you, then, Jule?" he asked.

She shook her head. "I shall have to think about it, Les," she said. "It is a most kind and generous offer. And I would not be able to ask for a gentler or more indulgent husband. But I need to think."

"Take your time, Jule," he said, getting to his feet. "No hurry. I'll still be willing next week and the week after. I just wanted you to know that you don't have to leave here and that you don't have to marry anyone who won't treat you right."

"Thank you, Les," she said, smiling. "I am going to stay here for a while and think. Do you mind?"

She watched him walk back to the house, the smile lingering on her lips. Now there was a definite and very wonderful offer for her to consider. But an impossible one to accept, of course. A wave of sadness rid her face of the last traces of her smile.

Dear Les. He was willing to marry her entirely for her own sake. Entirely for her own comfort and happiness. He would be the owner of Primrose Park as her husband, of course, but he would use it only to provide her with contentment. It seemed that he had no thought of using her. The very thought of Les's kissing her or holding her or being in any way intimate with her was ludicrous. She very much doubted that Les had even thought of consummating the marriage he had just proposed.

There would be nothing whatsoever in the marriage for Les. Except perhaps the satisfaction of knowing that he had secured her happiness. And there was nothing she could possibly offer him—except the affection she had mentioned to him. It would be impossible not to feel affection for Les. But nothing else. She would have nothing else to offer.

And so if she married him, she would be being as selfish and as mercenary as someone who would marry her just for the sake of owning Primrose Park. Freddie. That was why Freddie would marry her. Did he have as little else to offer her as she had to offer Les?

Julia sighed and felt the old familiar anger against her grandfather for putting her in this predicament and sorrow that he had left her so little freedom.

She needed exercise, she decided suddenly. Vigorous exercise. Swimming leapt to mind. But she would not feel free to swim until everyone went back home again. But there was the sudden numbing realization that when everyone else returned home this time she too would be leaving Primrose Park—forever. Unless she married one of the cousins.

Boating, then? But the boats were in the boathouse and too heavy for her to drag out unassisted. She would have to go in search of one of the gardeners to help her or else drag one of the grooms from the stables. It would take too long.

Riding, perhaps? She had ridden earlier in the morning but not so far as usual because it had looked as if rain was going to come down at any moment. She looked up at the sky. It was still gray with clouds, but they were too high to bring rain. It was just a dull day, that was all. She would go riding again, she decided, getting to her feet. She strode toward the house.

Had she met any of the cousins on her way inside and up to her room, she would have asked them to join her. But the hall and the stairway were deserted. Everyone, it seemed, was about some indoor activity since the weather made the outdoors uninviting. She rejected the idea of going in search of someone. She would prefer to ride alone anyway. She really needed to think.

And the deserted nature of stairs and hall made something else possible. Julia did not ring for her maid to help her into her riding habit. Instead she pulled on her breeches with a shirt and jacket, looked gingerly out from the door of her dressing room to make sure that the corridor had not suddenly filled with disapproving aunts, and darted out and

down the stairs and across the hall, almost holding her
breath the whole way.

Luck was with her. She met no one, and the grooms in
the stables were used to seeing her dressed as she was. One
of them saddled Flossie for her and she mounted—
astride—and made her escape from the stables unobserved.

Freedom! she thought as she made her way north of the
house at a canter. It was such a very precious commodity.
And Les could and would offer it to her permanently. She
would be foolish to reject his offer just because the arrangement would bring nothing to him. And just because she
craved more of a relationship than they could possibly find
together. And more of life than endless peace and comfort
at Primrose Park.

10

The Earl of Beaconswood left his cousins, Frederick and Lesley, when they decided to return to the house after a ride of a mere hour. He had not had enough exercise. Besides, he always enjoyed riding alone. Normally his life was a busy one. Solitary rides were a luxury and gave him a chance to think or merely to relax.

He was doing both on this particular morning. He was riding slowly along the bank of the lake—the trees made any faster pace unwise—enjoying the sight of the clouds reflected on its surface. He hoped that he would not see a swimmer. But surely even Julia would not swim this late in the day. Besides it would be a chilly pleasure on this particular morning.

He turned his thoughts resolutely away from her. By unspoken consent they had avoided each other quite successfully in the days since the walk out to the hill. And she had been behaving with something like decorum despite the fact that his mother had reproved her the evening before for growing rather noisy during a game of charades when they were all supposed to be in mourning for the late earl. But even he had been able to see that his mother had been rather unfair to her. After all, none of them were wearing mourning and almost all of them had been involved in the game. They were merely doing what his uncle had directed them to do in his will—enjoying the month together.

Julia had left both the game and the room without another word and a dampener had fallen on all their spirits. The game had gone only one more round. He had to admit—grudgingly—that Julia did add life to a party.

No, he did not want to think of her. He had had a letter

that morning from a friend in London. Blanche was going to Brighton for the summer. Horrocks was laying determined siege to her heart, his friend had written, and to her hand, and she was not discouraging him. But she had sent a message. Oh, no, that was not strictly accurate, of course. She was far too well bred to send him messages. But she had hinted in the way well-bred young ladies could excel at doing that she would wait to see if the new Earl of Beaconswood would put in an appearance at Brighton before making her decision. He was the favorite, it would appear.

In less than three weeks he would be free to leave Primrose Park. Perhaps she would still be in London. If not, he would know where she was and would be able to remove to Brighton himself without delay. If he wanted to. Following Blanche to Brighton would be tantamount to declaring himself.

Did he want to take such an irrevocable step?

He frowned and turned his horse's head into the grove of trees so that he would come out in the open meadows north of the house. He had had few doubts just a couple of weeks before. Was he having doubts now? Because he had not seen her exquisite beauty for a few weeks perhaps? Because now that the time was close he was realizing fully what a very irreversible step in life marriage would be?

He was not having doubts. He was longing to see Blanche again. He was longing to get away from this suspended life and back to his normal life. He was ready to move on to the next stage of it.

Another horse was cantering toward him across the meadow as he emerged from the trees. He might have thought that the rider was one of his male cousins, but he did not. He might have thought that it was one of the grooms. Certainly she looked enough like a boy with her boy's clothes and her manner of riding. But in fact he was not deceived for a moment. He had seen her riding thus many years before. And he was learning to expect the indecorous from Julia. Even at this time of the day when anyone might have seen her—his other cousins or his mother or his aunts. Or his uncles.

And he was learning to expect the tightening of muscles and the tensing of nerves. And the furious anger. And the urge to throttle. How dared she continue over and over again to fly in the face of convention? Good Lord, she looked—voluptuous. Her legs were long and slim. Not at all masculine. Never in a thousand years could he have mistaken her for a boy.

She saw him almost immediately and eased back on the reins so that her mare reduced its pace to a walk. Her own expression tightened for a moment and then unexpectedly she grinned—or perhaps not so unexpectedly for Julia.

"Where have you been for the last three mornings, Daniel?" she called as she drew closer. "It is amazing you were not there waiting to pounce the very first time—you or one of your five identical brothers. Less than an hour ago I was strolling in the parterre gardens just as a lady ought with Aunt Millie. And whom did I see? Freddie and Les, that's who. Now I have stolen away from being the perfect lady for a little time to myself, and whom do I see? You. Of course. Who else?" She laughed gaily.

Her flippant manner fanned his anger. "Julia," he said, "look at yourself. You are a disgrace to your family and your sex."

"I don't have to look at myself," she said. "There is no looking glass out here. And you do not have to look either, Daniel. You are returning to the house? I am not. Goodbye. I shall see you later if I cannot avoid doing so."

She was sitting very upright, looking quite relaxed and self-assured. Her thighs, spread wide across the saddle, controlled her mount with practiced skill. The earl swallowed and grew hot when he realized the direction his eyes and his mind had taken.

"You are going back to the house with me," he said. "Now, Julia. If we are fortunate we will be able to get you in through a side door and up the servants' stairs to your room before you are seen. I will have your word that you will not appear in these disgraceful clothes again while my family is in residence here."

His words were like a red flag to a bull, of course. He realized that even as he was still speaking. She raised her eyebrows and looked directly back into his eyes.

"You forget one thing, Daniel," she said, her voice cool and controlled. "I am not your property. Not even to the extent of being a member of the family of which you are the head. And I am not *on* your property either. If you wish me to go back to the house with you, you will have to take me there by force. I do not doubt that you will be successful if you choose to try, but you will not be unscarred. I can promise you that. As for the clothes, they are rather similar to yours though Weston did not make mine, of course. Are they really disgraceful? Are yours disgraceful?"

"A man's clothes are disgraceful on a woman's form," he said through his teeth. "Just as a woman's would be on a man. They are an open invitation, Julia."

"Are they?" She smiled and leaned slightly toward him from her saddle. "An invitation to what, Daniel? Are you having naughty thoughts—again? Your very proper lady love would be very shocked. Here is an invitation of another kind. A race. Race me to the stream?"

She did not wait for his answer or look back to see if he had accepted her challenge. She laughed, spurred her horse, and bent low over its neck as it bounded quickly into a gallop.

The stream circled around in a huge horseshoe northward from the hill east of the house and then southward to flow into the lake. There were two long meadows between where the earl was standing his horse and the stream. Two meadows full of potential dangers to the unwary and reckless rider. And two thick hedges bordering them. She would kill herself. It would be a fitting ending for Julia. She would break her neck when her horse stepped in a rabbit hole or when it failed to clear one of the hedges.

And he would carry the guilt of feeling responsible to his grave. Lord, this time he would wring her neck if he could get his hands about it before she broke it. He gave his horse the signal and went racing after her.

He was following her, she realized suddenly as she responded to the exhilaration of pounding hooves beneath her and wind rushing at her face. She was surprised. Or perhaps not. He would feel obliged to follow her just so that he might give her a thundering scold when the race ended. She did not turn her head though she wanted to laugh back at him again. She would need all her concentration if she was to maintain and even increase the pace she had set.

She did not usually gallop so fast over these meadows. Her grandfather's head groom had warned her not to but to reserve her more energetic rides for the park south of the house, which he could guarantee to be free of dangers. And she had never jumped these particular hedges, but only the lower, cultivated ones in the park. She did consider easing her pace, coming to a halt before the first hedge and grinning at him as if she had never intended to go farther. But the challenge had been issued quite unmistakably. Pride was at stake.

She would aim for the lowest part of the hedge without swerving too far off course. But there was no lowest part. It was all uniformly and alarmingly high and thick. She set her eyes on a part of the hedge directly in front of her, spurred her horse toward it, and concentrated on showing no sign at all that might convey nervousness to Flossie. She heard her mare's hooves brush twigs and leaves as they soared over.

And then she began to enjoy the race. She risked one quick glance back and laughed with excitement. He was clearing the hedge with perhaps a foot to spare. He was closer than she had expected. She would be fortunate indeed if she did not lose the race quite ignominiously.

He caught up with her when they were a little more than halfway across the second meadow. He rode dangerously close. She thought for one moment that he was going to try leaning across and grabbing her reins.

"Stop, Julia," he yelled. "Enough!"

If she had for a moment thought of not risking the second hedge, the thought was gone. She laughed once more. "Are you afraid I will beat you?" She called back without removing her eyes from the hedge ahead. It looked higher and thicker than the first. "Come on, Flossie," she urged, leaning farther forward across the horse's neck, lifting as much of her weight as she could from its back.

They went over together, side by side. By some miracle Flossie cleared the hedge, though the moment was to give Julia nightmares for several nights to come. The earl's horse, a massive stallion, had no trouble at all, of course, but Julia did not spare any attention to notice that. She slowed for the stream, patting Flossie's neck, wondering if her heart would stop pounding before cutting off her breathing altogether or before breaking right through her ribs.

A horse drew up beside her and she remembered her pride again. She flashed a smile. "A dead heat, would you say?" she asked. "We will have to try again some time, Daniel, to see who is really the better horseman."

She scarcely finished the words. Her companion had thrown himself from his own horse—there could be no better word to describe the way he dismounted—and was reaching up to grasp her ungently by the waist and drag her from hers. She came down in an inelegant heap—all arms and legs and indignation.

But before she could gather together either her dignity or her anger, a hand clamped on each shoulder hard enough to leave bruises and she was being shaken and shaken. Just like a rag doll with no chance to grab either her breath or her balance or fistfuls of his coat.

"You she-devil!" were the first words she heard, though many had gone before. "You might have killed yourself, Julia. Worse, you might have killed your horse. Do you have no sense of danger? No sense of responsibility?" The shaking continued so that she had no immediate chance either to reply or to marshal her thoughts.

"You are a dangerous child," he said, holding her still at last, clutching her shoulders even more tightly if it were possible, speaking directly into her face from only a few inches away. "Without thought, without conscience, without discipline. You are a wild uncivilized child. I have a mind to turn you beneath my arm and give you the thrashing with my riding crop that my uncle should have given you years and years ago. Or better still, with my bare hand."

She was afraid of him. For the first time she was afraid. He was within a whisker of doing it, she knew. And she could sense the power of his body through the strength of his hands. She was totally powerless in his grasp. There would be pain—he was furious and would not spare the weight of his hand. But far worse than the pain, there would be humiliation. Being spanked by Daniel. Just like a naughty child. She was not a child. She was a woman.

The realization that she was both in his power and afraid of him turned her to ice. "Take your hands off me, Daniel," she said. "I am not answerable to you for anything I do. And I did not force you to follow me, to turn my ride into a race."

"You did not force me!" He almost spat the words from between his teeth. He forced her closer to him so that she felt her breasts flatten against his coat and had to tip her head back. "You go out riding astride dressed like this and challenge me to a race across uneven ground and over unkempt hedges and you expect me to let you go? It is time you were taught a lesson you will never forget, Julia. A painful lesson."

"You did not follow me because you were outraged," she said. Her neck was aching already from the awkward angle at which she was forced to hold her head. "Or because you saw me as an unruly child in need of chastisement. Be honest with yourself, Daniel. You followed me because I am a woman. More woman than you have ever encountered before. More woman than you know what to do with."

The words seemed to speak themselves. In her voice. She listened, appalled, and stared defiantly into his eyes.

"My God!" His words were whispered, and she suddenly

found herself no longer frightened, but terrified. Mindless with terror.

Julia was quite blasé about the art of kissing. She had been kissed several times and by more than one gentleman and knew all there was to know about it. She even knew enough about it to realize that a gentleman she fancied or one with expertise could make the exercise a great deal more interesting than it had been in her experience.

But what followed was not, of course, a kiss. It was something she had never experienced and something she knew nothing about and something she had never suspected to be within the realm of anyone's experience. His mouth was open when it came down over hers, both his lips and his tongue demanding that hers open too. One iron-hard hand spread over the back of her head to prevent her from pulling back. But she had no thought of doing so or of resisting the demands on her mouth. She opened and was invaded. And invaded in her turn. She pressed her mouth back against his, fenced with his tongue in her mouth, followed it out and into his own, got her arms up somehow to circle his neck, pushed the fingers of one hand up into his hair to hold his head steady.

Everything became jumbled after that. If she had been able to think, she might have concluded that what happened over the next several minutes was more like a wrestling bout than an embrace. They fought each other, tasting, licking, biting, sucking, breathing in loud gasps, exploring each other with ungentle, unsubtle hands.

Julia could never afterward remember how they had got down onto the ground, and yet when she began to come partly back to herself, she opened her eyes and saw gray sky straight ahead. She was on her back on the grass by the stream, her jacket wide open, the buttons of her shirt all undone, her breasts aching from where he had been stroking and fondling them beneath her chemise.

His weight was half on her, one arm beneath her head, his mouth and his warm breath at her throat, one of his legs hooked over one of hers, holding it apart from the other.

His free hand was stroking down her inner thigh, on top of her breeches, and up again. And on up until his hand cupped her most private place and his fingers pulsed flat against her.

And the encounter changed tone. They both stopped fighting as if by mutual consent, although not a word had been exchanged. She tilted her hips, allowing his hand freer access. And she closed her eyes again as his head lifted and his mouth covered hers once more, open, wet, warm. Bringing pleasure. Bringing intimacy with his tongue, stroking aches and yearnings through her mouth and into her throat and breasts and on downward to be intensified by his hand.

He lifted his mouth away to kiss her chin and her throat. But they opened their eyes at the same moment and gazed with heavy desire into each other's eyes. There was a moment, Julia thought afterward, or perhaps the merest fraction of a moment, when all they saw was a mirrored self, a mutuality of need and desire. No more than a moment at the longest. And then he was sitting up beside her, his arms draped loosely over his knees, gazing out over the stream, and she was lying on the ground, doing up buttons with hands that felt as if they had been created with ten thumbs.

"That is the lesson, you see, Julia," he said quietly after what must have been a full minute of silence. "If you are not dressed like a lady, and if you do not behave like a lady, the chances are that you will not be treated as one. Be thankful that you will escape from here without being ravished."

The thing was, the very worst thing that had happened all morning, the worst thing she could ever imagine happening—the thing was that she could think of not a single reply to make to his words. They hurt like the stabbing of a dagger and they angered like the slap of a glove across the face. And they invited retaliation for their smug male double standard. But she could not marshal words scornful enough to speak. Her body was still crying out too loudly for him.

She lay where she was until she was sure that all her buttons were done up, and then she got to her feet without a word, walked over to where Flossie was cropping the grass in deep contentment, mounted with shaking legs that almost would not accomplish the feat, and rode off at a trot, in search of the gate leading into the nearest meadow. She did not look back.

Her throat was aching. She had to keep swallowing to get rid of the unfamiliar urge to start bawling. And her breasts were tender and aching against the cotton of her shirt and the coarse cloth of her jacket. There was a throbbing between her legs and along her upper thighs. And of course she was not even going to pretend that she did not understand either what was happening to her body or what had been happening down by the stream. Her body was still yearning for him. She had wanted him. She had wanted everything that a woman can want of a man. Had he stripped off her breeches, she would have allowed him the ultimate intimacy. Not only allowed it—she would have invited it, begged for it.

She had wanted him. Daniel. As she had always wanted him since childhood fantasies of Daniel as hero had been converted into girlhood fantasies of Daniel as lover. As she had wanted him since he came back to Primrose Park a few weeks before. She had always wanted Daniel—his attention, his approval, his admiration, his affection. His love. And because she had never been able to have any of those things, she had hated him and despised him and set out to shock him and outrage him. Just like a child who must win attention by being naughty if being good would not do it.

She hated herself. *Hated* herself. Craving the attentions of a man who was so prim and proper on the outside, so lustful just below the surface. Craving the attentions of a pompous hypocrite. She eyed the second hedge speculatively for a few moments, but good sense prevailed. In her present mood of agitation, she would doubtless come to grief if she tried to jump it. And that would be unfair to Flossie—as he had said. It was worse that she had endangered Flossie's life, he had said, than that she had endangered her own.

She hated him.

And she hated herself ten times more than that.

The earl did not turn his head to watch her go. Neither did he make any attempt to follow her until long after she must be back at home already. He sat and stared sightlessly at the stream.

He had just lost a battle he had been fighting for a few weeks, one he had first fought six years before. He had fought himself, his base human nature, and he had lost. He had always known that it was possible to lust after what one disliked and even despised. Had he not occasionally over the years, despite all resolutions to the contrary, made use of the services of whores? And despised his own weakness every time afterward?

But he had never dwelled on the guilt of those encounters. It was after all part of the sexual nature of man to need woman.

This was different. Julia was a lady and an innocent despite her behavior. The first time she had been only fifteen years old to his own twenty-three. A girl he had disliked and found completely lacking in manners and modesty. A girl who was only just budding into womanhood. One he had wanted with fierce heat. He had fought his own dual nature that summer and won. He was not even sure now if she had had anything to do with the fact that he had not returned for six years. He had never consciously thought so, but who knew what went on in the hidden chambers of the unconscious mind?

And now this year he disliked her and disapproved of her with many times the force he had felt all through her growing years. She was a woman now. She was supposed to be a lady now. Like Camilla. Like Blanche. His dislike of her was intense. But not as intense, it seemed, as his desire for her.

He had pursued her, she had said, not because she was a child in need of chastisement, but because she was a woman. Oh, God! He lowered his head until his forehead was resting on his knees. Could that be true?

God!

He had possessed many women, and had taken several of them with an energetic lust. He had never—not once—lost all touch with reality, been so absorbed with the woman in his arms that sensation had deprived him of thought and reason. Not once until just now, that was. If they had not by the purest coincidence both opened their eyes at the same moment, then . . . There was no need to complete the thought. She certainly would not have stopped him. And he was not going to throw all the blame on her for that, though he believed he had done so in what he had said to her before she had got up and left. If she had been mindless of her virtue, then he had been equally mindless of his self-respect.

God! Lord God. He was trying to keep his mind away from what he knew must be faced. He closed his eyes very tightly. No.

No. He would think of it later when he had had time to calm down. When he was able to think quite rationally again. Perhaps he would come to the wrong conclusions if he allowed himself to think now.

How could he come to the wrong conclusion? There was only one possible conclusion.

No. God! He scrambled to his feet and went in pursuit of his horse, which had wandered some distance away in search of greener pastures. He would think of something else, he thought as he mounted and settled himself in the saddle. He would think of Vickers Abbey and Willowbunch, his new properties, which must be visited sometime during the summer. He would think of Blanche. No, not of Blanche.

He would think of nothing, he thought, turning his horse's head in the direction of the house and looking along the line of the hedge for a gate. But of course it was impossible to think of nothing. He would think of the impossibility of thinking nothing, then.

11

The sun broke through the clouds and finally dispersed them altogether early in the afternoon, bringing with it brightness and warmth. Aunt Sarah decided that they should all stroll down to the lake and have a picnic tea brought out there later. Uncle Henry pointed out, a twinkle in his eye, that they hardly needed to organize an excursion to the lake as if it were a military exercise since it was a mere mile away from the house, but Aunt Sarah bent a quelling looking on him, and he held his peace and meekly fell in with her plans.

And so they all trooped down to the lake, two by two, just like the animals into the Ark, Frederick was heard to remark to Viola—very much sotto voce since Aunt Sarah had the reputation of possessing the sharpest pair of ears in the family.

Julia was dressed in flimsy white muslin with pink sash, slippers, and parasol. She had dressed with great care and tripped down the stairs and into the hall with determined gaiety. Whom should she choose as a walking companion? Gussie? But no, everyone must realize that she was not taking Gussie at all seriously as a suitor. Les? But she had not had time yet to think out her answer to his offer. Freddie was flirting with Viola, quite safely since Uncle Paul and Aunt Sylvia would not accept his suit in a million years. That left Malcolm.

And so all the way to the lake—it seemed more like five miles than one—she delivered a bright monologue on any and every topic that presented itself to her mind, one arm linked through Malcolm's, the other twirling her parasol above her head. She did not even pause to find out if perhaps he had some interest in making it a conversation. She talked faster and twirled harder and smiled more brightly whenever she fancied that the earl, who was escorting his mother, was glancing her way. But of course he was careful to do no such thing.

Malcolm was a good-looking man, Julia thought, if a trifle too tall and thin. He would surely make a steady and dependable husband. Perhaps he would never talk a great deal, but she always had enough to say for two. Perhaps it would work if she wanted it to. She wondered what it would be like to kiss him. Would he open his mouth? Would he draw her body right against his? Would he tear at buttons and put his hands where they had no business being? No gentleman had ever done any of those things to her except . . . Or would he set his hands at her waist or on her shoulders and touch closed lips to hers? As every gentleman who had kissed her except one had done.

Perhaps she should lure him off into the trees, she thought, and seduce him. It should not be difficult to do—to lure him among the trees, that was. But try as she would, she could not imagine being kissed by Malcolm.

"Malcolm," she said suddenly, breaking into her own monologue as they approached the lake, "have you ever been in love?"

He looked down at her and flushed. "I-I," he began and she was instantly sorry that she had asked him such a direct and such a personal question. Poor Malcolm was so very shy. "It depends on what you mean by the term, Julia."

"Is there more than one meaning?" She had never thought of it before. What did it mean to be in love? To want a man? She had wanted—oh, yes, quite voraciously—but her feelings could not at all be described as being in love. To feel deep affection for a man? She felt deep affection for Gussie—and for Les. She was not in love with either. To feel wonderfully, blissfully happy? She could feel that way when swimming or when gazing at a sunset. She was not in love with either the lake or the sun. "Oh, dear, I suppose there is. It is really a meaningless phrase, is it not?"

"L-love," Malcolm said and then paused to swallow—twice. "Love is wanting to be with someone all the time. It is accepting the other person with all good qualities and bad and not wanting to change any of them. It is wanting to give affection and approval and comfort and everything that is oneself, demanding nothing in return. It is—love is very difficult, Julia. It is an ideal, rarely achieved in reality because we are all selfish and imperfect beings. It is a dream, a goal, something to be aimed for."

Julia stared up at him. If she could string together all the words Malcolm had ever uttered to her, she did not believe they would be as many as he had delivered in this one speech. And they were words of unexpected wisdom and insight.

"Oh," she said. There was no man she wanted to be with all the time—except perhaps Gussie. There was certainly no man she could accept with all his faults and not want to change them. She would never be able to accept Freddie's gambling and womanizing or Les's eternal good nature or Malcolm's long silences. Or Daniel's stuffy sense of what was right and proper for that matter. She would never be able to give and demand nothing in return. What if she loved Daniel? It would be all give. All she would get in return was contempt and disapproval and demands that she change and become a lady. *If* she loved Daniel.

The sunshine was sparkling off the water of the lake. Daniel, Freddie, Uncle Paul, and Uncle Raymond were carrying the two boats from the boathouse.

"So being in love is not just the good feeling one gets when looking at or thinking of someone special?" she said.

"P-perhaps being i-in love is, Julia," Malcolm said. "But l-loving is something d-different."

Being loved by Malcolm would be something special, Julia thought in some surprise, looking at him with new and curious eyes as they seated themselves on a blanket with Uncle Henry, Aunt Roberta, and Stella—her in-laws if she were to marry Malcolm. It was a strange, unreal thought. Stella and Aunt Roberta were smiling at her and Uncle Henry was looking speculatively at Malcolm. Julia could feel herself flushing.

"The boats are out at last," she said brightly. "It is the first time this year."

"And I can tell that you are itching to be the first out in one of them, Julia," Uncle Henry said with a chuckle. "You had better go and secure two places, Malcolm."

Malcolm got to his feet and strode away.

"You are looking as pretty as a picture today, Julia," Uncle Henry said.

"And very bright and happy," Aunt Roberta said with a kindly smile. "Almost as if you were in love."

Julia twirled her parasol and smiled.

"I shall thoroughly approve, Jule," Stella said, "if it is with the right man. Mama and Papa are taking me to Brighton for a few weeks when we leave here. Is that not wonderful?"

"And you too, Julia, if you decide at the end of the month that you wish to make your home with us," Uncle Henry said. "It would be an arrangement that would suit all of us."

"Thank you," she said, blinking her eyes against the tears that wanted to rush there. "I have not made any decisions yet."

"Of course not, dear," Aunt Roberta said. "You still have almost three weeks to decide. There is no hurry at all. You must take your time and enjoy the choices that are yours."

"Thank you," Julia said again. But looking at them, knowing very well what they were thinking and hoping, she felt a wave of panic. She could not marry Malcolm. Of course she could not. Not in a million years. She would never be able to love him and, worse, she would never be able to make him happy. Malcolm, she thought, deserved to be happy.

Each of the boats held four passengers with comfort. Malcolm had secured two places in a boat with Frederick and Camilla. The earl was handing his sister into the boat as Malcolm brought Julia up while Frederick held the boat steady against the bank. Daniel obviously did not realize that she was to be the other lady passenger, Julia thought in some dismay as he turned quickly and extended a hand before he looked fully at her.

Meeting his eyes was one of the most painful things that had happened during the day. It was almost like a physical jolt, as if someone had placed strong hands against her shoulders and shoved her backward. She could not possibly set her hand in his, she thought, looking down at it and re-membering—of all things—that it had fondled her breast and pinched her nipple to tautness just a few hours before. She half expected him to snatch his hand away and save her from her dilemma, but he did not do so.

"I suppose you do not need help," he said at her hesita-tion, his eyes narrowing. "Foolish of me to think that you might, Julia."

She slapped her hand down onto his and waited for siz-zles to burn up her arm and into the rest of her body. But it was just a warm and strong hand closing about hers, dwarf-ing it. A hand that would hurt like the very devil if he ever made good on his threat to take her beneath his arm and wallop her. She looked defiantly into his eyes. He looked steadily back.

She scrambled into the boat with undignified haste, swaying it dangerously so that she shrieked and Daniel had to clasp her upper arm with his free hand to save her from pitching headfirst into the water. The spectacle she would have created in doing so did not bear contemplating. As it was all eyes had turned her way. She glared up at him, mor-tified by her clumsiness, as she seated herself beside Camilla. And good heavens, the hand that was only now re-linquishing hers was also the same one as had touched her in a place where she was almost too embarrassed to touch herself. On top of her clothing, it was true, but still and all. Good heavens.

"Thank you," she said tartly.

"My pleasure, Julia," he said, straightening up.

It was a great relief to have something to laugh over during the next few minutes. Frederick and Malcolm sat side by side and took an oar each. But try as they would, and no matter how much Malcolm frowned in concentration and Frederick whooped with mirth, they could not row in rhythm together or get the boat to go where they wanted it to go. Finally Frederick took the oars on the understanding that he would do the work until they reached the other side and Malcolm would row back.

But they got to the other side too quickly, long before Julia had recovered from the renewed agitation that had taken her a few hours to recover from just that morning. She did not want to go back so soon. She did not want to have him rushing to help Camilla out of the boat and feeling obliged to lend her a hand too. If she had to be that close to him again today, if she had to touch him again, she would explode. She would treat the whole family to the delightful spectacle of Julia having the hysterics and either hurling foul imprecations and fists at all and sundry or else sobbing beyond control and soaking every handkerchief that would be thrust at her. Neither prospect was in any way appealing.

"It is far too soon to go back yet," she said gaily when Malcolm offered to take over the oars.

"What do you suggest, Jule?" Frederick asked, smiling lazily at her. "Rowing in circles for the next hour?"

"I wish we could," Camilla said with a sigh. "It is lovely out here. And so very peaceful. But there are others waiting for the boat."

"I don't want to go back yet," Julia said. "There are too many people."

"What?" Frederick chuckled. "Too many people for Jule? I thought you thrived on having an audience."

"Well, there you are wrong, Freddie," she said. "I like being solitary especially when nature is so beautiful." She had a sudden idea. "Set me down on the bank here and I shall walk back."

"It is too far, Julia," Camilla said. "It must be all of two miles around the bank to the boathouse."

"Pooh," Julia said. "That is not far. The walk will help me work up an appetite for my tea."

Frederick laughed. "The aunts and Dan will have a collective fit if you are let off to wander alone, Jule," he said. "If you want to be eccentric enough to walk when there is a boat to recline in and look pretty in, then I shall play gentleman and come with you. It is Malcolm's turn to row anyway."

"I would not dream of inconveniencing you, Freddie," Julia said.

"It is no inconvenience at all, Jule," Frederick said, rowing the boat against the bank, scrambling out, and holding it steady against the side with one hand while extending the other to her. "In fact the more I think of the idea, the more merits it has." He grinned.

Julia looked down into the boat when she was standing on the bank beside Frederick. "Do you mind being abandoned?" she asked Camilla.

Camilla smiled back. "Not at all," she said. "Malcolm will take me back safely. I hope you do not get blisters, Julia."

"That was bad of Freddie," Camilla said. "You were her escort this afternoon, Malcolm. Would you have preferred to go with her yourself?"

He gazed at her for a while. "No," he said. "Should I have, Camilla? I would far prefer to be here with you. She will be more at ease with Freddie."

She laughed. "I am not sure that Mama or Daniel would approve of their going off alone like that," she said, "though I can see no harm in it when they have been brought up as cousins. And I cannot think that Freddie would hurt her despite his shocking reputation."

"Perhaps we should not have let them go," Malcolm said.

Camilla smiled. "Can you imagine stopping Julia from

doing something she had set her mind to doing?" she asked. "It was either alone or with Freddie."

Malcolm rowed in silence for a while.

Camilla closed her eyes and turned up her face to the warmth of the sun. "It is so lovely out here," she said. "And so peaceful, Malcolm. You are such a peaceful companion. One does not have to make a constant effort to keep a bright conversation going. I feel utterly happy."

"Do you, Camilla?" he asked.

"I have not felt happy since Simon's death," she said, "though I decided this spring to return to living. Unfortunately, when we were in Bath, Mama pushed any number of older gentlemen my way. She thinks that having experienced one unhappy love match, I cannot want another."

"Don't marry an older man, Camilla," Malcolm said. "And don't marry for less than love."

"I don't intend to," she said, smiling at him. "But I will think of all that later in the year when Mama wants us to go to London. For now I want to enjoy the summer and the lake and the sun. And your company."

"You can have that as often as you wish, Camilla," he said, "if it will bring you some happiness."

She smiled at him with gratitude and affection, and he smiled back.

Julia and Frederick walked for a few minutes in silence. The trees were denser on this side of the lake. The air was filled with the sounds of water lapping and birds singing and insects droning. It was wonderful.

"I thought Malcolm was the afternoon's favorite, Jule," Frederick said. "You were prepared to entrust him to Camilla's care?"

"It was not very kind of me, was it?" she said, lowering her parasol when she found it snagging on too many twigs and brushing against too many leaves. "Poor Camilla. It is well nigh impossible to hold a conversation with Malcolm."

"I don't think Camilla has that problem," he said. "They

grew up as close chums, you know, rather like you and Gussie. I think it was the general belief that they might end up together. But then Camilla fell for a military uniform."

Julia looked up at him in surprise. "Camilla and Malcolm?" she said. "No. They are both too quiet."

"Perhaps Camilla allows him to get a word in edgewise," he said.

"Meaning?" She looked up at him indignantly. "Meaning that I talk too much, Freddie?"

He chuckled. "Not for me, Jule," he said. "I can always shut you up when I have a mind to it."

"Well," she said, trying to remain indignant but laughing instead.

"So Malcolm is being rejected," he said, "and Gussie already has been. Dan has never been in the running. How did you take to Les's offer this morning?"

"I was moved," she said.

"Moved?" He raised his eyebrows.

"He is sweet and kind," she said. "Les knows how to give. In fact." She frowned. "In fact, according to one definition I heard recently, I think Les knows a great deal about love."

Frederick chuckled and set an arm about her shoulders. "And so do I, Jule," he said. His voice was lower suddenly, more husky. When she looked up at him, it was to find him regarding her from beneath half-lowered eyelids. "We were interrupted a week or so ago. I decided that maybe I should back off and let everyone else have a chance with you too. I think it is time to resume our—conversation. Don't you?"

Yes, she did. She had something she desperately wanted to forget and replace with another, less disturbing experience. "Yes, I do, Freddie," she said.

He stopped walking and turned her to face him, setting his hands at her waist. She spread hers over his chest and beneath the lapels of his coat. His muscles, she was relieved to find, were quite as solid as Daniel's. His chest was just as broad. He was a little taller. Her hands had to slide up a little farther to his shoulders.

"That's what I like," he said. "A willing wench." His dark eyes were smiling at her.

She felt a twinge of fright. But it was only Freddie. "I am not a wench," she said. "And I don't know quite what you mean by willing."

"What *are* you willing for, Jule?" he asked. His voice was low and he dipped his head to kiss her below one ear. He took her completely by surprise by nipping her earlobe with his teeth.

"Oh," she said, breathless. But she was not going to back off. She had a few ghosts to banish. And a future to secure. "I want you to kiss me, Freddie. Will you?"

She was walking into fire with her eyes wide open, she knew. They were quite hidden among the trees and miles from anyone. She reminded herself again that he was just Freddie. But she had a sudden and quite irrational longing to see one of the Daniel sextuplets come wandering out of the forest so that she could berate him for always being in the wrong place at the wrong time. He would look at her most scathingly for putting herself in such a compromising position, she thought. But she would be safe.

"Always willing to oblige, Jule," Frederick said, drawing her against him so that she could feel his size and strength and know her utter helplessness. He splayed one hand against her back below the waist and set the other arm about her shoulders. She lifted her face and waited for a repetition of that morning's experience. Except that Freddie did not have the dislike of her that would cause him to put an end to the embrace as soon as reason could see past lust.

But it was quite different. His lips were parted, as Daniel's had been, but his mouth did not assault hers. His lips caressed and teased, as did his tongue. She relaxed her own mouth and allowed him his will. It was—it was pleasant, she thought.

He kissed the end of her nose and gazed at her with those incredible bedroom eyes that would surely reduce to mush any woman who had not known him all his life and did not know that he was merely Freddie.

"Mm," he said. "More of the same, Jule? Or are you willing for something a little different?"

She was being given a choice? His arms were loose about her. She would be able to draw free of them if she wished and walk away. She lost her fear suddenly. He was not dangerous, as Daniel had been dangerous that morning.

"Maybe something a little different, Freddie," she said cautiously. "But not too different."

His eyes laughed at her before his mouth returned to hers. And his hands moved slowly, lightly, circling her upper back, smoothing over the sides of her breasts, cupping them gently. His thumbs feathered over her nipples. His tongue stroked over her lips, probed lightly up behind them.

It felt good, Julia thought, and quite unthreatening. She was enjoying the embrace. If he were not Freddie, she might be quite excited by it. It would be very possible, she thought, to become mindless with the pleasure of it. And so he would find her willing for a little more and a little more until . . .

Oh, yes, she thought suddenly, sliding her hands along his shoulders and admiring their rippling muscles, Freddie was every bit the expert that everyone said he was. The master seducer. He would not overpower with the strength of his passion. Not an innocent and potentially skittish partner, anyway. He would have infinite patience, leading on by slow and pleasurable degrees until he had what he wanted and his partner would be convinced that she had had what she wanted too—his worshipful love.

She was intrigued by this insight into a Freddie she knew of but did not know. A woman would not feel ravished or ruined by Freddie. She would feel beautiful and she would feel loved. She would feel that she was the one finally to entrap him and his eternal love and fidelity. Freddie's path through life must be strewn with broken hearts.

"Freddie," she said, setting a hand on either side of his head, drawing back her own, and then returning it to kiss him once lightly on the mouth, "that was nice. But I am not willing for any more."

"Nice!" He smiled lazily at her. "Faint praise indeed, Jule. But the rest can wait. I don't intend to rush you. I think you are worth waiting for."

And Primrose Park too, she thought and immediately felt mean for the mental sarcasm. He was being very gentlemanly—well, to a certain extent anyway.

"Do you?" she said. "Are you in love with me, Freddie?"

"I think," he said, bending his head to kiss her below the ear again, "I may surprise us both by being so before I am finished, Jule."

Which was, she had to admit, a clever answer. And a flattering one. And perhaps a true one. It was impossible to tell if Freddie was acting a part or for once in his dealings with women telling the truth.

"I like the way you kiss, Freddie," she said. "It is unthreatening."

His smile became a grin for a moment. "If I were you, Jule," he said, "I would never try to earn a living from paying compliments. I think we should marry. Soon. To hell with this monthlong game. Make us both happy. Marry me. Let me announce our betrothal today."

It was so very tempting. Freddie was by far and away the most attractive of her cousins—the eligible ones, anyway, and by far the most interesting too. And she would be happy with him. Until he gambled Primrose Park all away and until she began to have incontrovertible evidence that he was dallying with other women. She would never change him, she knew. She would only be changed by him. Changed for the worse.

"I don't know, Freddie," she said. "I'm not sure. I need more time."

He dipped his head and kissed her again, openmouthed, more fiercely than he had up to that point. She felt instant alarm, but he drew back almost immediately and smiled at her.

"Take all you need, Jule," he said. "I can wait. But the

siege is on, I warn you. I want you. For my wife. I think perhaps if I examine the state of my heart—something I assiduously avoid doing—I will find that I have already fallen."

"In love?" She could swear he meant it.

"In love," he said, releasing her and stooping to pick up her parasol, which she had dropped earlier. "But don't force me to examine my heart just yet, Jule. I am terrified."

They walked on, talking amiably about all sorts of inconsequential matters until they came in sight of the boathouse and the blankets and the gathered relatives.

"We could have the wedding here," Frederick said, having finished amusing her with an account of a curricle race between London and Brighton—one in which he had not participated, though Julia guessed that he must have bet heavily on its outcome. "It would be a lovely setting for a wedding, Jule."

"Yes, it would," she said. "Perhaps, Freddie. I need time."

"Granted," he said, smiling at her. "You are lovely, Jule. Lovely to look at, lovely to hold, lovely to kiss and to touch."

Even when one could recognize flattery for what it was, it was easy to be warmed by it, she thought. "Thank you, Freddie," she said, smiling back at him.

And then Uncle Paul was calling him to help steady one of the boats so that Aunt Millie could climb safely in, and he hurried away. Julia stood looking after him. What a pleasant hour it had been, she thought. It had quite restored her spirits, which had been severely bruised that morning. She felt quite genuinely cheerful again.

Until she saw the Earl of Beaconswood walking her way—obviously with deliberate intent.

12

At first when he saw the boat return with only two passengers instead of four, the Earl of Beaconswood had the horrid suspicion that she had gone swimming. Probably her pretty white muslin dress—for once she had looked like a lady that afternoon—was folded neatly at the bottom of the boat with her slippers and parasol. Or more likely, tossed into the bottom of the boat. Freddie—he could see that Malcolm was rowing—had gone with her. He shuddered at the thought of her appearing on the bank, in full view of the uncles and aunts and cousins—and his mother—as she had appeared to him early on a certain morning.

It was an enormous relief—for a while—to find out from Camilla and Malcolm that they had only gone walking, the two of them, having disembarked at the opposite side of the lake. Except that at the opposite side of the lake the woods were dense and in fact there were trees all around. The walk from the point at which they had disembarked must be at least two miles long. It would take them over half an hour even if they walked without stopping.

She would be alone with Freddie for more than half an hour—unchaperoned. The foolish, foolish woman. He could only hope that no one would notice, that everyone would assume that she was off walking somewhere with plenty of company. Did she care nothing for her reputation?

Freddie would not try anything with her, he thought, pacing the bank of the lake and smiling whenever he caught someone's eye and trying to look as if he were enjoying himself immensely. Freddie had some sense of what was right and proper, surely. But he himself had lost that sense during the morning and he had not even set out to fix her interest. Indeed, he did not even like her. But Julia had that effect on men. It was not just her prettiness. There were any number of pretty women around. She was just so damned attractive—and so recklessly available.

And then it happened.

"Daniel," his mother said, "where is Julia? Did she not go out in one of the boats? I did not see her return."

"Oh," he said, looking about him to see who else was absent at that particular moment. "She is off walking somewhere with Stella and Les, I believe, Mama. And Freddie."

"Well, that is strange," she said. "I did not see her come back. I hope this having power over the future of five gentlemen has not gone to her head. Julia does sometimes have a tendency to imprudence."

"She is strolling, Mama," he said. "As several other people are."

He hoped that she was. Half an hour had passed and there was no sign of her. He damned well hoped she was strolling. He hoped she was not . . . He had an unwilling image of her flat on her back by the stream, helping him undo her buttons, both pairs of hands fevered, and guiding his hand beneath her shift to her breast. As mindless with desire as he had been. And she was with Freddie. God!

And now she had caused him to lie to his mother. To cover up for her indiscretion. He stared broodingly out across the water until a boat cut across his line of vision and he was forced to smile and wave at two uncles and two aunts. Why had he lied? Why would he even want to cover up for her?

He looked to where she and Freddie would emerge from the trees when they came. There was still no sign of them. He was going to give them two more minutes and then he was going to go in search of them. If he found them in a compromising position, he would . . . He drew a deep, steadying breath. If Freddie had touched her, he would kill him. It was as simple as that. And if Julia had allowed herself to be touched, he would—he would do something to her. It alarmed him that he seemed so often to be contemplating violence against Julia. He was not a violent man. In particular he disapproved very strongly of using violence against women.

And then just when he was about to stalk off, they came. They were strolling arm in arm, looking perfectly cheerful and amiable. And looking remarkably tidy and unrumpled. But it had taken them almost an hour to walk two miles. Almost an hour.

Freddie was summoned almost immediately to help Aunt Millie overcome her jitters and get safely into one of the boats. Julia stood looking fondly after him. The earl felt the old familiar welling of irritation and even anger, especially knowing what he must say to her, what he had planned to postpone until the next day. He had learned from experience, though, that there was no point in putting off until another day what could just as easily be done today. It became no less difficult the next day, but sometimes more so.

She turned her head and saw him coming. He watched her smile disappear to be replaced by wariness and hostility. Her glance slipped away from his eyes to his mouth or his chin. She looked at him and yet she did not look.

"Where have you been?" he asked her. Not an amiable question. He could hear the iron in his own voice.

"Don't be tiresome, Daniel," she said.

"You were set down at the opposite side of the lake," he said. "The distance from there to here must be no more than two miles."

"If you knew the answer," she said, "why did you ask the question?"

"It took you all of an hour to walk those two miles," he said. "Longer. It is an hour since Malcolm and Camilla brought the boat back. What is the explanation?"

She lifted her eyes coolly to his. "Daniel," she said quietly, "if you expect me to be unladylike, I will be unladylike. You may go to hell."

He felt rather as if his face had been slapped. Except that blood seemed to be draining from it rather than rushing to it.

"Oh, good," a voice said from close by—too close by, "here come the picnic baskets. I am starved. Henry, dear, do let us go and be first in line. Julia and Daniel, you may fall in behind us." Aunt Roberta laughed.

"We will have this discussion somewhere else," the earl said, taking Julia's arm in a grasp that was not meant to be gentle.

"There is no discussion," she said. "And I have just completed a rather lengthy walk. I am tired and hungry, Daniel."

"You will come walking with me," he said, turning her in the direction of the trees and the house.

"What I will do," she said, "is make a scene, Daniel. I shall scream and have a fit of the vapors. Let us see how you will like that."

But he was in no mood to wonder if she was prepared to follow through on her threat. He had had enough. He had been plagued by her, tormented by her ever since his arrival at Primrose Park before the death of his uncle. She had even invaded his dreams, appearing in them flimsily clad and smiling and warmly inviting. Not that the dreams were nearly as powerfully erotic as the reality of that morning had been. It was time things were settled with Julia. It was time she knew what was what.

He propelled her forward and she came with him without any of the sounds of protest she had threatened. He relaxed his hold on her arm when they were among the trees and drew it through his instead. She pulled it free, but continued to walk at his side.

"Did he touch you?" he asked.

"You must have seen that my arm was through his when we returned," she said.

"Did he *touch* you?" His voice was vicious.

"Yes, he did." Hers was correspondingly cool and incensed him further. "He kissed me, Daniel. For perhaps ten minutes altogether. He does it quite differently from you, if you are interested in knowing. Gently and very expertly. He did not attack me."

"I did not attack you," he said to her through his teeth. "That would imply that you were my victim."

"Well, perhaps it was a mutual attack," she said. "I grant you that. It was rather strange, was it not, Daniel, considering the fact that our dislike of each other amounts almost to hatred and that we cannot talk to each other without quarreling."

"Julia," he said, "do you not realize how indecorous it was to walk so long alone with Freddie? And how dangerous?"

"He might have ravished me," she said. "I should have learned that lesson this morning, shouldn't I? But he did not do so."

"I would not have been ravishing you," he said. "You were willing."

She looked up at him and smiled. She was still maddeningly cool. "I was, wasn't I?" she said. "Does it not amaze you, Daniel, that we can be so attracted to each other on a purely physical level? That the body can be so divorced from the reason and the emotions?"

"It was your vulgar appearance and behavior that did it," he said.

"Was it?" She smiled at him again. "So you do not find me attractive now, Daniel? I have nothing to fear from you now?"

The trees were behind them. They were walking up the sloping lawn. He turned their direction so that they would come to the rose arbor.

"I hope not," he said. "I hope that this morning's experience will teach me that the consequences of behaving as less than a gentleman can be catastrophic. I should not have followed you."

"And missed the race?" she said. "I thought it rather exhilarating, Daniel. And fitting that we finished together with no clear winner."

"I must apologize to you for what happened this morning," he said. "I am deeply sorry, Julia, for the distress and dishonor I caused you."

She looked up at him with interest as they passed beneath the rose-laden arch into the arbor and were assaulted by the scent of a thousand roses. "That is very handsome of you," she said, "since you so clearly believe that the fault was mine. Wearing breeches and riding astride, it seems, are very provocative to a man."

"It was unpardonable of me to lose control," he said.

She seated herself on a bench, raised her parasol above her head, and gave it a twirl, looking at him the whole while. "I have to savor this moment," she said, laughing. "The Earl of Beaconswood apologizing to plain Julia Maynard. I did not think I would live to see the day. But alas, I cannot revel in the triumph of it, Daniel. You don't need to apologize. If we behaved wrongly, we were one as bad as the other. Which I suppose is not a great deal of consolation to you, is it? I am sure it must be lowering to know that you were ever provoked into behaving as badly as I. Let's forget it. Let's go back and see if there is any tea left."

It was tempting. Very tempting, considering the fact that she did not seem unduly upset by what had happened and considering the fact that no one else knew. But he could not give in to temptation. His upbringing had taught him never to do so but to behave rightly and properly and responsibly. It had taught him always to make amends whenever he did for some reason go wrong.

"You must marry me, Julia," he said.

Her parasol stilled and so did every part of her body. Until she laughed. "*What* did you say?" she asked.

"You must marry me," he said. "You have been compromised. Very severely so. I must give you the protection of my name."

She stared at him again for a few silent moments. And then the parasol was twirling again. "It must be the sun," she said. "We must send for a physician. Or it is Primrose Park. Having been here for a few weeks you are being enticed by its charms and wish to keep it. No, Daniel. A plain and simple and straightforward and quite unnegotiable no."

"You were alone with me," he said. "I embraced you in a manner that might be considered improper even in a marriage bed. You have no choice, Julia."

"Daniel," she said. The parasol was spinning so fast that it must be whipping up a breeze about her head. "You are too stuffy for your own good. You make the marriage bed sound like the dullest place in the world. And I do have a choice. Yes or no. Listen to my answer. It is no."

He should let it go. He knew that. He had done the honorable thing and been rejected. He had persisted and been rejected again. He should let it go and begin rejoicing in his narrow escape. He should begin allowing himself to think of Blanche again. Julia's answer was crystal clear. And knowing her as he did, he knew that there would be no shifting her.

"I must insist," he said. "Even apart from what happened this morning, Julia, you must realize that you need my protection. You admitted to me that the prospect of going to live with your uncle is less than appealing. And your marriage prospects here can be no more so. There is no one with whom you could be happy."

"Let me make myself clear," she said, "once and for all. I would rather go to my grave as a miserable spinster than marry you, Daniel. I would rather be dead. I would rather marry a dragon. And as for my other prospects, I have had two offers just today—two apart from yours, which was a command rather than an offer. I am giving serious and careful consideration to both."

"Who?" His hands clasped themselves tightly at his back.

"Les and Freddie," she said. "And you are not invited to comment, Daniel. You have no right to do so. I shall choose one of them and I will be happy with my choice."

"You will be miserable," he said.

"Then I will be miserable," she said. "Either way, it is

none of your concern." She got to her feet. "I am going back to the lake for tea. Are you coming?"

He stood and stared at her.

"On second thoughts," she said, "I have lost my appetite, and I do not much care for the prospect of walking all the way back to the lake at your side, Daniel. I am going into the house. Alone, if you please. I think even you will agree that it is unexceptionable for me to walk that far unescorted and unchaperoned." She turned and walked out through the other archway and on up to the terrace.

The earl watched her go without moving. Freddie. She was going to marry Freddie. She had refused him and was going to choose his cousin instead. She had said she would rather be dead than married to him. He waited for the sense of freedom, for the euphoria that was bound to follow on his escape from a dreaded fate. But he felt only—what?

Disappointment? *Disappointment?* Had she said yes, he would have been shackled to her for life. He would have been subjected to her bold, unconventional, sometimes vulgar ways for the rest of his life. He would have been subjected to permanent anger, frustration, outrage. He would have quarreled with her every day for the rest of their lives. No, he could not possibly be feeling disappointment. Did a man feel disappointed when he had just been reprieved from imminent execution?

He felt—hurt? Hurt that she would reject him with such vehemence and such scorn when he had agonized over his decision and come to it with such heavy reluctance? Hurt that she showed no gratitude? Hurt that she would choose Freddie or even Les before him? The whole world of man before him? He could not be feeling hurt.

But the thought had been there at the back of his decision. The consolation. The thought he had been quite unaware of until now and even now shied away from. The thought that when he married her the brightness, the exuberance that was Julia would be part of his home, part of his life. The thought that when he married her he would be able to complete what had been started that morning. The thought that he would be able to delight his senses with her alluring and passionate body. Not just once but over and over again through their lives. In his own bed, in his own home.

Yes, the feeling was disappointment, he decided as he turned and walked resolutely back in the direction of the lake. Disappointment that he was not after all to possess the most attractive female body he had ever felt drawn to. The only one for which he had felt an almost overpowering and persistently lingering craving.

He despised himself for such carnal desires. And after all he felt relief. It was a great escape he had just had. For along with that body, of course, came Julia. Not just her exuberance, but her unconventionality, her careless disregard for what was expected of her as a lady. And her hostility whenever he tried to confront her. She would not be a suitable countess. She would not suit him—or at least she would not suit the kind of person his position compelled him to be.

The fact that she was crying by the time she reached her room angered her more than anything else. It was the final straw. She slammed the door behind her, hurled her parasol across the room and followed it with her slippers, one at a time, and then with her bonnet. But she still felt no better. The tears had developed into sobs and after that there was no stopping the despicable self-pity. She threw herself facedown across the bed and howled and pummeled the bedspread with the sides of her fists.

The sheer insult of it! *You must marry me, Julia. I must insist.* Because he believed he had compromised her virtue that morning. Because even she must be encompassed by his cold sense of duty to what was right and proper. Not— *will you marry me, Julia? Please will you reconsider?* But— *you must marry me. I must insist.*

It was too much. It was just too much. Her mind and her emotions could not cope with everything that had happened in the course of one day. When Grandpapa had been alive, she had sometimes looked back on a day and been almost alarmed to find that she could not remember a single thing of any significance that had happened. She longed for a return of those days. Those blessedly quiet and rather dull days when there had been Grandpapa to read to and Aunt Millie to converse with.

And she longed for Grandpapa. Oh, to be able to go along to his room right now and tiptoe inside to see if he was awake. To sit quietly at his bedside if he were not. To fuss over him if he were.

Grandpapa! She wailed anew and felt doubly bereft when she remembered that all this misery was his fault. Because he had thought to force her into doing what he was convinced was the only thing that could make her happy—marriage. Men! They were all alike. They all thought that marriage was a woman's only salvation. *You must marry me, Julia.*

The morning's encounter had been deeply disturbing to her. Though she had spoken of it lightly to Daniel, she did not feel it lightly. She had tried to put it all out of her mind, get it into proper perspective by her encounter with Freddie. But it just had not gone away. It disturbed her to know that she and Daniel could have fallen into such a hot and intimate embrace. He had touched her naked breast. He had touched her *there* even though the fabric of her breeches had been between his hand and her flesh. She had wanted him with a terrible yearning that had not after all been all physical.

Oh, she had told herself that that was all it had been. She had told him that that was all. But it had been more than that. She had quarreled with him a little while ago when he was being autocratic, and she had spoken lightly and carelessly when the morning's doings had been mentioned. But she had known as soon as he had stepped close to her and spoken to her that she had been far more deeply affected than she had realized. That her emotions had been battered.

She had yearned for some kind words from him, for some sensible words. She had yearned to talk with him in-

stead of just sparring with him. That was all she and Daniel
ever did. Spar. Fight. Quarrel. She had wanted them to talk.
She had hoped . . . But she was as much to blame as he, she
knew. Perhaps more so. She had had her defenses up too,
making light of everything he said, being quarrelsome
whenever she could. She had not, she supposed, given out
very strong signals that she wanted a truce.

Just a temporary truce. Just long enough that they could
talk over the puzzling mystery of their behavior that morning. She needed some explanation, some understanding.
Some peace between them. She wanted him to go away.
She wanted her old life back. She wanted her grandfather
back.

Julia got up off the bed and went through to her dressing
room to blow her nose and try to repair some of the damage
to her face. She glanced in a looking glass and made a face
at the red-eyed, red-cheeked apparition who looked back.
She wanted her grandfather back, indeed! She would be
sniveling for her mother next.

He had apologized. Apologies did not come easily to
Daniel, especially when they were directed to her. But he
had done it. He had held out an olive branch and she had
slapped it away. She had even made fun of him. And yet
she was blaming him for arrogance and lack of feeling? He
had asked her to marry him. But no, he had not asked. He
had told. And it *had* been arrogant, all of it.

She had looked at him standing there in the rose arbor,
her emotions all raw and bruised, wanting reassurance,
wanting—sympathy. Wanting—oh, she did not know what
she had wanted. And all she had got was cold attention to
duty. He had been prepared to marry her because he
thought he ought. Was she being unfair to him? Julia eyed
with some misgiving the bowl of cold water she had just
poured and then resolutely plunged her face into it. No, she
was not being unfair.

She really would rather be dead than married to Daniel.

She came up sputtering, her eyes tightly closed, and felt
around for a towel.

Another thought arrested her movements, though, as she dabbed at her face with the towel. She had objected to his proposal because it was arrogant? Not simply because it was a proposal? How would she have reacted had it been made differently? If he had really asked. Would it have made a difference?

Would it? Was there any way on this earth that she would listen seriously to an offer of marriage from Daniel? She thought of him again as he had appeared in the arbor, framed by roses, the sun at his back, and there was a tightening in her breasts and an aching in her womb. Purely physical reactions. Pure lust. Except that there was an aching in her heart as well.

She thought determinedly of Freddie and his kisses. Wonderful and experienced and satisfying. Except that she could not really remember them. But they had been those things. She had thought so at the time. If only he were not Freddie. If only he were not someone she had known all her life, someone she could not think of seriously as a lover. But then she had known Daniel all her life too.

She thought of Les. Dear, kind Les, who would allow her to live at Primrose Park as she had always lived and would not inflict his company on her uninvited. Except that she did not want to live the rest of her life at Primrose Park as she always had. She wanted—something different. She yearned for something different.

Well, she thought suddenly, looking critically at her image again and deciding that the redness would no longer be noticeable to anyone who did not know she had been crying, so he had had enough of an effect on her to have her cowering in her room, had he? She would be damned before she would give him the satisfaction. She was going to go back to the lake if it killed her.

Besides, she thought, going through to her bedchamber again and picking up her bonnet and her parasol and pushing her feet into her slippers, she was starved.

13

There was not a great deal to be done in the village, but a summer at Primrose Park never seemed quite complete if the younger people did not spend a few hours there on at least one occasion. The main attraction when they were children had been the confectionary, which for some strange reason was a part of the milliner's shop. And they had always loved to wander in the churchyard reading the old tombstones—the girls had liked to sigh over the children's graves. And they had all liked to climb the bell tower, though that had been forbidden for two whole years after the vicar had complained to the old earl about the bell being rung in the middle of a Wednesday afternoon and throwing all the villagers into confusion. Daniel, only thirteen years old, and Frederick had been the culprits.

In more recent years the rest of the milliner's shop had had more attraction for the girls and the village tavern for the men. But the church and churchyard still drew them like a magnet.

They walked the two miles from the house to the village two days after the picnic at the lake. After a day of steady and heavy rain, the sun was shining again and they were all ready for exercise. Julia linked her arm with Augustus's without waiting for an invitation.

"Hello, Jule," he said. "Where have you been moping for a day and a half?"

"Must I have been moping," she asked, "just because I have been keeping quietly to myself? The rain made any outdoor activity impossible. I had some embroidery to work on and an interesting book to finish. Why are you grinning like an imbecile?"

"If you don't want to tell me why you have been moping," he said, "you don't have to. You don't need to tell ridiculous bouncers."

"How do you think I live when I am alone here with Grandpapa and Aunt Millie all the time?" she asked. "But I *have* been moping, Gussie. You are quite right. I had three marriage offers the day before last. What do you think of that?"

Augustus whistled. "All three of them?" he said. "Freddie, Les, and Malcolm? Is that a woman's dream come true, Jule? Which one are you going to accept? Or can't you decide? Is that the problem?"

"Not Malcolm," she said pointedly. "Daniel."

"Dan." He stopped walking suddenly and stared at her incredulously. "Dan offered for you? He must want Primrose Park quite desperately."

"Thank you, Gussie," she said, mortified. "I really needed that."

"Oh, sorry, Jule," he said. "It was not meant to be an insult. But we all know how Dan feels about you."

"He kissed me," she said. "Oh, that is a quite inadequate description of what happened. He did far more than kiss me. Gussie"—she spoke in a rush—"I have needed to talk to someone. I have run through all the aunts and all the female cousins in my head and rejected them all. I might have chosen Camilla, but she is his sister. May I talk to you?"

"I think you already are doing that, Jule," he said. "But I know what you mean. Fire away then."

She gave him a highly expurgated account of what had happened two mornings before when she had met the earl while out riding. "And then he took me up to the rose arbor from the lake in the afternoon," she said, "and apologized and told me I must marry him."

"Told you?" Augustus raised his eyebrows. "Now that

was a mistake. Sometimes Dan can show lamentable lack of sense."

"Yes," she said. "And then when I said no, I would rather be dead, he said he must insist."

"You said that?" he said. "About preferring to be dead? Not nice, Jule. He would not have liked that. So that is the end of it?"

"I suppose so," she said. "He has said nothing since. I suppose that means I have two offers to consider. Which should I accept, Gussie? Freddie or Les? They could hardly be more different from each other, could they? Who would ever guess that they are brothers?"

"Let's get back to Dan," Augustus said. "You sounded almost disappointed when you said 'I suppose so.' Are you?"

"Disappointed that Daniel has not renewed his offer?" She looked indignantly at him. "Or that he has not insisted further? Are you mad, Gussie? Daniel? I hate Daniel. I despise him. I would not marry him if he came with a gift of a million pounds. I would—"

"By George," Augustus said, "you *are* disappointed, Jule."

She stared at him openmouthed for a few moments. "If I am," she said at last, "it is because I have no further opportunity to cut him down, to give him a piece of my mind. Gussie, why did it always bother me that Daniel disapproved of me? Why could I never just thumb my nose at him and go on my way and forget about him? Why does it always hurt, even now, when he catches me doing something that perfect ladies would not do and looks along that aristocratic nose at me? Why do I want to hurl myself at him and scratch his eyes out? It should not matter, should it? All the rest of you seem to like me and accept me as I am. Even Camilla, who is so quiet and so dignified herself. And even Malcolm although he never says anything. But I don't feel disapproval coming from him. Why can't Daniel like me too?"

"Lord, Jule," Augustus said, "I think you had better take

a closer look at your feelings, girl. And if Dan forgot himself as far as to do what you say he did the other morning and then felt constrained to offer for you even though no one else had seen, then maybe he should do the same thing. By George, this is most interesting, you know. Dan. Who would have thought it?"

"Sometimes, Gussie," she said crossly, "you are no help at all. I have poured out my heart to you—my battered and very confused heart—and all you can do is utter imbecilic exclamations and give ridiculous advice. I tell you I would rather be dead than married to Daniel. I tell you I hate him. Can anything be plainer than that?"

"Not even the nose on your face, Jule," he said, grinning. "Or more to the point, the nose on Dan's face. Well, well."

Julia withdrew her arm from his, on her dignity. "Well, here we are in the village," she said, "and I am going to see if Miss Markham has any new bonnets in. Thank you for nothing, Gussie."

"Jule," he said fondly.

"Well really," she said, looking back at him, troubled, "I wanted you to tell me something sensible and comforting, Gussie. I am so confused that I have to look down occasionally to make sure that my head is still facing the same way as my feet."

He chuckled and rubbed two knuckles across her nose.

The Earl of Beaconswood had never understood quite what the fascination was with old churchyards, but it was something he and his cousins had always shared. It should have been morbid but was not. Perhaps it had something to do with history, he thought, with the realization that the village and the area around it had not sprung to life last week but had existed for hundreds of years. People had lived there and toiled and loved and died and left their descendants and names to live after them. Quite a number of the names on the tombstones still belonged to the villagers or the tenant farmers.

And of course there was his uncle and aunt's grave to be

paused over and to quell any high spirits for a few minutes. Sometimes it was hard to remember that his uncle had been dead for such a short while. Nothing in their dress or their behavior at the house was designed to remind them of that.

Julia lingered after the others, unusually subdued. She knelt down and touched the newly turned earth. The tombstone was not yet in place. It had been taken away so that the new details might be carved onto it. She was weeping silently, the earl realized, lingering too a little way behind her while everyone else made off in the direction of the church and its cool interior. He did not intrude on her for a few minutes and handed her a large handkerchief when she finally rose to her feet.

She looked up at him, startled and cross before taking the handkerchief and scrubbing at her eyes with it. "Well, why should I not shed a few tears for him?" she asked. "He was always good to me, Daniel. Too good perhaps. You always used to say he spoiled me. Perhaps he did. He gave me a great deal of love. I shudder to think of what being an orphan might have been like. I wish you would not creep up on me like that."

"I'm sorry," he said. "I should have allowed you some privacy."

"Another apology?" she said, making as if to hand back his handkerchief but changing her mind and stuffing it into her reticule instead. "I am going to call on Mrs. Dermotty. She will be hurt if I do not."

"The vicar's wife?" he said. "I intended to pay my respects too, Julia. I will come with you."

Both the vicar and his wife were at home, and the youngest of their children, a little girl with apple cheeks and blond curls who hid behind her mother's skirts on the doorstep of the vicarage. She was shy with the earl but peeped and smiled at Julia until Julia made a dive for her and scooped her up and twirled her around several times, sunny and laughing again while the child shrieked with laughter.

The earl had not intended to go inside, but both the vicar

and his wife were so very pleased to have callers from the house that he consented to take a cup of tea with them. And Julia was being dragged inside by the child to look at a new book her papa had brought her from Gloucester. Julia sat on the floor to look at it all through tea, one arm about the child, joining in the adult conversation too.

Normally the earl would have been scandalized. A young lady sitting on the floor while taking tea in the vicar's house? But she looked so happy as did the child, and the vicar and his wife looked so fondly at her and talked to her about so many people and events that the earl knew little about that he began to see that there was nothing scandalous about her behavior. For the brief span of their visit she was bringing a little ray of sunshine into the vicarage.

The same thing happened later when she announced her intention of calling upon Mrs. Girten and the Misses Girten, two sisters and a widowed sister-in-law, rather elderly and almost housebound, who would be hurt if they knew she had been in the village and not poked her head about their door—Julia's words.

He did not have to go with her. Indeed, she would doubtless be happier to be left alone. And he would be happier alone. But the others were sitting on the church wall or on the grass in front of it when they emerged from the vicarage and announced their intention of beginning the walk home. If he left her, the earl thought, she would have to walk home alone, and that would be most improper. Though he wondered how many dozens of times a year Julia walked alone to and from the village. He could not quite imagine Aunt Millie accompanying her unless the carriage was called out.

The Girten ladies were delighted to see him and preened and smirked and tittered and drew out all their best party conversation for his benefit. They sent for tea despite his protests that he had just finished a cup at the vicarage. But Julia they treated quite differently. Their smiles softened and became genuine when they looked at or spoke to her. They made no objection when she jumped to her feet to take the tea tray from their maid's hands and proceeded to pour the tea herself and hand around the cups and saucers. She should, of course, have left those honors to Mrs. Girten, but no one appeared offended. Indeed she was treated much like a favored daughter.

She would be missed, the earl could see, if she was forced to move away from Primrose Park. Mrs. Dermotty had talked to her about the summer fair in August and had seemed genuinely dismayed when Julia had talked vaguely about perhaps not being there this year. And the Girten ladies talked about the school closing for the summer and the usual presentations to be made on the last day. Again Julia had hinted that perhaps she would not be there. Apparently she usually played a prominent and a popular role in both events.

The earl bowed to the ladies on leaving. Julia hugged each of them and was hugged and kissed on the cheek in return.

"Come again, dear," the elder Miss Girten said to her. "You know it can never be too soon for us."

"And bring his lordship with you," Mrs. Girten said and tittered when she realized he had heard.

"Such a very handsome gentleman, my dear Miss Maynard," the younger Miss Girten whispered. "He has great presence."

Julia, the earl was interested to note, blushed.

And so, he thought as he offered his arm and she took it, they were doomed to spend the next half hour or so alone together on the walk home. Already the sunniness had gone from her manner again and she looked mulish, as if she was preparing to spar with him. Which was what they would undoubtedly do. They always did.

And yet he had just seen something he had never expected to see—a Julia he liked.

"I suppose," she said, "you stayed because you thought I was going to do something unspeakably vulgar if you were not there to stop me. Or because you thought it grossly improper for me to walk home alone."

"It would have been improper, Julia," he said. "Are you in the habit of doing it? Did Uncle and Aunt Millie allow it? It was very remiss of them."

Yes, they were back to their normal relationship. It felt quite comfortable, almost a relief. His emotions had been in turmoil for the past two days.

"Grandpapa was human," she hissed at him. "So is Aunt Millie. They have allowed me to live, to have some enjoyment out of life. You would squash the life out of me, Daniel, if you had your way. There would be nothing but sitting at home embroidering and taking tea with callers and walking outdoors with a maid or riding in the carriage. I could not live that way. I would suffocate."

"There are assemblies and balls and concerts and picnics and all sorts of legitimate ways in which to enjoy oneself, Julia," he said. "One does not have to be scandalizing the world by swimming in next to nothing and engaging in foot races and dressing in a manner unbecoming to one's sex and riding in a manner that invites a broken neck."

"I pity the woman you will marry," she said. "If she has any life in her when you marry, it will be sapped from her soon afterward. There is no room for spontaneity, for sheer joy in your life, Daniel. Only for what is right and proper. Only for what other people expect of you. I would rather be dead than subjected to such a fate. I did not speak impulsively two days ago. I meant it."

"Did you?" he said curtly. He was feeling that inexplicable hurt again. "I did not doubt for a moment that you meant what you said. I will not renew the offer, Julia, so you must not worry that you will be the victim of my repressive, killjoy ways. Someone else will, someone who perhaps will feel that life with me might be a desirable thing. Someone who will believe that I can perhaps bring her happiness."

"What is her name?" she asked.

He hesitated. He was no longer at all sure that he would be returning to Blanche. Somehow that relationship seemed to have been spoiled, almost as if he had been unfaithful to her. But then he had been, in intention if not in actual fact. He had wanted to possess Julia and had almost done it too.

"Blanche," he said. "The Honorable Blanche Morriston."

She was quiet for a while. "And will she be able to bring you happiness, Daniel?" she asked.

"I believe so," he said stiffly. "She is everything I have looked for in a wife."

She was quiet for so long this time that he thought the subject had been exhausted. But she spoke again. "Daniel," she said, "you used to be so different. I had forgotten a great deal since I was so young at the time, but I have thought about those distant years a great deal in the past few days. You were always into mischief. You even more than Freddie. You used to lead the way and he used to follow."

"I was a child, Julia," he said. "Or a boy, I suppose in the years you can recall. It is part of boyhood to get into as much mischief as possible, to get caught nine times out of ten, and to get thrashed most of those times. It is something one grows out of if one is to be a mature adult. I grew out of it."

"Too soon," she said. "When your father died."

"I had a mother and a sister," he said, "and a home and estate. And suddenly I was heir to an earldom and the estates and fortune that went along with it. I had to learn to take responsibility for all that, Julia. Perhaps I grew up sooner than I would have done otherwise, but it had to happen anyway. I was fourteen. Hardly a child."

"But all the light went out of you," she said. "All the joy. I can remember my bewilderment, Daniel, the summer you came back as the Viscount Yorke. You were like a different person inside the same body. I can remember that for those first two summers I was at Primrose Park you used to ignore me much of the time—I was a very young child. But sometimes you used to take me up on your shoulders to carry me around. And occasionally you would take me up before you on your horse to give me short rides. You taught me to swim, you and Freddie. I suppose you have forgotten that. You were my hero. I used to live for the time when you would come back."

Good God, the earl thought, was she speaking the truth? But he could remember the years when younger cousins had treated him worshipfully because he was older and taller and stronger than they. Julia must have been one of them for a few years. Her father and stepmother had still been alive and had neglected her shamefully. He had used to feel sorry for her. Yes, he could remember her launching herself into the lake and clinging, giggling, to him and Freddie while Susan and Stella and young Viola had hung back on the bank, terrified to take the dare that had been issued.

Julia had never refused a dare. It had been very easy to teach her to float and even to swim. She had bobbed like a cork in the water, totally without fear provided he or Freddie stayed close. God, he had forgotten. All those golden years.

"And then you came back," she said, "and you were cold. Not just neglectful. Young children expect that of older ones. And not even occasionally indulgent. Just cold and disapproving. And never joining in any of our games if they smacked of mischief. And always I was the one in trouble with you. Because I was a girl, I suppose, and liked to keep up with the boys. I could never do anything right in your eyes. Never. I came to hate you, Daniel. I was never so glad as when you stopped coming. But I did not set out to say this. Somewhere I lost track of what I *was* going to say. Oh!" She jerked her arm from his suddenly and turned sharply away to fumble in her reticule. Out came his crumpled handkerchief. "An insect must have flown in my eye. Now both eyes are watering. How ridiculous!"

"Let me see," he said. But she slapped his hand away from beneath her chin.

"Don't touch me," she said. "Don't touch me, Daniel."

He swallowed and felt all his emotions raw again, as they had been for the last two days. He wondered why she was crying. For a lost childhood? For a lost hero? For the fact that he had returned to bring shadow back into her sunny world? He waited until she blew her nose and announced that the horrid insect was gone.

"The point I was going to make," she said, starting to walk again, ignoring his arm, "was that you were robbed of something, Daniel. I don't know if it was just circumstances that were to blame or if it was Aunt Sarah, perhaps, demanding too much of you too soon. You were too young to know that doing your duty did not prevent you from also having fun out of life. You don't have fun, do you? Not ever?"

He wanted to do violence to something or someone. They had emerged from the tree-lined section of the driveway. The house was in sight, fortunately. They did not have too far to go.

"What do you call having fun?" he asked, and he could hear the anger in his own voice. "Riding neck or nothing across uneven fields and jumping thick hedges? Swimming in the raw? Climbing trees? No, of course I do not indulge in any of those things, Julia. They are childish or dangerous or can bring great embarrassment to others."

"When done in private?" she said. "On one's own property? Of course one would not climb a tree in Hyde Park or swim—in the raw or even in a shift—in the Serpentine. Even I did not get into any trouble when I spent a Season in London, you see, Daniel, though I ached for more freedom sometimes. But when you are alone or with people to whom you feel close, don't you ever have the urge to shed your titles and your duties and even your adulthood? Don't you ever want to run down hills shouting your lungs out? Don't you?"

He had a vivid mental image of her racing down the steep side of the hill, shrieking and keeping her balance by the sheer effort of will and of himself catching her at the bottom and twirling her about. And wanting to kiss her.

"Oh," she said crossly. "I hate being given the silent treatment. You don't, do you? You don't even know what I am talking about. Do you?"

Everything snapped in him suddenly and he clamped one hand on her wrist, not even knowing with his conscious mind why he did so or what he intended to do next. But he turned off the path, taking her with him, and strode across the lawn in the direction of more trees and the lake. Julia trotted along at his side, not saying a word. His conscious mind knew that he was walking too fast for her, that the gentleman in him would cause him to reduce his pace. But his unconscious mind drove him on until they were deep into the trees, not far from the lake.

He stopped at an oak tree, an ancient oak that appeared not to have changed by so much as a twig in fifteen years and more. Except that its lowest branch seemed lower to the ground, perhaps. He looked up at branches and footholds that were impressed indelibly upon his memory even across the span of so many years. A tangible and unchanged link with childhood.

"Climb!" he said tersely, releasing Julia's wrist. He looked at her for the first time since his control had snapped back on the driveway. She was wearing a flimsy and very feminine muslin dress and a straw bonnet. "I don't doubt that you can do it even dressed as you are. Climb."

She looked at him for a few moments, her expression blank. And then she dropped her reticule, removed her bonnet and dropped that too, slipped off her shoes, and turned to the lowest branch. She held up a staying hand when he would have helped her.

She climbed and he climbed after her.

14

She was a little frightened if the truth were known. She did not know at first if he intended her to climb the tree so that he could stand below and lecture her again. Perhaps he hoped she would get stuck there so that he could walk away. And when he had first taken her by the wrist and dragged her in the direction of the trees, she had thought that perhaps he intended to continue where he had left off down by the stream. One never knew with Daniel. Certainly he looked grim enough to try anything.

But she climbed. The order had been almost in the nature of a dare after he had looked over the unsuitability of her clothes for such an activity and had told her to climb anyway. She was soon aware that he was coming up after her. To push her off? That was the most ridiculous thought she had ever entertained. After thinking it, she climbed higher than she had intended to go, and then seated herself on a broad branch, setting her back firmly against the trunk. She watched him come up behind her.

She would not speak. He must be the first to do that. If they must sit there in silence for an hour, then so be it. She was not going to say a word. She thought about two days ago—about the embrace they had shared, about his apology and marriage proposal later. She thought about the day before when she had avoided him and everyone else too as much as she possibly could. And about Gussie's disturbing words on the way to the village. And the strange comfort of finding Daniel behind her in the churchyard and the strange novelty of having him with her as she paid calls on some of her friends.

But she had been right in what she had said to him on the way home, she thought. Perhaps she should not have said it aloud, but she was not sorry. He had been robbed, probably by Aunt Sarah, though she had not labored that point. He had been robbed of the sort of adult he would have grown into if he had not been forced into too much responsibility too soon. He would still have acted responsibly. Obviously it was in his nature to do so. But he would also have been as carefree and as charming as Freddie.

He climbed up onto a branch that was on a level with and almost parallel to the one she occupied and moved out along it, turning eventually and surprising her by lying down full length on it, one booted foot raised, one arm behind his head. He stared upward through the higher branches of the tree to the sky.

"We used to play here as children," he said. "Maybe not in your time. I can't remember. And then I used to come here alone as a boy when the rest of you were off playing somewhere else. For hours on end I used to lie here in this exact spot and just stare at the sky. I used to climb trees even after I was the Viscount Yorke, you see."

Julia hugged her knees and rested her chin on them. She said nothing. Somehow it seemed important not to say anything.

"My father was a wastrel," he said after a lengthy silence. "Did you know that, Julia? Probably not. Children tend not to know such things, and families tend not to talk about them. Even I did not know until after his death. He was vital, charming, athletic—and devoted to gaming and womanizing. Does the description remind you of someone? He left behind him an estate so heavily mortgaged that there seemed almost no way of saving it, and a widow who was embittered and anxious for the future of her children. Especially perhaps for that of her son, who resembled his father in both looks and character to a remarkable degree."

Julia closed her eyes and moved her forehead to her knees. She was not sure she wanted to hear this. But she could not stop him. Or would not do so.

"Young as I was," he said, "I understood the situation. I

understood that only I stood between my mother and my sister on the one hand and ruin on the other. More than ruin in my mother's case. Destruction. She seems to be a strong person, doesn't she? She can be very harsh and opinionated. But she was very close to total collapse for a long while after my father's death. I was her anchor to sanity, she used to tell me, not realizing what a heavy burden she was laying on a boy's shoulders. She loves me and Camilla to distraction, you see. For years we were all that gave meaning to her life."

I came to hate you, Daniel. Julia could hear herself saying the words just a short while before. She wished she could recall them now. Oh, her wretched mouth. She wished she had not spoken at all.

"And so I learned," he said. "In addition to my school work I learned how to be a viscount, how to manage an estate on the verge of ruin, how to be the head of a family. I learned how to be the sort of man whose womenfolk could depend upon him. Women are the most helpless members of our society, you know. Not through any fault or weakness of their own, but because they are at the mercy of men—physically, economically, in almost every way. And men can be blackguards."

He stared upward at the sky until Julia thought he must have forgotten about her. But she did not think of moving or of climbing down to the ground again.

"And yes, you are right, Julia," he said at last. "I was young. The only way I could cope with the demands of my life was to stamp out of it everything that might have diverted me and hurt my mother and my sister. And yes, you were always the brunt of my anger almost more than anyone else."

"Why?" She spoke at last.

"I don't know." He drew his arm from beneath his head and set it over his eyes. "Perhaps because I saw you as more helpless than most women, more at the mercy of men. There was your orphaned, dowerless state, though I always believed that my uncle would look after you. His will was cruel to you."

"He owed me nothing," she said. "I had rejected all the gentlemen who showed interest in me during the Season that Grandpapa financed. And all the gentlemen he brought here for my inspection after that. He tried to see me securely established before his death."

"And perhaps I could see you on the way to your own destruction," he said. "The only hope for someone in your position seems to be to live by all the rules. You live by none of them."

"You exaggerate," she said.

"Yes." He thought for a while. "I do. Other people—the villagers and the family here—are very fond of you. But they have no responsibility for your future, Julia."

"Neither do you," she said.

"No." He sat up at last, carefully, and looked down. "No, I don't, do I? Are you going to be able to get down from here?"

"There are no crumbling stairs between here and the ground," she said. "And I am not wearing slippery slippers. I have called myself all kinds of fool since that incident, by the way. Why did I not simply take off my shoes and stockings? I would not have needed either your assistance or Gussie's. And I would not have made such a cake of myself."

She lowered herself carefully to the branch below as she talked. But descending from a tree when one was wearing a costly and flimsy muslin was not a speedy business. He was waiting on the ground by the time she stepped onto the lowest branch. He reached up his arms for her, and it seemed petty to refuse his help. She set her hands on his shoulders while he set his at her waist, and allowed him to lift her to the ground.

"Julia." He kept his hands at her waist when she was down and standing very close to him. His face was beside hers. If she turned her head, their noses would collide or their mouths would meet. She did not turn her head. "Promise me one thing. Promise me that you will not marry Freddie."

She was almost ready to promise him the moon and a

few stars for good measure, especially when she was standing like this within the aura of his physical magnetism. But
nothing had really changed. He had explained things to her
that she had never dreamed of, things that helped her understand why he had changed so completely in the course
of one year and why the fun and the laughter had gone out
of his life never to return. And she understood better perhaps why he had always been so hostile to her. But the hostility was still there nevertheless. And she was still in no
way answerable to him.

"Freddie is not your father, Daniel," she said. "No one is
ever an exact replica of someone else. And I have made no
decision yet about whom I will marry. If anyone. I think
perhaps I will marry no one but retain at least a part of my
freedom."

"That is not an answer," he said. "Promise me."

"I can't promise anything, Daniel," she said.

"You mean you won't." His tone was hard again.

"I mean I won't," she said quietly.

"Because it is I who ask you," he said.

And he turned his head and set his mouth to hers and
kissed her fiercely and openmouthed for several long moments while her mind spun off into space and she clung to
him, all the aches of the past two days suddenly focused
again in the one embrace. With a man who had offered for
her and whom she had rejected. With a man who disliked
her and whom she hated—*had* hated. With a man who
could make her want to cry and cry for no discernible reason at all.

He released her suddenly, and she felt bereft and disori-
ented. He was stooping down to pick up her bonnet and her
reticule and straightening up to hand them to her. His eyes
were hard. "You are a foolish woman, Julia," he said. "You
would rush to your own destruction just to spite me, would
you not? Perhaps I should urge you to marry him. Perhaps
then you would feel obliged to reject him."

She slid her feet into her shoes and tied the ribbons of
her bonnet beneath her chin with hands that did not feel
quite steady. "I will do what I consider right for myself,"

she said. "I am not your mother or your sister. You do not need to burden yourself with my care, Daniel."

She turned to walk back in the direction of the house, and he fell into step beside her. He did not offer his arm. They walked all the way back without speaking a word.

Frederick stood at the top of the horseshoe steps whistling. But it was an enforced cheerfulness that he displayed, for the benefit of the servants in the hall behind him. He was not feeling cheerful. His eyes were narrowed on the driveway as it emerged from the trees.

Interesting, he thought. Why would they be making off in the direction of the lake instead of coming directly back to the house? Why indeed? Judging from the way those two apparently felt about each other, they should have been taking the shortest route back so that they could be rid of each other.

And why had Dan attached himself to her in the village even to the extent of visiting with her people who could mean nothing whatsoever to him? Frederick could not feel convinced by Camilla's argument that as the new Earl of Beaconswood Dan felt obliged to make himself agreeable to some of the leading families of the village. Primrose Park did not belong to him, after all. Unless he intended that it would.

Dan had whisked her away from the lake the afternoon of the picnic too, when Frederick had intended to press his advantage and take tea with her. And neither one of them had come back in a hurry.

Could he have underestimated Dan? Frederick wondered. Was it possible after all that he was interested in Jule or interested in Primrose Park? Was it possible that he was indeed a contestant for her hand, a crafty one? And was there even a glimmering of a chance that Jule would favor him? The lure of a countess's title and the other properties and all the rest of the fortune must be strong. Not that he would expect Jule to be swayed by such considerations. But would the lure of Dan, a man who had always disliked her and whom she had always hated, be equally strong? The attraction of opposites? The love/hate relationship?

It seemed altogether possible.

Frederick left off whistling in order to grin. But neither the expression nor his amusement lasted long. Normally he would welcome a worthy opponent and long odds. They would add uncertainty and excitement to the game. But unfortunately the game had just become too desperate a one, winning it just too crucial to his well-being.

He had been right to feel unease when one creditor had found him at Primrose Park. For of course now others had found him there too. One particularly nasty letter had been awaiting him on his return from the village. It was from a creditor who had lost both his patience and his sense of humor. Either the Honorable Mr. Frederick Sullivan would pay up immediately, it seemed, or he must bear the consequences. And the sum in question was enough to make Frederick break out in a cold sweat.

The only way he could save himself from the humiliation of throwing himself on his father's mercy—and even his father's considerable fortune would be dented by the payment of all his debts—or from the disaster of debtors' prison was to persuade Jule to marry him. Soon. Before the month was out. All the pleasure involved in the game of courting her was gone, for the game could no longer be played at his leisure. And it must be won.

And so damnation to Dan and his sly courtship, if indeed that was what he was involved in. Dan had quite enough already. More than enough. And he had no expensive habits as far as Frederick knew. Besides, he had the young and lovely Miss Morriston waiting for him in London. A man ought not to be allowed to become too greedy.

Frederick waited for a while, but the two did not emerge from the trees again. Whatever they were doing down by the lake, they were taking their time about it. He had to make a conscious effort to restore the accustomed good humor to his face before turning to enter the house.

* * *

Julia was late for dinner. Not that she was so busy in the late afternoon that she left herself insufficient time to change and tidy herself. She was not busy at all, in fact. On her return from the lake, she withdrew to the conservatory and curled up on the window seat with the curtain pulled across to hide her from anyone who happened to stray there. She clasped her knees and stared sightlessly out over the rose arbor. And thought.

And realized something all in a rush. Something characteristically stupid. And impossible. And totally undesirable. She only wondered if it had always been so or if it had happened more recently—since his arrival at Primrose Park just before Grandpapa's death. Or even more recently. Perhaps as recently as that afternoon. Had she fallen in love with him just that afternoon and merely because of the story he had told her? Or had that story just revealed the truth that had been in existence before that?

What truth? It could not be the truth, surely. It would be just too utterly ludicrous. It was just that he had aroused her sympathies. And like all women—foolish women, and foolish of herself to so generalize—she had fallen in love with a rather sad story. Or rather with the man who had told it.

Yes, of course it was ridiculous. Too stupid even to be considered with any seriousness. She would laugh at herself in the morning when she had had time to sleep on it—if she slept, that was. Or else she would have put the afternoon's experience into proper perspective and realized that she could sympathize with a man without falling in love with him. Indeed, it would be a pleasant realization to wake up to. For the first time since her early childhood she would perhaps be able to like Daniel. Understanding could breed liking.

But it was no good. There was no point in trying to be sensible. She should know that from experience. Emotion—intuition—was always more powerful than good sense. She knew it for a fact, then, and she knew that a good night's sleep, even if such a thing were to be had, would not change that fact. This was what she had always

known would happen to her one day. It was what she had
awaited for so long. It was the reason she had rejected half
a dozen suitors. She had always known that one day she
would love, and that she could not marry unless or until
that happened.

It was stupid and unreasonable and not at all desirable.
She had no wish whatsoever to be in love with Daniel, but
in love with him she was. Yes, she might as well admit it
finally in words even if she did not speak them aloud.

She loved Daniel. The words sounded strange. Impossible to believe. Strangely heartwarming. Daniel!

And so everything was spoiled. Any hope she might
have had that she could stay at Primrose Park was gone.
Any hope that she might have been able to remain a member of the family that had always seemed hers but had
never actually been hers was gone. She would not now be
able to marry any of the cousins—not Malcolm or Les or
Freddie. And certainly not Daniel. For even if he could be
induced to renew his offer—and he had said that he would
not do so—she would not be able to accept him. Him least
of all, for it would be impossible to marry a man who did
not love her when she did love him. Better to marry Freddie, who would not demand love, or Les, who would not
expect it.

Except that she could not marry either. Or anyone. Ever.
Perhaps that was being a little melodramatic. Perhaps love
that was not fed died eventually—in a year or ten years or a
hundred years, perhaps. Perhaps if that happened she would
be able to love again. Perhaps she would even be able to
marry. Who knew? There was always hope for happy end-
ings, she supposed, as long as one still lived and breathed.

She was going to have to talk with Freddie and Les. She
was going to have to reject their offers. She was not sure if
she needed to explain to Malcolm since he had not yet
made her any sort of an offer. But in order to tidy up loose
ends she supposed that she should. She was going to have
to do it all within the next day at the longest and then try to
persuade Mr. Prudholm to come back early. There was no

point in prolonging speculation within the family when her mind was made up irrevocably.

She must start thinking about her uncle and aunt and their family in the north of England. She must start accustoming herself to the fact that she was going to be there soon. Perhaps it would not be as bad as she expected. After all, she was not a child to be making a nuisance of herself. She was an adult and could be of some use. Anyway, out of sheer pride she would probably take some sort of employment.

It was all a matter of turning her mind in that direction. There was no point in going into the mopes because life was not handing her a neat happily-ever-after ending on a platter. Life rarely did, she supposed.

Why had he kissed her, she wondered, when he was angry with her for refusing to promise not to marry Freddie? And such a hot and fierce kiss? But there was no point in trying to guess Daniel's motives for anything. And there was no point in teasing her memory with such titillating details—that and the embrace by the stream. She wondered in some disgust how long she would feed her love-starved heart with those two particular memories. She had an image of herself as an aged spinster nodding over a winter fire and remembering that once upon a time she had been kissed and a little more than kissed by a man who had been capable of turning her knees to jelly.

It was not a very pleasant or a very dignified image. And if she was not much mistaken, the dressing bell had rung some time before and she was going to be late for dinner if she did not make great haste.

But it was too late even for great haste to be of much help. And so she was late for dinner and won for herself a scold from Aunt Sarah as she slid onto the one vacant chair, a frown from Daniel, a smile and nod of sympathy from Aunt Millie, and a wink and a grin from Freddie.

Malcolm supposed that he should be feeling disappointed or chagrined or—something negative. Julia was the first woman with whom he had seriously considered matrimony. And yet she was telling him in that candid way that was peculiar to her that she had decided she was not going to marry anyone in the foreseeable future. She had called him over after dinner to the pianoforte, where she was picking out a tune on the keyboard with one finger.

"You have not offered for me, Malcolm," she said, "and you have given no positive indication that you intend to do so before the month is over. But I thought you should know, anyway. I cannot choose a husband under such circumstances, and I do not think it fair for you or any of the others to choose a wife this way. I am going to tell Mr. Prudholm, perhaps tomorrow, that Primrose Park can be given to that charity of Grandpapa's choice."

Malcolm seated himself on the stool beside her, and she looked anxiously into his face.

"You are not offended, Malcolm?" she asked. "Either by my rejection or by my assumption that you meant to offer?"

"No, Julia," he said, feeling quite at ease with her for perhaps the first time in his life. "I am not offended. And I thank you for saying this to me privately like this."

"I have to tell Freddie and Les too," she said, pulling a face. "They actually have made offers. This is really a dreadful coil. I wonder if Grandpapa is sitting somewhere in a corner of eternity having a good laugh at the way his joke is turning out."

Malcolm looked gravely at her. "I think your grandfather wanted the best for you, Julia," he said. "I think he would be sad at your decision, but I think he would respect it too. As I do."

"Thank you, Malcolm," she said, setting a hand on his sleeve. "You are kind. Oh, here comes Les. I might as well get this all over with this evening, I suppose." She smiled brightly as Lesley approached the pianoforte. "What a warm evening it is, Les. Don't you think so? Take me out onto the balcony?"

She smiled and got to her feet and Lesley offered his arm and drew her out through the French windows. She was utterly charming, Malcolm thought. For the past few years he had fancied himself a little in love with her, but he knew now that his feelings had always been more admiration and affection than love. He had never felt more relieved in his life than he felt right now. He should be feeling depressed, perhaps, but he was not. He was feeling elated. He knew that there never could have been a relationship between him and Julia. She was a bright star who would have made him feel dull and awkward for the rest of his life.

He looked about the drawing room, wanting uncharacteristically to share his mood of exhilaration and his newfound sense of freedom. His eyes came to rest on Camilla, who was seated with his mother and Aunt Millie, listening to the latter talk. He met her eyes and smiled. She smiled warmly back.

Camilla. She would understand his feelings. She would enjoy celebrating with him his escape from a possible marriage that would have brought no happiness either to Julia or to him. And she would appreciate the fact that Julia had rejected him without waiting for him to offer first. She would share his amusement over that detail.

She looked up at him and smiled again when he crossed the room to her side and waited for his mother to finish what she was saying.

"Would you care for a stroll outside, Camilla?" he asked. "It is a lovely evening if the air coming through the French windows is any indication."

"I would love it," she said, getting to her feet. "I don't believe I even need a shawl."

Aunt Millie smiled and nodded her encouragement.

"Dear Camilla," he heard her say as he led Camilla away, her hand through his arm. "It is high time she found herself another beau, Roberta."

They were words that spun around in Malcolm's head as he led his friend down the stairs and through the hall to the front doors.

15

Lesley had been very decent about the whole thing, Julia thought as she looked about the drawing room after coming in from the balcony. But then she would have expected no less of Les. He had merely smiled and told her she must do what would make her most happy, and no of course he was not disappointed to have lost Primrose Park. He had only wanted it as a home for her. Perhaps he would travel, he had told her. He had been thinking about it and thought that perhaps he would go to Italy for the winter. He had looked excited at the prospect.

Dear Les, Julia thought, locating Frederick with her eyes and making her way across the room toward him, he deserved to be happy. She was glad she had helped him realize that he could do what he most wanted to do.

"Freddie." She touched him on the arm. He was talking with Gussie and Uncle Henry and Daniel, of all people. She did not look at Daniel. "May I have a word with you?"

"More than one if you wish, Jule," he said, jumping to his feet and grinning down at her. "Outside? Malcolm and Camilla are strolling out there too, but I imagine we can avoid them if we try hard enough."

Uncle Henry chuckled, and Julia even more diligently avoided looking at the earl.

"I saw you talking with both Malcolm and Les," Frederick said when they were on their way downstairs. "You have made your decision, have you, Jule?"

"Yes, I have, Freddie," she said. She felt far more nervous with him than she had felt with either of the other two.

She did not know how he would take it. She rather believed
he had his heart set on acquiring Primrose Park.

"Well," he said, looking about him as they descended the
horseshoe steps outside, "we seem to have lost Malcolm
and Camilla without even having to try." He patted Julia's
hand before raising it to his lips and looking down intently
at her. "Put me out of my misery, Jule. What have you decided?"

"That I am going to marry no one," she said quickly.
"This competition, or whatever it might be called, was not a
good idea of Grandpapa's. I cannot choose a husband in
such haste merely to save myself from being at the mercy
of my father's relatives, whom I scarcely know. And I
don't think any of you should be in competition with one
another for my hand and for possession of this property.
There is something sordid about it, Freddie. I am going to
send for Mr. Prudholm tomorrow and get him to put a stop
to it all even before the end of the month. My mind is made
up."

"Ah," he said quietly as they strolled along the terrace,
"you have saddened me, Jule."

"Because you have lost Primrose Park?" she asked.

He smiled down at her, his eyes lazy beneath drooped
eyelids. They were quite devastating eyes in the moonlight,
Julia thought. "Yes, because of that," he said. "I cannot
deny that it was the initial attraction of this whole thing,
Jule, though I was never sorry that you would come along
with it. But as the days have passed I have come to realize
that my priorities were wrong. To hell with Primrose Park.
It is you I want."

"You love me?" The trouble with Freddie was that she
knew him only as a cousin and former playmate. She knew
nothing of him as a lover except that he was very accomplished and very successful. It was impossible to know
what was sincerity and what was flirtation or even seduc-
tion. Not that it really mattered to her decision. But she
would like to know. Was she hurting him?

"You will force me to say the words, Jule, won't you?"

he said. "The most difficult words in the English language for a man to say. And you will force me to say them when they are useless, when you have already rejected me. Yes, my dear, I love you, I am afraid."

"Oh, Freddie," she said, frowning, "are you telling me the truth? Don't tease me if you are not. I would not hurt you for the world. I am far too fond of you."

They had come to the end of the terrace and had stopped walking.

"Will it make a difference," he asked, "if I pour out my heart to you, Jule?"

She shook her head.

"Then I'll not do so," he said gently. "And if it will make you feel better, I will tell you that my words were all cha- rade, that in fact I feel nothing for you but a deep affection. There. Better?"

"No," she said, turning so that they could stroll back again. "But I am sorry if I am hurting you, Freddie, and sorrier still if you are making me feel bad for nothing. What will you do for the summer?"

"I have not thought of it," he said. "Go to Brighton, per- haps. But what about you, Jule? Have you really rejected all of us? Dan too?"

"Daniel?" Her brows shot together as she looked up at him.

"I thought perhaps he was a contestant after all," he said. "He has spent a considerable amount of time with you in the past few days, Jule."

"I hate him," she said vehemently. "You know that, Freddie. I always have. I would rather be dead than married to Daniel."

" 'The lady doth protest too much,' " he said quietly.

"Freddie!" She withdrew her arm from his so that she could punch it. "Don't be horrid. Oh, don't, please."

"I must admit," he said, "that I will be able to endure los- ing you far more cheerfully if Dan doesn't get you instead. You would not enjoy life a great deal with Dan, Jule. I could give you far more fun."

"I know," she said. "But I have to put an end to this dreadful game, Freddie. As soon as possible. It seems that Mr. Prudholm has gone home to Gloucester for the month. I hoped he would have stayed at the village as he did during the last weeks of Grandpapa's life. I hoped to be able to summon him tomorrow and get this all behind me. But it will be a few days before I can send a message to him and before he can come. I just hope he does not delay. Each day is going to be an agony to me, and I suppose it will not be pleasant for you or Les either. Perhaps not even for Malcolm."

They came to a stop again at the foot of the horseshoe steps.

"Gloucester is only twenty miles or so away, is it not?" he said. "It would be quicker to go to him and explain in person rather than send a letter by messenger, would it not, Jule?"

"I suppose so," she said. She laughed suddenly. "Can you imagine Aunt Sarah's face and the faces of the other aunts if I went galloping off to Gloucester on Flossie? Wearing my breeches? And can you picture Daniel's face?"

Frederick took both her hands in his. "You don't need to go alone, Jule," he said. "There are plenty of people here to go with you. I'll go with you. If we leave early in the morning, we can be back by nightfall. Perhaps with Prudholm in tow. The next day all this unpleasantness could be over for you."

"You would do that for me, Freddie?" she said, squeezing his hands. "Even though you will be the loser? You are kind."

"Not really, Jule," he said. "I know better than to argue with you once you have made up your mind. And if it is to be all over, then I would prefer to have done with it as soon as possible too. Every day spent in company with you now that I know I cannot have you will be something of an agony to me too, you know."

"Oh, Freddie," she said, "don't say things like that. Besides, we cannot do it. For riding off in a carriage with you will be seen as even worse than riding off alone—in breeches."

He clucked his tongue. "Of course," he said. "Even I realize that, Jule. You did not think I meant you and I alone, did you? Les or Gussie will come and one of the girls. I'll arrange it all tonight and we can be ready to leave early. A private little excursion for four to Gloucester. We had better keep quiet about it, though, or everyone will want to come and the whole thing will become rather unwieldy. And some of our relatives may try to persuade you out of calling Prudholm back early. Just leave it all to me. Agreed?"

She thought for a moment. But it really was a splendid idea. She wanted to be away from Primrose Park, away from all the people who had been family to her through most of her life. Away from Daniel. She could not bear to wait longer than necessary now that she had realized she was going to have to leave them all soon enough anyway. Better to get it over with as soon as possible.

"Agreed," she said, squeezing Frederick's hands again and standing on tiptoe so that she might kiss his cheek. "Thank you, Freddie. You are turning out to be a true friend after all."

He stood back and released her hands, smiling ruefully. "Perhaps you had better not touch me too much, Jule," he said. "I have not had a great deal of practice at resisting ladies I want, you know."

"I am sorry," she said, taking a step back herself. "Shall we go inside?"

"I think we had better, Jule," he said. "Eight o'clock breakfast tomorrow?"

"I'll be down," she said, "and ready to go as soon as we have finished eating."

Malcolm and Camilla had crossed the terrace and descended the steps to the formal gardens. They strolled along the gravel walks, arms linked.

"Julia spoke with me," Malcolm said. "She has decided

not to betroth herself to anyone this month. She feels that it would be wrong."

"Ah," Camilla said quietly. "Are you disappointed, Malcolm? Were you still planning to offer for her?"

"I was not sure," he said. "But I am not disappointed. I don't think Julia would have been happy with me. I am too dull a fellow."

Camilla smiled up at him. "More to the point," she said, "is that you would not have been happy with her, Malcolm. She would have unwittingly made you feel dull, and you are not. I am glad that she has rejected you though sorry if you are hurt in any way."

"I asked you out here with me," he said, smiling ruefully, "because I wanted someone to help me celebrate."

She laughed.

"I have always admired Julia's high spirits," he said. "I even fancied myself a little in love with her though I know now that I was not. We would have nothing to offer each other. I fancied myself in love once before. And I think perhaps I was not deceiving myself that time because I liked her too and she liked me and she was one of the few women in my life with whom I always felt at ease."

"But it did not work out?" She looked rather sadly at him. "I am sorry, Malcolm. You must have suffered from her loss. She married someone else?"

"There was a betrothal," he said. "But he died. She was very much in love with him. After her betrothal and after his death I persuaded myself that what I felt was affection, not love. She is still my friend."

They walked in silence for a while. "Malcolm." Her voice was almost a whisper. "Whom are you talking about?"

"Perhaps it would be better if I said no more," he said. "Perhaps I have already said too much. I would not want to lose a dear friend. Except that it has been two years, Camilla, and you said yourself that it is time for you to live again."

"It was me you loved?" Her voice was trembling.

"Present tense," he said. "I was wrong about Julia and I was wrong about my real feelings for you. But I did not realize it fully until this evening. I don't want it to spoil our friendship, though, Camilla. I should have said nothing just as I did when we were growing up."

She stopped walking and turned to look at him. "You were always my hero," she said. "I even used to sigh secretly over you during my growing years and admire your height and your lovely blond hair. But you were always so quiet and somehow unattainable. And then I met Simon and fell head over ears for him. You became my friend—or remained my friend, I should say, after all the silliness had passed. Or what I thought of as silliness, Malcolm." She set her head to one side and continued to look at him.

"You would prefer that we remained as just friends?" he said. "Perhaps it would be as well."

"Simon is dead," she said. "I did love him dearly, Malcolm. But he has been gone for longer than two years and I have love to give. It is fairly bursting from me. And I need to be loved. Now, in the present, not just in the past. Life is to be lived. Now. I want warm, living arms to hold me."

He touched his fingertips to one of her cheeks. They trembled slightly. He lowered his head and touched his lips to hers. "Mine will hold you forever if you want them to," he said.

He could see the tears swimming in her eyes as she smiled at him and slid her arms up about his neck. "Yes, I do, Malcolm," she said. "Oh, yes, please, I do."

He kissed her again, wrapping his arms about her and drawing her close against him. And feeling so brimming over with happiness that he could have cried too.

"You will marry me, then?" he asked her when he finally lifted his head.

She nodded, smiling, and he could tell that she would not trust her voice.

"I'll talk to your brother, then," he said. "Now, Camilla? Shall I do it now?"

She shook her head. "Don't let's go inside yet," she said.

"I want to be alone with you for a while longer, Malcolm, to savor the wonder of this night."

He kissed her briefly once more. "You think it is all right for you to be out here even longer with me when you are unchaperoned?" he asked her.

She laughed softly. "I am twenty-four years old, Malcolm," she said. "I am no girl." She set her cheek against his shoulder and sighed. "Oh, you are so wonderfully warm and alive."

"Let's go and sit by the fountain, then," he said. "We'll stay out a little longer. I'll talk to Daniel later. I shall probably stammer over every word."

Camilla laughed again as they walked toward the fountain, their arms about each other's waist. They sat on the bench below the fountain, looking out over the darkened, moonlit garden, scarcely talking. She nestled her head on his shoulder and he set an arm about hers.

They were unintentional eavesdroppers to parts of the conversation between Frederick and Julia, especially the last part, which was spoken just above the fountain.

"She is very brave," Malcolm said when the couple had gone back inside. "She has spoken to all three of us this evening—I left her with Les when I came to invite you outside. Poor Julia. It cannot have been easy to do."

"I think she is wise to end the month early," Camilla said. "And yes, I admire her decisiveness, too. It is so typical of Julia. I am not surprised that she has decided not to marry. I have always thought that she is something of a romantic. I think Julia wants to love the man she will marry. I hope she finds what she is looking for."

"Is the journey to Gloucester wise?" he asked.

"In a party of four?" she said. "I think it quite unexceptionable. Kiss me again before we go inside, Malcolm. And assure me that I am not going to wake up soon to find this all a dream."

He smiled and kissed her again.

* * *

It was going to be a very tricky business, Frederick thought, and just as likely to fail as to succeed. Eight o'clock was very late to have set for breakfast. There were all sorts of chances that a few other early risers would be in the breakfast room. Of course he had urged secrecy on Julia and the chances were that she would see the wisdom of keeping her mouth shut. But seven o'clock would have been altogether a more comfortable time to be eating.

But he had not been able to suggest seven because then the rest of the plan that had been developing in his head would have seemed even less believable than it was going to sound anyway. It seemed altogether possible that Julia would not fall for the story. Especially if she came down to breakfast early or if she went out early riding, as he knew she sometimes did.

Frederick did not have a good night's sleep. It was a mad plan. There were far too many things likely to go wrong with it. Only by the sheerest miracle would it succeed. And yet even the faint chance that it would work did not bring him any comfort. He felt like the worst villain who had ever stalked the earth. He just could not go through with it, he told himself. Devil take it, it was Jule who was to be his victim. He had always been fond of Jule.

And then he thought of his astronomical debts and his creditors waiting like birds of prey to pounce on him and drag him off to debtors' prison. And of his father hearing about it and coming to his rescue, that look of sorrow on his face that Frederick dreaded more than any other expression his father was capable of. He felt clammy with cold sweat.

No, he would have to go through with the plan and hope that somehow miracles could still happen for a black-hearted villain like himself. Perhaps it would succeed.

He consoled himself for the possibility that it would indeed succeed by telling himself that he would make her happy. He would give up his gambling and he would give up other women and devote himself to making Jule happy. Yes, and pigs might fly too. But at least she would be better off than she would be stuck up in the wilds of northern England with relatives who did not want her.

The miracle happened inch by inch. Frederick was pacing the breakfast room soon after half past seven. Julia did not arrive there until a couple of minutes before eight. And it seemed that she had just got up and had had to hurry to get ready.

"I was so late getting to sleep, Freddie," she said, "what with one thing and another swirling through my head and refusing to leave it so that I could rest, that I slept in. I almost never sleep beyond six o'clock at the latest."

It was better than he could have hoped for.

"I have eaten already," he said, though he had been quite unable to do any such thing, "and sent orders to have my carriage and horses prepared. We can leave as soon as you have eaten, Jule. Remember, if anyone should come in here before we leave, we must say nothing. The more I think of it, the more I am sure they would all try to dissuade you from going to Prudholm's if they knew about it."

"I shall say nothing, Freddie," she said. "I am quite determined to go. Who is coming with us?"

He chuckled. "Les and Stella," he said. "I did a most foolish thing, Jule. Stella was quite furious with me. I told them that breakfast would be at seven. That was what I thought I had told you until you did not turn up at seven and I remembered I had told you eight."

"Ouch!" Julia said, settling herself at the table with two slices of toast. "Stella would not have liked that. She is a notoriously late riser."

Yes, that was why Frederick had chosen her.

"Did she go back to bed?" Julia asked.

"No, actually," he said, chuckling again. "Les persuaded her to take some morning exercise since we will be spending so much of the day in the carriage. They set off walking in the direction of the village almost half an hour ago. We are to pick them up there with the carriage."

"Stella out walking at half past seven in the morning?" Julia said, laughing. "I shall tease her about this one for years to come. We must not keep them waiting, then, Freddie. I shall eat fast."

There was a moment of anxiety when the door opened and Uncle Paul put his head around it and then came on inside.

"Ah, other early risers," he said. "I hate eating alone."

"But I am afraid I am going to have to leave you within five minutes, Uncle Paul," Julia said. "I have promised to go riding with Freddie and he is standing there pretending to look patient so that I am almost choking on every mouthful."

Uncle Paul seemed quite without suspicion. And they met no one on their way to the stables and no one there except a few grooms. Frederick had been holding his breath. Dan sometimes rode early, he knew, and anyone else might take it into his head to do so too on this of all mornings.

"Poor Stella," Julia said as the carriage pulled out of the stableyard and made its way onto the driveway. "She is going to be in a very cross mood unless the walk and the morning air have revived her spirits. It is a good thing it is Les who is with her. He is so very good-natured."

"Yes," Frederick said, looking rather tensely from the windows, hoping for the final part of the miracle. "Les won't mind." He was wondering how Julia was going to react when she found that there was no one to be picked up in the village.

She reacted predictably. She peered out of the windows as the carriage entered the village and exclaimed in surprise at the fact that they were nowhere in sight.

"They must have grown tired of waiting," Frederick said, "and walked home a different way."

"Don't be foolish, Freddie," she said. "And why is your coachman not slowing down? Tell him to slow down."

"I already told him not to, Jule," he said quietly, the end of the village street having been reached and all the houses left behind.

"You told him—?" She looked around at him with sudden suspicion, but with no fear in her face. Good old Jule.

"What is this, Freddie? Stop this carriage instantly. I am going home."

"No, Jule," he said. "We will go alone together. It will be easier that way."

"They were never coming with us, were they?" she said. "It was all lies. Freddie, I hate you. And I won't do this. I know I do some ramshackle things, but I won't do this. I'll not be alone with you all day. I would be ashamed to show my face at Primrose Park again." She got to her feet and banged the side of her fists against the front panel.

His coachman did not slow the carriage.

"Jule," he said, "sit down." He did not believe he had ever felt so wretched in his life.

She turned to look at him again, her eyes wide, her cheeks flushed. "We are not going to Mr. Prudholm's, are we?" she said, surprise in her voice. "You are kidnapping me. Aren't you? I am your prisoner. You are going to try to force me to marry you. Oh, Freddie, they must be huge debts."

"I'll make you happy, Jule," he said. "I'll make you fall in love with me. It will be better than your uncle in the north of England."

"Goddamned bloody hell it will be better!" she said, causing him almost to laugh for a moment. But he did not believe he could laugh to save his life. "I'll not marry you, Freddie, if we ride about the countryside for a whole month. I still have to say yes, and I will never say yes. You might as well save yourself the trouble of being shut up with my temper for a long spell. I'll never marry you."

"You will have no choice, Jule," he said, trying to possess himself of her hand. But she snatched it back and then cracked it painfully across his cheek.

"You are not only going to compromise me, are you?" she said, her voice shaking—more with rage than with fear, he thought. "You are going to rape me. Aren't you?"

"I would far prefer it to be just a compromising, Jule," he said unhappily. "And it would not have to be rape. I can make you want me."

She looked at him long and hard before settling back in her seat and folding her hands in her lap, apparently calm.

"It will be rape, Freddie," she said. "I will not give you the comfort of thinking that it may be something else. It will not. Will it be tonight? In Gloucester?"

"Yes," he said.

"I may still not marry you, you know," she said. "Only if you get me with child. I suppose you could keep me long enough to make sure that that does happen, but it will not be soon enough, Freddie. I have to be betrothed to you within the next two weeks and a few days. I'll not consent before that time. You may have me if you are capable of begetting children, but you will not get Primrose Park. You might as well take me back, you know."

He said nothing and made no move to change his orders to his coachman. She would marry him, and she would agree to it before the deadline. Once he had taken her virtue—Lord God, was that what he was planning to do to her? Once he had done that, she would see that she had no choice. Besides, he would make her fall in love with him. He would use all the charm and expertise of years on her and she would not be able to resist him.

But it would be rape nonetheless, a part of his brain that he would just as soon have ignored told him over and over again during the silent hours that followed.

16

Nobody really missed them at first. It was true that Aunt Millie commented on the fact that dear Julia was not at breakfast, but Uncle Paul, who had eaten earlier but came back to the breakfast table anyway in order to enjoy the company, explained that she had gone riding with Freddie. It seemed a fairly unremarkable fact except that she had no business riding alone with Freddie or any other man. But the earl frowned only briefly. He would think about it later, he decided. There were other things to take his mind this morning.

Like the unexpected offer for his sister he had had from Malcolm late the previous night and her even more unexpected happiness. If only he had opened up the eyes in his head, the earl had decided, he would surely have seen in which direction the wind was blowing. Camilla had always been fond of Malcolm and it had been very obvious since spring that she was over the death of Captain Styne and ready for love again. And she had spent more time with Malcolm in the past week or so than with anyone else.

The earl was delighted. So was his mother as soon as she remembered that Malcolm would be a baron someday. Though that was a little unfair to her. She wanted both her children to marry well, but first and foremost she wanted their happiness. She happened to believe that happiness was more likely to result from a good marriage than from an unequal one. And Camilla was now, after all, the sister of the Earl of Beaconswood.

So the betrothal, and its announcement at breakfast of all places because in a family it would be impossible to hold

such a fact secret until a more appropriate time for an announcement, took most of the earl's attention. He had determinedly put out of his mind all the turmoil of his own
emotional life.

Julia. The almost unconscious maneuvering that had en-
abled him to spend most of the afternoon alone with her the
day before. The strange need to justify himself to her. The
hurt rather than anger he had felt when she had refused despite everything to promise not to marry Freddie. The kiss
he had been unable to resist. The anxiety—*anxiety?*—he
had felt when he saw her speak with Malcolm and Les and
then witnessed her asking Freddie to walk outside with her.
Everything was pushed to the back of his mind, to be dealt
with later. He owed Camilla his full attention. And he really did rejoice in her joy. He had been the one who had
had to deliver to her the news of her Simon's death in battle. It was a day he did not care to remember.

It was only after breakfast, when the general family excitement had died down a little or been carried to other
parts of the house and Camilla and Malcolm had gone off
somewhere together, that the earl's thoughts returned inevitably to Julia. Where was she? He wandered in and out
of all the daytime apartments and even strolled out onto the
terrace, but there was no sign of either her or Freddie. The
earl could not be sure when Uncle Paul had had breakfast.
He had not thought to ask him. But whenever it was, the
two of them must have been gone for a few hours.

He stood on the terrace and clenched his hands into fists
at his sides. He could remember all too clearly another ride
Julia had taken with a man and the way it had developed.
Was the same thing happening between her and Freddie?
She had freely admitted that Freddie had kissed her at the
lake—for all of ten minutes.

She was making up to Freddie. Quite recklessly. She was
going to marry him. Just out of spite. Though perhaps that
was a rather conceited idea. Freddie was a marvelously
handsome man and had a great deal of charm and skill in
his dealings with women. Julia would not have a chance

against him if he turned the full force of that charm on her. It was altogether possible that she really was in love with him.

He could kill, the earl thought. And stopped to consider the feeling. Why? Because Freddie was taking advantage of an innocent woman and he himself felt responsible for her? He was not, as she had been at pains to remind him more than once. And Freddie meant honorably. He would marry her. That was the whole point of his pursuit of her. There was no rationality, then, in this murderous mood.

And yet reason could not dispel it. He could kill Freddie, he thought. If Freddie had touched her or persuaded her into a marriage that she would regret, then . . .

The thought could not be pursued. Camilla and Malcolm were coming toward him from the direction of the stables, and he unclenched his fists and smiled. But they were not smiling in return. Camilla looked anxious.

"There is something wrong, Daniel," she said. "We thought we should speak to you about it."

He raised his eyebrows.

"Freddie's carriage is gone," Malcolm said. "And so are Julia and Freddie, of course. But no one else."

The earl felt instant alarm.

"We overheard them last evening," Camilla said, "planning a journey to Gloucester for today. Julia wanted to visit Uncle's solicitor and persuade him to come back early. I think she has decided not to marry any of the cousins."

"The woman needs throttling," the earl said through his teeth. His hands were back in fists again.

"But she refused to go alone with Freddie," Camilla said. "He was going to arrange it so that another couple went with them. They wanted to do it all secretly so that no one would dissuade Julia from doing what she had decided to do."

"But no one else is missing," Malcolm said. "All the girls are here and so are Les and Gussie. And all the uncles and aunts, of course. Even Julia's maid is still here. Camilla checked."

"God!" the earl said.

"They must have gone alone after all," Camilla said. "The earliest they can arrive home is this evening. By that time Julia will have been dreadfully compromised. I can't understand it, Daniel. She seemed quite adamant about not going alone with Freddie. And she seemed equally determined that she was not going to marry him."

"The trouble with Julia," the earl said, "is that she will not recognize that rules and conventions apply to her just as much as to anyone else. It doubtless seemed more convenient to her this morning that just the two of them go. To Gloucester, did you say?"

Camilla nodded. "I think we should do something, Daniel," she said.

"Of course I must do something," he said. "I am going after them. Perhaps I can cover up for the fact that she has been alone with him all day."

"I knew you would say that," she said. "I will come too, Daniel. Don't say no. Think about it. It would be just as shocking for everyone to see that she has been with two gentlemen all day. You will need me if we are to avert dreadful scandal."

"We had better leave without delay," Malcolm said. "We can discuss the story we will tell when we are on the way. And we will hope that we can find them easily when we get to Gloucester so that they will not after all come driving home alone tonight."

The three of them hurried toward the stables without delaying to go inside to change clothes.

They talked as they traveled in the earl's carriage, devising a story they might tell to explain the disappearance of five of them in two separate carriages for a whole day, wondering why either Freddie or Julia would behave so irresponsibly. Camilla confessed herself very puzzled over Julia's behavior since the night before she had seen the full impropriety of traveling alone with Freddie. Malcolm agreed that something did not seem quite right.

"Daniel," Camilla said eventually, her voice troubled,

"Freddie would not have tricked her into coming alone with him, would he? Or forced her?"

The earl closed his eyes. The ghastly suspicion had been growing in his mind too, and yet behaving recklessly and without thought was so typical of Julia.

"Can he be so desperate for Primrose Park?" Malcolm said. "Can his debts be that bad? It seems to be common knowledge that Freddie does play deep and gets himself into trouble on occasion. Would he do this to Julia, though?"

"I find it hard to believe of him," Camilla said. "He has a reputation for wildness and he has always been up to some mischief during the summers, even since he has grown up. But Freddie is no villain. But then Julia is not so lost to all conduct as to do this. I just don't understand."

The earl surprised them all suddenly, himself included, by pounding one fist against the door frame and splintering wood.

There were too many emotions chasing themselves about in her head for her to feel as terrified as she knew she should be feeling. Freddie was going to rape her, she told herself. When they reached Gloucester, he was going to take an inn room and keep her there for the night so that she would be thoroughly compromised, and for good measure he was going to rape her.

She should be blubbering with terror. Instead she sat like a marble statue, staring sightlessly from the window of the carriage. It was her own fault. She should never have believed that ridiculous story about Les and Stella walking to the village. She should never have set foot inside the carriage without a female companion right there beside her. She had only herself to blame. And she could not hope to be pursued and overtaken in the nick of time. No one knew they were going to Gloucester. No one would have reason to guess even after they were missed and it was discovered that Freddie's carriage was gone.

It was Freddie. That was what made the whole thing so

totally unbearable. She supposed it would be unbearable whoever had taken it into his head to kidnap and rape her. But it was definitely worse knowing it was Freddie. Freddie! Her playmate from childhood on. Her partner in mischief on innumerable occasions. She had always liked him. More—she had always had a deep affection for him. He had seemed like a real cousin. During the summer months of her life he had sometimes seemed more like a brother.

If she could have any choice under such ghastly circumstances, she would choose to be riding now with a stranger, with an evil and sinister stranger, one she could hate without qualms.

It was deeply distressing to hate Freddie in all earnest. And perhaps to be tied to him in hatred for the rest of her life. For despite what she had said to him earlier, she was not sure that she would be able to hold firm against marrying him once he had had her virtue. She could only imagine what she would feel like afterward. She could not know with any certainty since what was going to happen was quite outside her experience. But she feared that after all she might feel constrained to marry him.

She shuddered inwardly at the thought. She would never be able to like Freddie after tonight. Or to feel affection for him.

She supposed he would take her back to Primrose Park the next day, provided she had promised to marry him. He would doubtless make up some story about what had kept them in Gloucester overnight but would pacify the relatives by announcing that he was doing the honorable thing and marrying her. They would all be satisfied.

Daniel would be there. He would look at her with contempt and loathing. Daniel! Her hands began to twist themselves in her lap, but she stilled them. She would not give Freddie the satisfaction of knowing that she was upset in any way.

Daniel. She swallowed and heard a gurgle in her throat.

They rode around and around the streets of Gloucester

when they arrived there for what seemed to be hours and probably was. Frederick started talking again.

"I feel like the very devil, Jule," he said. "Don't make me do this. Just say you will marry me."

"You *are* the very devil, Freddie," she said, looking steadily back at him. "I am only sorry that it is so. And as for the rest, you are wasting your breath."

"You know that you are going to have to marry me after today," he said. "Why not just forget about your stubbornness and save us both some distress?"

"Will it distress you to rape me?" she asked. "Good."

He was silent again for a while. And then he touched his knuckles to her cheek and smiled at her and tried to use his charm on her. She leaned away from his hand and looked at him stonily.

"Let me make one thing clear to you, Freddie," she said. "You are not going to persuade me or coax me into anything no matter how long and skillfully you try. I will fight you every inch of the way. You will not be quite unscathed at the end of this night, I believe. I have no doubt that you will overpower me in the end. Indeed you are big enough and strong enough to do so without getting badly hurt yourself, I daresay. But you are going to have to fight for whatever you get. That is all I have to say."

"Jule," he said, "you would enjoy it. You could be happy with me. You *will* be happy with me."

"I could be happy in hell with the devil too," she said, "except that I happen not to like the thought of roasting for the small matter of an eternity."

"You are making altogether too much of this," he said, smiling again and using his bedroom eyes on her.

She turned her head to look out of the window again and they lapsed into another lengthy silence. Almost she could wish that he would put an end to the delay and have his coachman take them to some inn. What was going to happen was inevitable. It would be almost a relief to have it over with. Though she would fight him like a vixen. She had not lied about that.

"Jule." She turned her head to look at him. His elbow was resting on the windowsill, his hand spread over his closed eyes. "I can't do this, you know."

She said nothing. She did not realize that she was holding her breath.

"I can't do it," he said again, removing his hand and looking across at her, his eyes mocking. She guessed that they mocked himself rather than her. "I thought I could. I thought I was desperate enough. But I can't."

She hardly dared hope.

"Lord God," he said, "what have I come to? How low is it possible to sink, Jule?"

"Pretty low, Freddie," she said. "But I think there are perhaps limits for someone who is basically decent."

"Basically decent," he said. "Me?"

"Yes, you, Freddie," she said, and hope surged like fresh blood through all her veins. "But you have sunk pretty low today. I am not sure I will ever be able to forgive you."

"I don't think I would expect you to." His smile was twisted. "But I am going to have to offer for you anyway, Jule, after we get back to Primrose Park and the storm has broken over our heads. You are going to have to marry me."

"I am expected to behave with impropriety," she said. "This will only seem a little worse than my usual type of escapade. I will not marry you, Freddie."

He sighed. "We will be fortunate to get back by nightfall," he said. "Should we find out Prudholm so that at least it will seem that we had a reason for coming here?"

"Yes, please," she said, turning back to the window. "I want him to come to Primrose Park as soon as possible so that all the business concerning Grandpapa's will can be finished and I can be on my way to my uncle's."

"Jule," he said, his voice quiet and almost pleading.

But she did not respond. Soon, if she held her breath and did not hope too hard, they would be on their way back to Primrose Park. She did not care how late they arrived there. She would be safe again. At home again.

For the first time since they had left home that morning she felt like crying. She fought the tears with dogged determination.

The problem was what to do when they reached Gloucester. Should they find Prudholm's chambers first of all to find out if Julia and Freddie really had been there? Or would they merely be wasting more time doing that? Lord, those two had had a head start of at least two hours, perhaps longer. Should they immediately start searching all the inns in Gloucester? How many inns were there anyway? Just one or two or a dozen or more? None of them were familiar with Gloucester.

And what if they were not there at all? What if Freddie had taken her farther, stopped at a country inn instead? Or what if he had not taken the Gloucester road at all? The earl felt rather like vomiting at the very real possibility and hoped that neither of his two companions would voice his own doubts. But Freddie had no reason to believe that anyone suspected his destination. He would have no reason for changing it merely to throw pursuers off the scent.

Lord, if Freddie really had abducted Julia in the hope of forcing her to marry him, the pursuit might be hours too late. The earl sat looking impassively out of his window. He did not know quite what he would do if that were the case. He did not know and he did not care to think about it. He would act from instinct when the time came, he supposed. When? Not if? He suppressed a shudder.

Then just when they were all feeling anxiety because they were nearing Gloucester and had come to no satisfactory agreement on how they would proceed, the carriage slowed and the earl's coachman shouted down to him that another carriage was approaching that looked remarkably like Mr. Sullivan's. And now that it had drawn even closer, he could see that Carl was driving it. Carl, the earl assumed, was Freddie's coachman.

He did not wait for his own carriage to come to a complete stop. He opened the door and vaulted out into the roadway and stood in the path of the other carriage, which was already drawing to a halt. He leapt without thought at the door of the carriage and dragged it open. And found himself glaring into the set, pale face of Julia. She was staring back at him with wide eyes. He looked beyond her to Freddie, whose face was expressionless.

Suddenly anxiety and fear and even terror disappeared. Or rather, were converted to a different emotion—white-hot rage.

"Get out!" he almost whispered. He was vaguely aware of Malcolm jumping into the road behind him and helping Camilla down. Then he made his words redundant by reaching inside, taking Julia by the waist, and lifting her out none too gently, setting her down on the road in front of him. "There had damned well better be a good explanation for this."

Frederick stepped down behind her. "There is," he said. "Jule wanted to summon Prudholm back to Primrose Park early and I accompanied her. Now we are on the way home, the task accomplished. The man is coming tomorrow."

The earl drew a slow breath, not taking his eyes off Julia. She was still very pale. She looked stubbornly back at him.

"It is true, then?" he said. "That really is what today has been all about? And you came alone together?" He injected as much ice into his tone as he could. It was not difficult. It was an icy fury that he felt.

Her eyes held his for a few moments and then slipped to his chin. She raised them back to his nose, but then she let them fall all the way to his boots. She said nothing. Altogether she was most unlike Julia.

"Don't go blaming Jule for anything," Frederick said. "I persuaded her that it would be better not to bring anyone else. No harm has been done, Dan. We should still be home before dark if we do not stand about in the roadway conversing like this."

"Camilla," the earl said, moving his gaze to Frederick, who was looking quite as pale as Julia, "take Julia back to my carriage, if you please, and start on the way home. Malcolm, you will accompany the ladies? And explain to Julia what story we are to tell when we get back to Primrose Park?"

He was surprised that she did not argue or make any resistance. He expected her at least to make a token protest against his trying to tell her what to do. She stepped around him, her eyes still lowered, and disappeared from his sight.

He waited for a few minutes until his carriage had turned in the roadway and was moving off in the direction from which they had come, watching Freddie the whole time. His cousin remained pale and expressionless, as unlike Freddie as Julia had been unlike Julia. They were not just two people caught out in a minor indiscretion. Freddie and Julia of all people would have brazened that out. There was a great deal more to it than that. The earl felt himself grow cold.

"We will talk about this on the way back," he said, stepping closer. "If you have touched her, Freddie, I will be hard put to it not to kill you."

"I have not," Frederick said.

"But you have compromised her unpardonably," the earl said, "or would have done so if we had not arrived to somehow patch things up. There is a story we are all going to tell when we get back. All of us. You included, Freddie."

Frederick nodded.

"We had better not delay longer, then," the earl said.

Frederick half smiled. "You might as well do it, Dan," he said. "It will clear the air a little before we have to travel together in this carriage."

"You are right," the earl said, and he felled Frederick with one hard right to the jaw. There was no fight, though the coachman looked on with hopeful interest. Frederick was not even unconscious. He got to his feet after a mere few seconds, his legs only slightly unsteady, and gave his cousin the same half smile.

"Feel better?" he asked, turning toward the carriage.

"No," the earl said curtly.

"A pity," Frederick said. "Neither do I."

17

Julia felt as if she crawled rather than walked to her bed. She did not believe she had ever been more exhausted in her life. Or more depressed.

They had arrived back when it was already almost dark and had walked into a veritable wall of questions and anxious inquiries as soon as they set foot inside the house. They all smiled and smiled and told the same story, that Camilla and Malcolm had taken it into their heads quite on the spur of the moment to drive to Gloucester to find a jeweler and a betrothal ring and had dragged Daniel off with them to make all proper. And then when they were already in the stables waiting for the carriage to be ready, they had met Freddie and Julia, who had decided to go with them since Julia wished to pay a call on Mr. Prudholm. They had completed the latter errand, but alas there were no suitable rings in Gloucester.

There had been a chorus of protests from cousins and even a few uncles and aunts who were offended at having been left out of such a secretive excursion and a few scoldings for not having left word of where they had gone, but their story had not been questioned. Scandal had been averted.

Frederick had caught at her wrist when she was coming up to bed. He had been smiling that twisted half smile.

"I don't expect you to forgive me, Jule," he had said quietly, for her ears only, "but I am dreadfully sorry for what happened. It will haunt me for a long time to come."

"I hope it does, Freddie," she had said, looking at his hand rather than at his face. He had a bruise on the left side of his jaw, acquired when he had been standing too close to the carriage door when opening it. She wondered if that was what had really happened.

She did not think she would ever be able to forgive him, though he must have a conscience, she thought, or he would not have found himself unable to go through with his final plan.

Julia burrowed beneath the blankets though the night was warm, and curled up into a ball. She felt hurt and used. Daniel had said nothing to her. He had not even looked at her. His face, when she had glanced at it, had been hard and pale, even when he was smiling for the benefit of the relatives. She would have welcomed even one of his famous pompous scolds rather than the silence. But he, of course, thought her guilty of a dreadful indiscretion—dreadful even for her. She had made Camilla and Malcolm promise to say nothing.

Julia burrowed even farther beneath the bedclothes. She had gone all to pieces as soon as she was alone in the carriage with them—body and limbs trembling, teeth chattering, tears flowing. The whole humiliating scene. She had huddled in a corner refusing to say a word beyond the repeated assertion that nothing was wrong until Camilla had come to sit beside her and cradle her head on her shoulder and rock her just like a hurt child. Julia hated to remember.

Then it had all come pouring out. All the sordid details. All her terror. And then she had become terrified anew. Terrified that they would retell the story back at Primrose Park and Daniel would feel obliged to challenge Freddie to a duel and put a bullet through his brain or something dreadful like that. And there would be all the ghastly unpleasantness of Aunt Eunice and Uncle Raymond's discovering how villainously their son had behaved. She would just die, Julia had thought, if she became the cause of such disruption within the family.

And so she had made them promise that they would say not a single word to anyone, least of all to Daniel. After all, she had pointed out when they had seemed unwilling at first to promise, Freddie had relented and he had been taking her home again. No real harm had been done.

No real harm had been done. Julia emerged from the suffocating heat of the blankets to rest her head on the pillow again and stare upward at the canopy of the bed. Mr. Prudholm had agreed to come on the following day. The day after tomorrow she should be able to leave. She could leave it all behind her forever and start a new life. Grandpapa, Primrose Park, the family. Daniel.

Daniel. She would be able to forget about him. Everything about him. She would be able to put it all in the past and start again. There was some excitement in the thought. It was always exciting to start a new life. She supposed.

Daniel.

She slid into a deep sleep.

He watched from the window of his bedchamber as she left the house and set off walking in the direction of the lake. It was very early. He had expected to have to wait until after breakfast to get her alone so that he might have a private talk with her. But he had hoped that perhaps she would be up and out early as she frequently was. Especially on this morning he had hoped that she would find herself unable to sleep.

She would be going swimming, he thought. She probably needed the cool water and the exercise after yesterday's ordeal. It was amazing that she had held herself together so well last night. None of the rest of the family could have suspected that she had been through a worse hell in the course of the day than any woman should be required to face during a lifetime. She was a remarkable woman.

She had, of course, gone to pieces for a while in the carriage with Camilla and Malcolm. But only for a while. Then she had pulled herself together and insisted that they promise to say nothing about what had happened to her. Camilla had been very reluctant to tell him the story until he had told her all that Freddie had told him. Freddie must have wanted some sort of absolution. He had told everything. And of course he would go unpunished beyond that one punch to the jaw since the whole thing must be kept strictly secret from the rest of the family and battered faces would require explanation. But then the earl rather suspected that Freddie would punish himself quite adequately.

The earl waited a full ten minutes before going after Julia and even then he did not walk fast. If she had gone for a swim, then he would allow her the privacy in which to enjoy it—for a while anyway. But when he arrived at the lake, it was sparkling and very empty in the early morning sunshine. There was no one on the bank either. He looked right around the lake, but there was no one. She had gone somewhere else. He had missed her.

He would have to wait until after breakfast after all, he thought, disappointed. He sat down on the bank for a few minutes, but he was restless and was soon walking back to the house again. Perhaps he would go for a ride. It would pass some time and use some energy. He did not know what made him glance up as he passed a short distance from the old oak tree. A rather wistful memory of two afternoons before, perhaps?

She was on the branch he had occupied then, lying full length, face down, her arms folded beneath her head. He did not think she was aware of his presence.

"Julia," he said softly when he had walked up to the base of the tree.

She did not move. "Go away, Daniel," she said. "Please go away."

She was in his tree. On his branch.

"Shall I come up or will you come down?" he asked. "We need to talk."

For a few moments he did not think she would answer him. Then she lifted herself to a sitting position and began to climb down, without once looking at him. She looked weary and dejected, quite unlike Julia. His heart ached for her. He did not help her when she reached the lowest branch. He let her jump down to the ground.

"Well," she said when she was there, standing in front of

him. She did not look up at him or attempt to step back. "Go ahead, Daniel. It was scandalously indiscreet of me. I can be only thankful that you had the presence of mind to come after me and that Camilla and Malcolm knew where we had gone. I *am* thankful. There. How is that for humble pie?"

"I know what happened," he said quietly. "Freddie told me."

"Did he?" He watched her swallow. "Did you give him the bruise?"

"Yes," he said.

"So you can't really scold me too much after all," she said. "Except for being foolish enough to believe that Les and Stella were waiting for us in the village. But you can still say 'I told you so,' Daniel. You were perfectly right about Freddie, of course. Go ahead and say it. I am sure you are longing to."

"Julia," he said softly, and he touched the backs of his knuckles to her cheek.

She jerked her head back. "Don't touch me," she said. "Please. I would rather you did not."

"You are planning to tell Prudholm that you are going to marry none of us?" he said. "That is why you have summoned him here?"

"Yes," she said.

"Why?" he asked.

"Because I am tired of this whole mess," she said, looking up at him at last, her eyes miserable, her voice passionate. "I hate it, Daniel. I have hated it all. I have wanted to grieve for Grandpapa. I have wanted everyone to be together just as we always have been during the summers. I have wanted the comfort of that one more time. I didn't want all the rest of it. This horrid thing with Freddie would not have happened if it had not been for the stupid will. And now I have lost him forever. I was fond of him."

"My uncle wanted what was best for you," he said. "He loved you, Julia. He would be upset if he could see how miserable his will has made you."

"I know he loved me," she said. "I don't need you to tell me that. But he just did not understand women, Daniel. Men generally don't. Marriage for the sake of security and position is not enough for us, or not enough for me anyway. There has to be love. I could not marry a man I did not love or one who did not love me. And so I will never marry. For men do not know what love is."

"Oh, we do," he said. "Perhaps we do not recognize it so fast and perhaps we are more hesitant than women to own to it. But we know what love is, Julia, and it is a desirable ingredient of marriage for us too."

"I don't want to talk about love or marriage," she said. "I am going to the north of England, perhaps as soon as tomorrow. And I am going to become a governess or a lady's companion. So it does not matter to me any longer how women feel or how men feel or what they each want of marriage. It just does not matter anymore. And I would be obliged if you would leave me now, Daniel, for I am feeling despicably close to tears and I will hate myself forever if I cry in front of you."

He set his hands on her shoulders and drew her firmly against him so that her face was buried among the folds of his neckcloth. She stiffened immediately, but she did not try to push away. After a short while she relaxed and started to cry. He wrapped his arms about her and rocked her until she fell silent again after several minutes.

"I didn't want this to happen," she said, her voice still miserable. "I didn't want any of this."

"This?" he said. "This situation at Primrose Park? Or this specifically with me?"

She sniffed and he handed her his handkerchief.

"I don't think either of us did, did we?" he said. "Nor did we expect it. But it has happened anyway."

She looked up at him with reddened, suspicious eyes. "What are you talking about?" she asked.

He clasped his arms behind her waist. "You and me," he said, "falling in love."

He expected her to argue. She opened her mouth to do so

but then shut it again. And gazed at him with naked longing in her eyes.

"I think we have gone through enough days of open denial, haven't we?" he said. "It is time we admitted it to ourselves and to each other, Julia."

"You hate me," she said.

"Love is very similar to hatred," he said. "They are both passionate extremes of feeling, easily confused with each other. I have just been using the wrong word. And you too."

"I could never please you," she said. "You disapprove of everything I do."

"Because I have envied you your freedom and high spirits," he said. "You are going to have to teach me to relax and have fun again, Julia. I used to be expert at it but I will have to relearn the skills."

Once more she opened her mouth only to close it.

"I love you, Julia," he said. "Just as you are, with all your unconventional spontaneity. And since I have decided that love must be an essential ingredient of my marriage, you see, I want you to marry me. Will you?"

"It is just because of what happened yesterday," she said. "It is just that you feel obliged, as you always do—"

"If you must talk, Julia," he said sharply, "at least talk sense. That is utter nonsense as you are well aware."

"There," she said accusingly. "You would be forever scolding me."

"Yes," he said, "whenever you talked such nonsense. I don't expect a tranquil marriage with you, Julia. I would fully expect that we will quarrel frequently. But I don't want to live without you. Life would be dull. It would be without love. And without fun."

"Oh," she said.

"Well?" He gazed down into her eyes.

"I decided I could not marry any of the others," she said, "because none of them was you, Daniel. Because I could love only you."

He smiled at her.

"I will marry you," she said. "But I think you will be sorry."

He laughed. "No, I won't," he said, lowering his head and kissing her openmouthed as he had been longing to do for days.

"Daniel," she said when they finally came up for air. Her smile was radiant. "Oh, Daniel, we will be able to keep on coming here for the summers, won't we? Sometimes? Just for the sake of nostalgia?"

"Every summer," he promised. "We will invite everyone here as always, Julia, and bring our children here. There is one thing I am going to do, though. On our wedding day. I am going to give you Primrose Park as a wedding present."

Her eyes widened.

He grinned at her. "I do not want to have you throwing in my teeth every time we quarrel," he said, "the accusation that I married you only for the property."

"I wouldn't," she said. She chuckled. "How nasty you are, Daniel. You are taking away from me what could have been my most powerful weapon."

And then he kissed her again in an embrace that soon enough had far more than just their mouths and tongues involved.

"Too public," he murmured eventually against her ear, lifting her dress to cover the breast he had exposed to kiss and fondle. "And too soon. We have to leave something for our wedding night, Julia. But God, how I want you."

"Is it still early?" she asked, buttoning up his shirt again with reluctant fingers. "Or is that really the noonday heat beating down on us?"

"I think the noonday heat is coming from inside us," he said, nipping her earlobe and straightening up again.

She was smiling impishly at him. "It is still early?" she asked. "How about a swim, then? It would feel wonderful, Daniel."

A swim? Together? Julia in her chemise, he in his breeches? It would be quite shockingly improper.

She was laughing.

"I'll beat you to the lake," he said, turning and racing away, taking quite unfair advantage of the surprise that held her immobile for a fraction of a second.

And then she shrieked and came after him.

The family was gathered in the drawing room again. But this time they were not all dressed in black, and this time the servants were not present.

And this time Julia sat in the front row, her head bent, her hands twisting each other with nervousness. She was wishing she had not agreed to the suggestion Daniel had made earlier that morning. But then she would have agreed with anything he had suggested after they had swum and frolicked and splashed each other and kissed until they sank to the bottom and then spluttered to the surface and kissed some more. And shrieked with laughter. Or rather, she had shrieked. Daniel had merely laughed.

Oh, it had been so wonderful to hear him laugh again, to see his eyes dance with merriment, to see his dark hair plastered to his head with wetness and water droplets on his bare chest. It had been wonderful beyond imagining. Yes, she would have agreed to anything.

Mr. Prudholm cleared his throat and everyone fell silent. Julia twisted her hands and drew a steadying breath. And then he was explaining that she had summoned him back early since she had made her decision and he had been able to find nothing in the wording of the will to say that they had to wait the full month. He would await Miss Maynard's decision, then.

Everyone awaited her decision with bated breath.

There was a dramatic way of doing this, she thought. She was sure that was what Daniel had had in mind that morning when he had suggested it.

"I am going to marry Daniel," she said so quickly and so quietly that aunts were craning their necks from all directions.

"What did she say?" Aunt Eunice asked in a stage whisper.

"*What* did dear Julia say?" Aunt Millie asked aloud.

"Julia did me the honor this morning of accepting my hand in marriage," the earl said distinctly.

The room erupted in sound and the poor solicitor was left for several minutes to cough in vain. Julia had not realized that there were quite so many relatives until each of them felt compelled to hug her tightly. Only Frederick held back, that characteristic half smile on his lips.

Aunt Sarah kissed both her cheeks in addition to hugging her. "I am so glad, Julia, dear," she said. "I always did say that the property should be kept all together in the hands of the Earl of Beaconswood. I am glad that you saw that too. I shall be delighted to welcome you into the family as my daughter-in-law."

"Sisters," Camilla said, tears in her eyes. "I am so happy, Julia. And I know you will make Daniel happy. You better than anyone."

Mr. Prudholm's cough became insistent.

And so Primrose Park was Daniel's, Julia thought, seating herself and looking down at her hands again. His hand came across to cover them, and she turned her head to smile at him. He had changed places with Uncle Henry so that he might sit beside her. But he was going to give it to her as a wedding present. Not that it would matter. She would always think of it as theirs rather than hers. But it warmed her heart anyway that he was going to do it. Now she would never be able to feel even the most niggling of doubts about his motive for marrying her.

How she loved him! she thought. She could cry with joy and probably would too and die of mortification if she did not distract her mind by concentrating on what Mr. Prudholm was saying. He was reading from a codicil to Grandpapa's will.

" '. . . And so, if you have any doubts about your choice, Jule,' " Mr. Prudholm read, sounding not at all like Grandpapa, " 'then tell whichever of my nephews it is that you have changed your mind. Send him home. Primrose Park will be yours, my dear granddaughter, if you do not marry, and your husband's if you do. So you see, Jule, you have only love to gain by marrying. My solicitor has been directed to give you two days in which to make your final decision.'"

Mr. Prudholm paused and looked directly at Julia. Everyone was waiting with bated breath again. She had a death grip on Daniel's hand, she realized suddenly.

"I am not going to change my mind," she said. She turned her head to look up at her betrothed. "Whatever you give me or do not give me as a wedding present."

And then the unthinkable humiliation happened as Gussie and some of the uncles cheered irreverently. Julia's face crumpled and she hid it quickly against Daniel's broad shoulder just as an inelegant sob hiccuped past her lips. They were tears of happiness she shed, not only because Daniel loved her and they were going to be married, but because Grandpapa had loved her too and had given her the most precious gift of all—her freedom. Even so it was mortifying in the extreme to be bawling—though she was not quite doing that—in front of all the family.

And then Daniel behaved with such shocking and unexpected impropriety that her tears stopped as if by magic. In full view of the whole family and his late uncle's solicitor, he encircled her shoulders with one arm, lifted her chin with the other hand, and kissed her mouth.

"Daniel," she hissed, deeply shocked. "Everyone will *see*. This is most improper. You are never improper."

"Give me time," he said tenderly. "I have a good teacher, love."

And while Gussie whistled and Mr. Prudholm coughed and Aunt Millie sniveled, he repeated the impropriety. He kissed her again.